SINFULLY TEMPTED

The Five Deadly Sins
Book 2

Kathleen Ayers

Dragonblade Publishing, Inc. is an imprint of Kathryn Le Veque Novels, Inc.
P.O. Box 23
Moreno Valley, CA 92556
ceo@dragonbladepublishing.com

Produced in the United States of America

First Edition August 2023
Print Edition

ARE YOU SIGNED UP FOR DRAGONBLADE'S BLOG?

You'll get the latest news and information on exclusive giveaways, exclusive excerpts, coming releases, sales, free books, cover reveals and more.

Check out our complete list of authors, too!

No spam, no junk. That's a promise!

Sign Up Here

www.dragonbladepublishing.com

Dearest Reader;

Thank you for your support of a small press. At Dragonblade Publishing, we strive to bring you the highest quality Historical Romance from some of the best authors in the business. Without your support, there is no 'us', so we sincerely hope you adore these stories and find some new favorite authors along the way.

Happy Reading!

CEO, Dragonblade Publishing

Additional Dragonblade books by Author Kathleen Ayers

The Five Deadly Sins Series
Sinfully Wed (Book 1)
Sinfully Tempted (Book 2)

The Arrogant Earls Series
Forgetting the Earl (Book 1)
Chasing the Earl (Book 2)
Enticing the Earl (Book 3)

CHAPTER ONE

L ADY TAMSIN SINCLAIR pushed her body flush against the wall of
Lady Curchon's drawing room, willing herself to disappear into
the walnut paneling. Escape from this affair was impossible; she felt
much like a poor fox trapped in a hunt with a trail of hounds following, but Lady Curchon's offered far less places to hide. Not a bloody
hollow tree trunk in sight.

No matter how much time had passed since the scandal of
Tamsin's parents, or how much coal had been found at Dunnings, the
Sinclair family remained notorious. The product of the union between
a former actress and the Earl of Emerson, she and her siblings were
considered ill-bred. Uncivilized. Mannerless.

Sins.

Unfortunately, Tamsin and the rest of the Sinclairs had done nothing to dissuade society from such an opinion.

The mere thought of Dunnings brought back the taste of boiled
cabbage to Tamsin's tongue. Cabbage had been one of the few things
that grew at the tiny estate, and it seemed as if the horrid vegetable
had been served at every meal. Tucked away in an obscure area of
Northumberland, Dunnings had been a convenient spot for the eldest
Sinclair, her half-brother Bentley, to hide his unwanted family from
the rest of England. Now Bentley was dead, and Tamsin's older
brother Jordan had inherited the title. Which left Tamsin...well *here.*
At a ball hosted by Lady Curchon. To be gawked at by the curious

wishing to catch a glimpse of the ill-bred daughter of the reviled former Lady Emerson.

Poor Mama.

No one ever recalled her with any fondness. It was fine for an actress to become an earl's mistress. But *not* his countess. Mama had committed an unpardonable sin.

Tamsin slid further down the hall, keeping her eyes lowered and skirts pulled back, hoping no one would glance in her direction. Or if they did, pay her as little attention as possible. The scandal of Tamsin's parents should have died down years ago, but the vindictive nature of Lady Longwood kept the tale alive. Lady Longwood was a sour, bitter woman who detested every Sinclair, but particularly Tamsin.

I look so much like Mama. The old harpy can't tolerate it.

The Dowager Viscountess of Longwood was the sister of the *first* Lady Emerson, Pauline, Papa's first wife and mother to Bentley. Pauline was often sickly, keeping to her bed more often than not and leaving Bentley to the tender care of her sister. After Pauline's death, Lady Longwood blamed Mama. Her vitriol and dislike for the Sinclair family poisoned Bentley against his half-siblings. The loathing of Lady Longwood had only grown worse since his death.

A taint. Sins, if you will. Born of an unfortunate, distasteful union.

Lady Longwood sneered her disdain for the Sinclairs to an acquaintance at this very ball only moments ago. If not for her continued verbal assaults on Tamsin's family, the scandal of Tamsin's parents, among some others—

She paused and took a deep breath recalling her own role in the Sinclair family's poor reputation.

—might well have stayed in the *past*, where it belonged. Instead of being dredged up to be examined once more. But Lady Longwood refused to allow her bitterness to rest.

Tamsin had been strolling among Lady Curchon's well-dressed guests, trying not to stand out, determined not to do or say anything which might draw attention when she'd nearly run into Lady Longwood's silk-clad back. She'd halted immediately, so close the aroma of the other woman's perfume caught in her nose.

Cloying and overly sweet.

Nothing at all like the lady wearing it.

Tamsin's first thought was that Lady Longwood should *not* be in attendance. The Season was, for all intents and purposes, *over.* Lord Longwood, the dowager viscountess's son, had already departed for the country and the assumption made he'd taken his harpy of a mother with him.

Yet here she was. Destroying what little enjoyment Tamsin had gleaned from Lady Curchon's ball. Which wasn't a great deal, mind you.

Attendance at Lady Curchon's this evening was sparse, mainly limited to those who had delayed their departure to the country for one reason or another. Had the crowd been larger, perhaps on the same level as the event Lady Curchon hosted a few months ago, Tamsin might have been able to go unnoticed. But with fewer guests to hide behind, Tamsin might be spotted by Lady Longwood at any moment.

I should have stayed home.

Indeed, she should have, but Miss Maplehurst, elderly chaperone and great aunt to Jordan's wife, Odessa, insisted Tamsin attend. Aunt Lottie, as she'd asked to be called, promised Lady Curchon's event this evening would be of little note. Barely attended. And Tamsin needed to practice the much-lauded skill of polite conversation. Fan waving. Lowering one's eyes for the purpose of modesty or flirtation.

Ugh.

There were better ways to spend one's time than learning how to properly bat your eyelashes. If Aurora, her younger sister, hadn't been making her debut next year, Tamsin wouldn't have bothered with such social niceties. Tamsin had long ago decided that not only did she not suit society, but society did not suit *her.* At twenty-six, she was firmly on the shelf and in no danger of making a match. Spinsterhood loomed before her. Dunnings had taught Tamsin to survive, but not how to be a lady. Her formative years were spent challenging gentlemen with large purses to horse races, which she usually won due to the distraction of her opponents.

Tamsin rode astride and in leather breeches.

The point being, she won quite a few purses, which in turn, helped keep the Sinclair family fed. She hadn't time to practice her manners and perch properly on the edge of a settee while sipping tea. But there was still hope for Aurora. Her sister deserved to have her place in society. One Aurora had been denied for far too long.

A wave of guilt, old and endless, filled Tamsin.

She would do anything to ensure Aurora's future, even if it meant pretending to be something she was not. A lady.

Tamsin continued to dart down the hall, using the vivid plume of feathers springing from the coiffure of Lady Longwood as a marker of sorts. Lady Longwood was holding court among a group of expensively dressed matrons, likely dissecting the prospects of every young lady who had failed to make a match this Season. Her cruelty echoed across the half-empty room, earning nervous bursts of laughter from her audience.

Horrid woman.

Tamsin resumed her journey, deciding that the gardens would be her destination. Hiding behind a shrub seemed cowardly, and she rarely, if ever, ran from a fight, but Tamsin had promised Jordan to rein in her behavior. Do nothing rash. Do not allow herself to be provoked. Dampen her overprotective instincts. Society already believed Tamsin to be uncivilized, ill-mannered, and far too brazen. There was no need to prove them right.

Far more difficult than it sounded.

Jordan was recently wed and in residence at River Crest, the family estate, with his new bride. Tamsin had no desire to interrupt his long-deserved happiness with another uproar caused by the reckless actions of his sister. She'd resolved to stay quiet. Beneath notice. Refuse to allow Lady Longwood to get beneath her skin.

Hiding was her best hope to avoid contact with the old witch.

Tamsin peered around the corner, searching unsuccessfully for Aunt Lottie. The elderly woman had drifted away some time ago, headed in the direction of the refreshment table though she'd promised to stay glued to Tamsin's side. Aunt Lottie was a lovely woman. Aurora and Tamsin both adored her. They had both been grateful when she offered to stay in London with them, while Jordan saw to matters at River Crest.

But Aunt Lottie was a *terrible* chaperone.

Not that Tamsin required the services of a chaperone, and not only because of her age. Tamsin had dispensed with her virtue long ago having given it to a sea captain. There was nothing left to protect. Aurora, however, was another matter.

A gentleman passed Tamsin, attractive and well-dressed. His gaze dragged over the green striped silk she wore, lingering on her bosom. A not uncommon occurrence no matter how modest her necklines. A froth of lace decorated the edge of the bodice and Madame Theriot, the modiste who had created the gown, assured Tamsin the decoration would hide the rise of her breasts. An impossibility. Tamsin was far too well-endowed. Gentlemen had been leering at her bosom since she was fifteen.

Yes, and remember how that ended.

The fingers of her right hand immediately curled into a fist. Thumb on the outside, as Jordan had taught Tamsin when they were children. All three of her brothers liked to brawl and Tamsin had learned at a young age how to use her fists, or throw a rock and hit a mark. Her aim was excellent. She could defend herself from unwelcome attention and was not shy about doing so.

A good punch to the stomach would get this gentleman to move on.

And cause a scene. She could almost hear Lady Longwood cackling with glee.

Tamsin slowly uncurled her fingers and smoothed out her skirts. Aurora's come-out must not be ruined by the impetuous behavior of her older sister. When Aurora should have been playing with dolls and planning tea parties, Tamsin's sister had been scratching in the dirt to grow cabbage.

Because of me.

"I don't believe we've been introduced." The gentleman gave Tamsin a polite bow. "I am—"

"Oh, there's my chaperone. Apologies, my lord," she said in a rush, cringing at her timid, mouselike tone before hurrying away. What Tamsin wanted to do was to discourage his leering with a scathing rebuke and possibly a fist to his midsection, but that would be unwise. Such reserve was difficult for Tamsin. As was holding her tongue. She had been speaking her mind for years. Now she was trying to enjoy ratafia and wearing layers of petticoats.

But it was a sacrifice willingly given for Aurora.

Tamsin kept moving in the direction of the doors leading out to the terrace, giving up the futile search for Aunt Lottie. She'd find her after cooling off a bit. The best course of action at present was to be anywhere Lady Longwood was not.

And get some air.

Lady Curchon's home was *sweltering.* One would think that fewer guests in attendance would keep the air flowing, but the evening was overly warm. Tamsin's skin beneath the striped silk and multiple layers of undergarments was uncomfortably damp. A puff of cool air beneath her skirts would be most welcome.

A tiny breeze lifted a strand of hair across one cheek, bringing with it the scent of roses.

Tamsin was not meant to be with the snobs inside, all reeking of excess amounts of pomade or poor hygiene. There wasn't even anyone worthy of a polite conversation, should she be inclined to practice. Out of doors was where Tamsin was most content. She yearned for the country. Even when she visited the park, the air smelled of soot or something equally unpleasant. The city was noisy. Crowded. She missed fresh air and the chirping of frogs at night.

And there was a great deal less judgement in the country.

All conversation paused as Tamsin's slippered foot stepped onto the terrace. The half-dozen guests enjoying the night air paused in their whispered conversations. Heads turned in Tamsin's direction, observing her with curiosity. Someone snapped a fan. Skirts rustled.

"Broke his nose without a qualm."

Tamsin sucked in a lungful of night air at the words but kept her gaze focused on the gardens.

The breaking of the Marquess of Sokesby's nose eleven years ago had been warranted, though no one else agreed. She hadn't known who he was at the time, not that it would have mattered one whit. Tamsin had been fifteen and enjoying an ice at Gunter's, which did not entitle Sokesby to grope her person. Nor be offered the position of mistress by some overprivileged lordling. Papa had just died. Bentley was horrible. Tamsin merely wanted to enjoy the day, her ice, and not have Sokesby's hand grab her breast.

She'd punched him right in his perfect, aristocratic nose.

The crunching sound was much louder than Tamsin anticipated.

As were Sokesby's screams. Half of London must have heard him.

Tamsin pressed a hand to her midsection as she hurried down the path into the gardens, trying to staunch the guilt that seemed to bleed out of her whenever she recalled that day.

She'd broken the nose of a duke's heir, and Bentley had banished them all to Dunnings the following day.

Had she not been so rash, not made a spectacle of herself, Bentley might have listened to reason. As the family was escorted to the coach waiting to take them to Northumberland, Lady Longwood had hissed into Tamsin's ear.

"Bentley told me only last night that breaking Sokesby's nose was the

final straw. Your presence can no longer be tolerated."

If not for her, Aurora would have had a proper childhood. Drew wouldn't have become a gambling rake. Malcolm wouldn't be wandering about the Continent after leaving the army. Jordan wouldn't have had to take on the responsibility for his entire family at eighteen.

And Mama wouldn't have died.

Marching past two ladies both eyeing her as if she were some sort of wild animal invading the sanctity of Lady Curchon's garden, Tamsin headed directly into the relative safety of the rose bushes. She was no dull nitwit, terrified to walk on her own. There *were* torches. Plenty of couples lurked about Lady Curchon's manicured flower beds whispering to each other.

As she strolled down the path, one of those amorous couples came into view, or rather their outline, barely visible beneath a tree. Wet, slurping sounds were followed by a girlish giggle.

Ugh.

It wasn't that Tamsin was opposed to romance or having a kiss stolen. She had taken a lover at the age of nineteen. But the cooing nitwits beneath the tree with their polite declarations of affection didn't suit her. She preferred a man who bluntly stated his intentions rather than one who used flowery language to make his point.

The path curved to the right, moonlight sliding along the well-tended beds of flowers. Taking a deep, cleansing breath, Tamsin immediately coughed at the taste of London invading her tongue. She might never grow accustomed to it.

Settling on a bench near a spray of wisteria, Tamsin glanced down the path in the direction of the house. She had a clear view of the terrace, but the wisteria surrounding the bench gave her some privacy. No one could see her at this distance unless they made a great effort to do so. The closest torch only spilled a small, muted halo of light a few feet from her. Assured she wouldn't be seen, not even by the shadowy couple she'd passed earlier, Tamsin lifted her skirts.

Cool air whispered around her ankles. Nothing had ever felt so wonderful. Grabbing the froth of silk, lace, and petticoats, she dared to raise her skirts further while lifting her feet. A small groan left her as the night breeze slid up her stockinged legs. One slipper dangled off the edge of her toe. Dare she kick her slippers off completely?

Tamsin peered through the wisteria in the direction of the giggling woman and her companion. She could no longer see them, only hear their whispers and the smacking of lips. They probably hadn't even noticed when she walked by. Figures moved about on the terrace, but no one seemed concerned she'd disappeared into the gardens.

Petticoats, she mused, tossing up another mound of fabric to her thighs, were useless at best. Only good for giving your skirts a decent shape. There had been no multitude of petticoats at Dunnings because such things were deemed frivolous and a waste of good coin. Tamsin spent her days in riding breeches and one of Jordan's old shirts. Breeches afforded the wearer a great deal of freedom. Corsets, Tamsin had recently decided, were the invention of the devil. Slippers, nothing more than a bit of silk with a heel. Worthless. She missed her boots.

Existence at Dunnings had been fraught with challenges. And while she enjoyed sleeping on clean sheets that weren't threadbare and having a roof above her which wasn't in danger of collapsing, Tamsin did miss her freedom. But it was a small price to pay for all that the Sinclairs had gained with Bentley's death, which included a wealth of coal beneath the crumbling foundation of Dunnings. Despite her half-brother's success at bankrupting the estate of the Earl of Emerson, the Sinclairs were wealthy once more. Or would be once the coal was excavated.

Something toyed with the hair atop her head, plucking along the thick strands before disappearing.

Startled, Tamsin turned sharply, chin upward, surprised to see a pair of wings flash in front of her eyes. A moth. The wings fluttered once more before her nose, then broke away, sailing toward the torch.

"Are you looking for the moon?" Tamsin raised a finger and pointed up at the glowing orb in the night sky. "No, not me," she insisted as the moth returned to circle her. "You're going in the wrong direction."

The moth ignored her advice, returning to settle itself delicately on Tamsin's calf. The pale cream wings with their unusual pattern of spots, stretched and trembled, but the moth didn't fly away.

"You are the best welcome I've received thus far in London," Tamsin whispered. "I am pleased to make your acquaintance." She kept her leg still, not wanting to startle the moth whose presence brought her an odd sense of comfort.

Tiny legs stuck to her stockings as the moth carefully scaled to the top of her knee, where it once more seemed to settle.

It took a few moments of admiring the moth before Tamsin noted that the cool breeze at her back had stopped. The aroma of bergamot filled the air around her, mixing with the scent of roses. There was just the slightest rustle of leaves at her back. Her neck prickled in warning, alerting Tamsin to a presence behind her.

If it was the gentleman who'd attempted to speak to her earlier, Tamsin would make certain he would regret his decision to follow her.

"Do not move." A deep murmur met her ears.

Tamsin stayed perfectly still. Not out of fear, but out of shock that she might possibly be accosted in Lady Curchon's garden. Her legs were completely and improperly exposed. Perhaps the idiot gentleman from earlier assumed her stance to be an invitation of sorts. She would soon dissuade him of that notion. Twisting slowly, she peered into the darkness.

A grunt met her ears as a looming, monstrous form took shape, erupting from a large shrub to her left. The enormous mass, shadowy in form, sank directly to the ground and proceeded to crawl on four legs towards her.

Was it an animal of some sort?

No, it or rather he, had spoken to her. But her assailant appeared malformed. *Misshapen.* Could he not walk upright? The shape was far too large to be the gentleman who'd ogled her bosom earlier.

Another giggle came from the pair of lovers down the path and Tamsin breathed a sigh of relief she was not completely alone. If this horrid creature attacked, she would scream.

But everyone on the terrace would hear.

She was trying to *avoid* attention, not attract it. The last thing Tamsin needed was to cause a scene. Not with Lady Longwood just inside.

"If you don't get away from me," she hissed in a low, menacing tone, "I will defend myself."

Undeterred, a giant hand stretched towards her exposed legs.
Good God.

Odessa, her sister-in-law, insisted that London was populated by hordes of unfavorable elements. Criminals. Deranged individuals. Unnatural creatures. Tamsin herself was cursed with a vivid imagination. The fault of a mother who had once been an actress and adored make believe.

She flicked one of her useless slippers in the direction of the creature, satisfied when the heel clipped what appeared to be a chin.

The moth took flight, hovering above Tamsin before once more settling just above her knee.

"Do. Not. Move." The dark voice commanded in an icy tone.

Creatures, not even the sort Odessa claimed to inhabit London, didn't speak with a crisp accent.

"Don't you dare touch me," she whispered. "Or I will kick you."

The massive paw stretched towards her. A dark head settled far too close to Tamsin's legs. Warm breath slowly glided up her calf to the hollow of her knee. Hair tickled the inside of her thigh. Something sharp—

Teeth? her mind asked hysterically. Had he bitten her?

—pricked the silk of her stockings. The misshapen lump of shoulders rose between her thighs.

Tamsin's foot shot out, her heel catching her shadowy assailant in the jaw. Pity. She'd been aiming for the nose.

A gurgle of surprise left the beast.

Tamsin curled both hands into fists, which unfortunately, released her skirts and in turn, trapped the creature beneath her voluminous petticoats. His hot breath trailed along the inside of her legs, far too close to her—

"Don't touch me you monster." Tamsin punched, fists pounding against a stretch of muscled shoulder.

"What is wrong with you?" The muffled question came from beneath her skirts.

Tamsin punched harder, hitting the side of his head.

"I demand you stop this instant." The words vibrated between Tamsin's legs. Her assailant had become hopelessly tangled in the mass of petticoats. "I've no interest in your underthings. Or you, for that matter. Dear God, release me."

Tamsin did not comply. All she had wanted was a breath of cool air and she had been attacked. Her foot made contact with the solid wall of his chest, kicking furiously to force him away.

"You've crushed the *colostygia pectinataria*. You careless chit," came an annoyed snarl.

He backed away from her on his arms like a crab, her skirts trailing over his head.

No mere assailant or shadowy beast but a man. An overly large one. Long legs attached to massive thighs stretched all the way beneath the bench on which Tamsin sat. A tangled mass of pitch-black hair spilled over his forehead and cheeks, obscuring his features.

"Do you imagine your underthings," the snobby, upper-crust accent sounded like cut glass, "are more important than the *colostygia pectinataria?*"

The lords in Parliament likely dictated bills in that same clipped tone. But that didn't give him license to assault her.

"You attacked me." Her fist was still clenched. "Forced yourself beneath my petticoats."

"I didn't ask you to lift your skirts, did I? You already had them up and around your ears."

"I—" she sputtered.

"You what?" The man loomed over her. He was very tall. Somewhat...lumpy, though she couldn't tell if he was ill-formed or merely rumpled. One massive hand was curled protectively around something. The moth, she supposed.

"Ruined. Because some *nitwit*," he flung the word at Tamsin, "thought I wanted a peek at her underthings."

"What else would I possibly think? And keep your voice down," she whispered. "You were lurking about. Hiding in shrubs. Popping out with no warning."

"Take a good look at me." The gigantic form turned slowly about. "Do you honestly think me capable of sneaking up on anyone? And I gave warning. I asked you not to move."

"Is it dead?" She nodded to his hand. Was he a gardener? Or a naturalist? Why on earth would he be in Lady Curchon's garden while she was hosting a ball?

"Quite," he snapped back without looking at her. "I was attempting to collect a specimen which you have now ruined." He moved behind her into the darkness, kneeling to place the moth on the ground. If he didn't move, it would be easy to mistake his form for an untrimmed shrub. Or a small tree.

How long had he been watching her?

Bending, she picked up her discarded slipper and slapped it back on her foot. A caustic rebuke was forming on her lips for her unwelcome companion, though she doubted he'd care to hear it. She meant to remind him that a gentleman should alert a woman to his presence *before* digging beneath her skirts, accidentally or not. Her fingers relaxed, no longer afraid she was about to be attacked. At least by the moth collector.

"Like mother like daughter, I see. I'm hardly surprised."

Tamsin lifted her head at the familiar, disdainful tone.

The outline of two women were before her on the path, stopping just beneath the circle of light from the torch, their faces shadowed.

Lady Longwood and her eldest daughter. The truly terrible one. Helene.

"My daughter overheard the entire sordid episode," Lady Longwood trilled.

"I've no interest in your underthings. Or you, for that matter. Dear God, release me. That is exactly what I heard, Mama," Helene recited the words Tamsin's assailant had spoken.

"Trapping a gentleman. Well, I suppose you must, given your reputation. Very much like your mother." A satisfied smile stretched Lady Longwood's mouth.

"Imagine my surprise at bearing witness to your sordid tactics." Helene wagged a finger at Tamsin. "Fentwell and I were horrified."

"Was that your husband cooing to you in the darkness?" Tamsin kept her tone polite. "I must offer him my condolences on your marriage."

Helene laughed. "Such brave words from a trollop."

Of all the rotten luck. Tamsin had escaped the house to avoid Lady Longwood, only to be found by Horrible Helene instead. This entire evening had been a complete and utter failure, proof that Tamsin did not belong in polite society.

"The pity, Lady Tamsin, is that your sister will be making her come out next year," Lady Longwood said in a sugary tone. "I suppose it will be less successful now. But what else could she expect from a sister whose antics gave Bentley no choice but to send her away from

London?"

"Her legs were spread, Mama, as she sought to coerce that poor gentleman. She pounded on his shoulders. Writhed on the bench. Like some doxy." An ugly grin stretched across Helene's sharp features.

Tamsin swallowed, willing the panicked flutter of her heart to stop. Aurora. This would destroy any hopes of her entering society. "My lady—"

"*Repugnant.* But your mother was much the same."

A rustle came from the shrub behind her, and Tamsin said a silent prayer that whoever he was, he had the decency to remain silent and not show himself. For all she knew, he *was* Lady Curchon's bloody gardener.

"Your eyesight is as poor as your manner," Tamsin said to Helene as she crossed her ankles, ensuring her legs and slippers were appropriately covered. The silk of her stockings was torn, punctured by whatever sharp implement her moth-loving assailant carried. "I think you've had too much ratafia, Helene. Are you certain that was your husband with you under the tree?"

"Trollop," Helene snapped. "Just like the actress who became a mistress then a countess."

Everyone in London was aware of the origins of Tamsin's mother. There was no need for this shrew to belabor the point.

"And ambitious. Her mother was a masterful seductress and doubtless taught her well." Lady Longwood peered at Tamsin. "I find it difficult to look at you."

"Then I beg you, my lady." Tamsin made a twirling motion with her fingers. "Do not subject yourself further."

Lady Longwood straightened with a resigned sigh. "I fear I cannot, in good conscience, leave you to wander about without informing our hostess Lady Curchon of your behavior. I'm sure she'll want to personally see you out." She cocked her head at Tamsin. "She'll be distressed over the situation, but Lady Curchon had to have expected

15

something unsavory may occur given your presence. She should be far more discerning in her invitations."

"I agree," Tamsin replied with a pointed look. "Considering you are here, I can't imagine she took much thought with the guest list."

I have ruined everything. Again.

"Get up." Lady Longwood fairly bristled with anger. "We'll go find Lady Curchon together."

"I am quite comfortable where I am."

If this vile woman wished to parade her about the other guests, shaming her in front of everyone present, she could do so without Tamsin's assistance.

She glanced in the direction of the terrace, noting the small crowd gathered at the edge, peering into the garden. One young lady was even leaning over the marble balustrade, short of leaping onto the path to view the proceedings.

"Agreed. It will be much more entertaining to have Lady Curchon's footmen toss you out." She gave Tamsin a pitying look. "I fear I cannot stay silent about your picadilloes. I must warn everyone the danger of issuing you an invitation. Or your sister."

The cruelty of Lady Longwood, the absolute *hatred* she held for Tamsin colored every word. She would destroy Aurora's happiness without a second thought.

"Helene is mistaken." Tamsin lifted her chin. "As you can see, there is no gentleman hiding in the garden. Too much ratafia." She wiggled a finger at Helene.

"I heard you. And him," Helene insisted.

The shrub behind Tamsin rustled again.

Please let it be a squirrel.

"Don't worry, darling. I believe you." Lady Longwood bared a hint of teeth. "As will everyone else. I'll be sure and spread the news of your adventures before I depart London. Another example of the Sinclair lack of breeding. But I suppose your family doesn't have much further to fall now that your brother has had the bad sense to wed

Angus Whitehall's daughter."

Tamsin looked Lady Longwood right in the eye, refusing to give an inch. She would not allow her family to suffer this woman's hatred without fighting back. In fact, she could not. "You are a sour, *miserable* creature. If your pathetic sister was anything like you, it is no wonder my father wandered."

Lady Longwood's nostrils flared, eyes widening in outrage.

"You vile—I will destroy every Sinclair. An eradication of the vermin which has infected society. I will personally ensure your sister doesn't receive one dance at her come out. And Odessa Whitehall will *never* be received as Lady Emerson. If I *ever* find out who had the bad sense to sniff beneath your skirts tonight, I will shred *his* reputation into tiny bits and blame you for all of it."

Tamsin's form on the bench bent back just slightly, absorbing the horrible words. Her defiance had made things that much worse, as usual. Why hadn't she just gone meekly when Lady Longwood ordered her out?

The massive, shadowed form once more stepped onto the path, but this time, took a position just beneath the torch so that he was clearly visible. Purposefully, Tamsin thought.

He is not what I expected.

Overly large, of course. Broad of shoulder and chest. The mop of hair atop his head was a shaggy snarl of blue-black. Like a raven's wing. Pale, silvery eyes flashed above a bold slash of cheekbone. His clothing was expensive. Finely tailored.

Well, yes. Given his size, it would have to be.

But rumpled and wrinkled, given he'd been crawling beneath shrubbery. Dirt clung to his eveningwear. A diamond, nearly as large as a quail's egg sat atop the stickpin shoved through his poorly tied cravat.

So not Lady Curchon's gardener unless she pays an incredibly high wage.

The sharp end of the stickpin poked out of the silk at an odd angle.

That is what tore at my stockings. Not teeth.

"You would dare shred *my* reputation?" he said in such an icy tone goosebumps formed along Tamsin's arm.

Only the very powerful possessed such an arrogant manner. Or viewed others with such aloof disdain.

Lady Longwood paled. Her hand went to her throat. She appeared close to fainting.

Horrid Helene grabbed her mother's arm.

In unison, both women went down into a perfect, polite half-curtsey.

"Your Grace," Lady Longwood murmured. "I did not realize you were in attendance this evening."

A duke. Splendid. She'd managed to punch yet another one. Though Sokesby had only been the heir of a duke when she punched him, still—

"Now you do." The chilly tone sounded once more, like the snarl of an angry bear. "Please. *Continue* to shred my reputation. I would hear your opinions for myself. As would my mother."

Lady Longwood went a ghastly white color. She looked as if she might be ill.

"I've heard your thoughts on my cousin."

"Your cousin, Your Grace? But I—" Lady Longwood stuttered.

"Did you not realize Lady Emerson is my cousin? You do not seem well-informed, madam. Given how you flaunt your place in society, I had thought you would be."

Lady Longwood's glance fell on Tamsin with absolute hatred. "An oversight, Your Grace."

Tamsin's eyes trailed over the giant dressed in his rumpled, horribly expensive evening clothes. There was only one duke in all of London who would come to the defense of the former Odessa Whitehall and claim her as a relation. Or be searching for insects during a ball.

The Duke of Ware.

The *brother* of the lord whose nose Tamsin had broken so many years ago. Odessa's oddly eccentric cousin. He was reputed to be a naturalist of some sort. Solitary. Difficult. Liked moths a great deal more than people. That was all Tamsin could recall. She had hoped to make his acquaintance under better circumstances.

This night continues to become worse.

She and Ware had never met. Didn't know each other. Their association by marriage was tenuous at best.

I boxed his ears.

"There you are, Your Grace." Lady Curchon appeared, skirts floating about her ankles as she hurried down the path towards them. A polite smile sat firmly fixed on her lips. "Did you find your moth?"

Aunt Lottie rushed behind in her wake, silver curls bouncing about as she struggled to catch up.

"A moth." Lady Longwood glanced from Tamsin to Ware, her shoulders tightening as she regained some of her previous manner. "The duke was in the gardens looking for a moth?" Disbelief colored her words.

"I am an entomologist, madam." Ware took a menacing step in Lady Longwood's direction, his big form somewhat terrifying in the light of the torch. "Why else would I be here?" He pulled out a small glass vial from his coat and shook it before her shocked gaze. "The garden is filled with *colostygia pectinataria*."

"Your Grace, forgive me—" Lady Longwood sputtered. "While I'm certain *your* presence is without fault, for your reputation is impeccable and your honor above reproach, I fear the same cannot be said of Lady Tamsin."

Helene nodded. "I heard you struggling to get away from her."

Ware cocked his head and shot Tamsin a look before returning to Helene. "Do you think me unable to defend myself? I am twice her size."

"Do you understand, Lady Fentwell, how preposterous that sounds?" Lady Curchon trilled.

"You may not be aware, Your Grace, due to your long absences from society and devotion to your research," Lady Longwood placed a hand on Helene's arm, "that this is the young lady who was responsible for the incident at Gunter's." She cleared her throat. "So many years ago. Have you any idea what sort of—" Lady Longwood abruptly stopped speaking, perhaps realizing how condescending she sounded.

"Do you think me so obtuse, madam? So unintelligent? That I must need you to inform me of pertinent facts?"

Lady Longwood stiffened. "I meant no disrespect, Your Grace."

"Lady Tamsin was enjoying the night air. I came upon her while seeking to obtain the *colostygia pectinataria*."

"It was a lovely moth," Tamsin spoke up. "But with the appearance of Lady Longwood and Lady Fentwell, I fear the moth was grievously injured. I do apologize, Your Grace."

Lady Longwood shot her another look of undisguised loathing. She looked about to hiss at Tamsin like a wet cat.

"Is there anything else you wish to convey, madam?" Ware said in a bored tone. "I find this entire affair to be tiresome."

Tamsin thought there was a great deal more that Lady Longwood wished to say, but she wisely kept her mouth shut. Odessa had said that while Ware didn't care to be a duke, he had the manner of one at times. Such arrogance was rarely learned but bred into a gentleman.

"No, Your Grace," Lady Longwood murmured, defeated.

"Then I bid you good evening." Ware gave a dismissive flick of one big paw.

"Good evening, Your Grace. Lady Curchon." Lady Longwood chose to ignore Tamsin and Aunt Lottie. Taking hold of Helene's arm, she made her way back to the terrace, wisely waving away the curious, and disappeared back into the house.

Once the garden was quiet once more, Lady Curchon cast a baleful eye at Tamsin. "I knew it was a mistake to have you here."

"She will not remain silent," Aunt Lottie murmured. "Lady Longwood. This will be a scandal of epic proportions."

"I didn't—" Tamsin tried to explain.

"Silence, Lady Tamsin. You've done quite enough." Lady Curchon put a hand to her temple. "This is an utter disaster. The gossip will spread like wildfire and become the topic of nearly every house party over the entirety of the summer. I can already hear it echoing around Bath. What were you even doing in the garden alone?" She stopped before Tamsin. "Were you seeking an assignation?"

"With him?" she said in disbelief, shaking her head. "I was overly warm. I needed air." Tamsin clutched at her skirts. "A moth landed on my knee. The duke attempted to retrieve it." She looked at Ware for confirmation, but he seemed to have lost all interest in the conversation.

He was holding a pencil and writing something down in a small notebook, facing the moths circling the torch. He gave them his back, completely absorbed.

"Or did you follow him outside, hoping to compromise yourself? Perhaps Lady Longwood's assumptions are not far off the mark."

Tamsin gasped. "Are you joking?"

Ware finished whatever he was scribbling, shut the tiny book, and placed it into the folds of his coat along with the pencil.

"Calm yourself," he said to Lady Curchon. "I followed a *colostygia pectinataria*, which landed on Lady Tamsin's knee. In the attempt to retrieve the specimen, *she*," he stated in an accusatory tone while eyeing Tamsin, "attacked me. There is a propensity towards violence within her, as I believe we are all aware. But no *impropriety*. I became aware of her identity while she boxed my ears. The manner of her fists was familiar." He regarded Tamsin with annoyance. "Did you recognize the nose? Looks exactly like my brother's before you broke it."

"You were *beneath* my skirts," Tamsin returned, angry and utterly mutinous over the entire situation. Must she be reminded of that terrible day at Gunter's at every turn? She had done many questionable things since then; why couldn't one of those be held up as an example of her behavior? "I had no idea who you were," she continued. "Just some large, brutish creature on his knees plucking at my stockings—"

"Not another word," Lady Curchon hissed. "Do not even breathe. This is far worse than I—" She pinched the bridge of her nose.

"An accident." Aunt Lottie spoke up. "Certainly nothing devious."

"Yes, a rather unfortunate accident," Lady Curchon snapped. "One I shall have to fix. Somehow."

"If she had just remained still." Now that Ware was closer, Tamsin could see that his eyes were not as pale as she first assumed but more the color of tarnished silver. Lovely. If they hadn't been filled with so much disgust for her. "Had she not caused such a fuss—"

A fuss? He'd been pawing beneath her skirts for his bloody moth. Tamsin's mouth parted. A squeak of fury came out.

"You sound like a rodent of some sort." Ware rolled his eyes at Tamsin. "A mouse or a vole. Do you even know what a vole is? Probably not. You don't strike me as having any common sense else you would have stayed still when I commanded you."

Tamsin popped up from the bench, fists clenched once more. "You monstrous, moth-hunting—"

"Enough." Lady Curchon moved between them. "I must speak to His Grace alone. Miss Maplehurst, if you would please escort your charge home." Her words grew icy. "Call upon me tomorrow. I should have a solution by then."

"Yes, my lady." Aunt Lottie stood. She took Tamsin's arm, pausing before Lady Curchon and Ware. "Alice—"

"Tomorrow." Lady Curchon crossed her arms. "I will have things settled." Her eyes were filled with dislike as they took in Tamsin. "I hope."

CHAPTER TWO

HAYDEN REDFORD, DUKE of Ware, Marquess Sokesby, and a list of other titles he couldn't be bothered to remember, watched his aunt pace back and forth along the garden path, her frustration and despondency apparent. Poor Aunt Alice. She had taken her role of protecting him seriously when he was a child of six and was loathe to relinquish it.

"Were you beneath her skirts?" she asked.

"Yes, but only to retrieve the specimen," he explained, a bit defensively. There were times when Auntie Alice reduced him to no more than the chubby little lordling he'd once been. "*Not* to take liberties. I would never do such a thing."

Hayden had a well-defined sense of honor. A remnant of being the son of a notorious debaucher of women. And while he hadn't intentionally sought to be beneath Lady Tamsin Sinclair's skirts, he also didn't regret it. The sight of her exposed legs, skirts lifted up her thighs had nearly struck him dumb as he followed the moth.

"My God, if it were anyone else but her." She shook her head. "Lady Penelope is inside. The duchess has been hoping for a match between the two of you, but once Lady Penelope's mother hears the gossip—*why* could you have not asked her to accompany you outside while you looked for your butterfly?" A small sound left her. "The duchess will blame me for this, Your Grace."

"Moth. *Colostygia pectinataria*," he corrected her. "And my mother is on the Continent at present." Hayden didn't bother to add that Mother's traveling companion was also her lover. A Bavarian count. "I've made no offer for Lady Penelope."

"She is perfect for you," his aunt insisted.

Perfectly unappealing. Lady Penelope possessed little intelligence and her laugh sounded like the braying of a sheep. Hayden had only begun to take up the reins of his title. *Reluctantly.* And while marrying was his duty as a duke without heirs, Lady Penelope would not have been his choice.

"We could have solved a variety of problems had you been caught with anyone else. Or merely stayed silent instead of frightening Lady Longwood half out of her wits. You should have allowed Tamsin Sinclair to twist in the wind."

"I am not a small child in need of your chastisement, madam," he said curtly.

His aunt stopped pacing. "Apologies Your Grace. But do you not see that if I do not find a way to fix this you could well end up wed to that girl? Which cannot, under any circumstances, occur. She is a Sinclair. Broke your brother's nose. Lord knows she probably was in the gardens for an assignation when you happened upon her. Or worse, she sought to entrap you."

"She didn't even know I was in the gardens, my lady." Hayden exhaled. "I was only thinking of the moth." He'd forgotten all about the bloody moth as soon as his eyes caught on the delicate arch of Tamsin Sinclair's naked foot. The curve of her knee. God help him, her *thigh*. Trapped beneath her skirts, the scent of warm woman and jasmine had made Hayden's head swim. More intoxicated than he'd ever been on spirits.

Hayden's mouth, of its own accord, had skimmed the inside of her thigh.

Then she boxed his ears. Soundly.

When Hayden finally came to his senses, scrambling away from beneath her skirts, he'd been struck speechless at the sight of her. The magnificent bosom heaving with anger, the shining mass of chestnut curls and—*Good lord*—a face that put Helen of Troy to shame.

"Nothing improper transpired." He gazed at his aunt, wondering if she could hear the lie.

Hayden had wanted to put his mouth on every inch of that jasmine-scented skin. It had been a nearly primal urge. He'd thought he'd grown immune to the calls of his baser instincts, but that was not the case. The last time he'd felt so savage had been, ironically, the first and only time he'd seen Lady Tamsin Sinclair.

"Lady Longwood will not be put off, Your Grace. She detests Lady Tamsin and wants to destroy her, and in doing so, will bring shame to you. I fear that if no action is taken, you will be declared much the same as your sire."

He bristled. "I will not be compared to the other males of my family." A deep well of distaste filled him at the thought of being his father's son.

"Nor do I wish you to be." Her tone turned cajoling and soft. Much like the aunt he'd worshipped as a child. "If she were another girl, one of good breeding, I would be the first to insist you do the honorable thing and wed. But wedding Tamsin Sinclair is out of the question. And it becomes much more complicated because her brother is married to Odessa."

"*My cousin.*" Hayden stated with conviction. "And your relation as well, though you will not admit to the connection."

"You should not have admitted to it either," his aunt snapped. "Had I known you would form such an attachment to Odessa, I would never have brought you with me when I visited my dear Emily."

Hayden ignored his aunt's diatribe. He'd heard most of it before under different circumstances. Odessa's mother, Emily, had been his aunt's favorite cousin until she wed the notorious, lowbred Angus Whitehall, known more for lending money to impoverished titles than his legitimate business activities. Odessa had been shunned by her mother's family who considered her unacceptable. And Hayden, an odd, chubby child who was far too intelligent for his own good, was declared strange by the previous Duke of Ware. A bond had formed between them because they were different. Living on the fringe of everyone else's existence. They weren't actually blood relatives, but Odessa was Hayden's closest friend and he her fiercest protector. They were both related to Lady Curchon, so it was only natural to declare themselves cousins.

"Neither Odessa nor Emerson would thank me for allowing Lady Tamsin to be torn apart by Lady Longwood even if I was inclined to do so. Which I am not." Jasmine once again caught in Hayden's nostrils along with the heat of her skin beneath his lips. "If I must make such a sacrifice and wed her, I will do so." A wispy press of desire rolled over his torso at the thought.

"Do not say such things, Your Grace. Do not even give voice to it. Her mother was an actress and then her father's mistress before they wed." His aunt shook her head. "She broke Thompson's nose. Her reputation is poor, and she is given to brazen behavior. There is no circumstance under which she is suitable, especially for you. But— your connection to Odessa may be the key."

Hayden watched her pace back and forth, tapping her finger against her lips, pausing only to glance in the direction of the terrace which was now deserted.

"I will not have Odessa maligned. Nor Lady Aurora."

"Who?" Lady Curchon stopped before him.

"Emerson's youngest sister."

"Oh, yes." His aunt waved her hand as if Lady Aurora and her entire future were of no import. "I think I know what we must do. It will silence the gossip and harm no one's reputation, especially yours. Your unwelcome relationship to Odessa will now prove useful. And most everyone knows you have no interest in such things."

"What things?"

"Dalliances. Assignations and the like. You are of a scientific bent and thus pay little attention to things of a flirtatious manner."

Not entirely true. He was greatly interested in Tamsin Sinclair, for instance. But when he was faced with an aunt and mother, both united in their determination to have him wed as soon as possible, it seemed easier to pretend he cared for nothing but his research. Hayden was exhausted at having young ladies paraded before him.

"So this is less a dalliance more a…vague sort of attachment. One that might well fade over the summer months." His aunt came towards him. "You are marginally related, after all, through Odessa's marriage to Emerson. Perhaps you share common interests. It is unfortunate that after retiring to the country, you realized your attachment was more of a friendly nature and because you realized the duchess would never approve." She clapped her hands. "That is exceedingly neat, is it not? Tidy. But it will require an effort on your part for a short time."

"What sort of effort? I am nearly finished with my research and can't afford to be distracted." Even if the distraction was Tamsin Sinclair.

"If you ignore Lady Tamsin, tonight will be regarded as a sordid indiscretion on your part, which will upset the duchess and damage your reputation. She'll be viewed as no better than a harlot. *But*—if we make it appear that there is something undefinable between the two of you, a friendship of sorts, or a vague attachment that will merely run its course over the summer—" She shrugged. "Then your association tonight becomes much more innocent in nature. Lady Longwood will still gossip, but society will be less likely to listen. Miss Maplehurst and Odessa will have to be informed in case of questions and it will mean you'll have to be in Lady Tamsin's company." She placed a hand on his arm in assurance. "Briefly. And she'll have to agree. I can't imagine that she would not, although I do not think Lady Tamsin gives a fig for her reputation."

"Tell her you will sponsor Lady Aurora."

His aunt made a sound. "I do not think—"

"It would be wise to do so, aunt. It will convince her. And Lady Aurora is completely innocent and does not need her future ruined because of my careless behavior. It was an accident."

Somewhat.

Lady Curchon took his arm and nodded. "Very well. Then let us begin this charade."

CHAPTER THREE

T AMSIN SAT IN the drawing room of Emerson House with Aurora having tea and practicing decorum. Earlier, it had been dancing with their instructor Monsieur Pierre, a slim Frenchman with a tiny mustache hovering like some sort of caterpillar above his lip. Aurora took to heart each complicated step she was taught, but Tamsin flailed about miserably in a hopeless manner. At least according to Monsieur Pierre who deemed her unteachable. The dance instructor despaired of Tamsin *ever* dancing at a ball, which was just as well because after Lady Curchon's event earlier this week, Tamsin wasn't sure she wanted to ever attend another gathering of the sort.

Andrew, smiling and dressed in a coat the color of newly turned earth, had popped in during the dance lesson, offering to partner Aurora. He declined to dance with Tamsin because, as he said, he valued his toes. Her brother *did not* flail about but moved gracefully around the room, delighting Monsieur Pierre.

House parties, Drew advised Tamsin as he waltzed by her with a wink.

Andrew attended a great many house parties, shooting parties, and fox hunts, though the only hunting her brother ever did was beneath a woman's skirts. He was bound to run afoul of a jealous husband one day or perhaps find himself accused of cheating at cards, something else he was rather good at. Not the cheating, but card playing. Drew was on his way out of London once again with a group of acquaintances all destined for a month-long house party in Bath. He had graciously offered to escort Lady Penthwaite whose husband was far too elderly to make the trip.

And far too old to tup her properly.

Drew was definitely a rake. A gambler. Completely charming and irresponsible. Harmless, really, unless you were a husband about to be cuckolded or were poor at whist. He'd found a group of like-minded gentlemen and spent his time flitting about enjoying himself. Tamsin didn't deny Drew his pleasures. Truly. And she was vastly relieved he would not be in London if and when a scandal broke out concerning the Duke of Ware. Her brother might be inspired to defend her honor.

"My dears." Aunt Lottie appeared in the doorway, silver curls bouncing against her temples. "How was your dancing lesson? Has Monsieur Pierre already departed?"

"A short time ago." Aurora set her teacup down. "He proclaims my steps flawless. Perfect. I will not embarrass myself when I come out."

At least one of them would not. Tamsin was another matter entirely.

She looked down at her own cup of tea thinking of Lady Longwood's diatribe. If that harpy had her way, Aurora's come out would not be the lovely occasion her sister hoped for. Instead, it would be ruined by speculation about Tamsin and Ware. How the *ton* would laugh over the irony of Tamsin first breaking the nose of one brother and possibly having seduced the other.

She eyed the older woman as Aunt Lottie took a seat beside Aurora. Nothing more had been said to Tamsin about Ware. If Lady Longwood was busy painting her as some sort of ambitious trollop, not a whiff of such talk had made its way to the house on Bruton Street. Not that they had many callers save for Mr. Patchahoo, the family solicitor. Aunt Lottie had written to Odessa, but Tamsin and the older woman were both in agreement Jordan should *not* be told.

He was busy restoring River Crest and overseeing the start of the mining operation at Dunnings. Jordan didn't need to once more bear the brunt of his sister's reckless behavior. At least, not yet.

"Wonderful," Aunt Lottie said, placing an arm on Aurora's shoulder. "You've worked so hard, dearest. I have it on good authority that Mrs. Cherry is of a mind to reward you. Currant scones. Warm and just out of the oven."

"Currant is my favorite." Aurora popped off the settee without another word and hurried to the kitchens as Aunt Lottie must have known she would.

"A proper young lady would have summoned a maid to bring the scones to her," Aunt Lottie said with a resigned sigh. "I'll have to remind Aurora. But not today. There is much we need to discuss. As you know, I have called upon Lady Curchon. She has advised me on a solution to our problem."

"I had been hoping my oversized, rude problem would simply go away."

"Not with Lady Longwood casting speculation about what her daughter may or may not have seen or heard at Lady Curchon's. And do not refer to the duke in such a way. Ware has agreed to heed his aunt's advice. I am suggesting you do as well."

"I see." Tamsin folded her hands in her lap. "I am to be sent away." She had prepared herself for this instance. There didn't seem to be any other recourse. "I agree with Lady Curchon that it would be better if I disappear from London and never return. My family can publicly denounce me. Ware can claim I threw myself at him." Her fingers twisted. "I will become a pariah, which I must say is unfair given the duke is to blame."

"Good lord, you've grown dramatic." Aunt Lottie took up a biscuit. "Must have been all those plays your mother had you perform when you were a child. Though I suppose such skills are going to come in handy."

"It is no great punishment to reside in the country for the remainder of my days, Aunt Lottie. Truthfully, I don't care for London. If I stay away long enough, everyone will forget there ever was a Lady Tamsin Sinclair. I will be the shamed spinster who is only trotted out on rare occasions. It won't be so bad, I suppose. At least I can ride in breeches and not worry overmuch what anyone thinks. But I will request that Ware not be welcomed to River Crest. Given the circumstances."

"No one ever truly forgets, Tamsin. I would know because that's what *I* did," Aunt Lottie informed her. "Ran off to the country to settle into life as a scandalous spinster until Odessa's mother took pity on me. It isn't nearly as much fun as you would imagine. I took up knitting and even that didn't help. And Odessa will always welcome her cousin no matter what has happened. There is another way."

A deep sigh of resignation left Tamsin. This would be worse than becoming a pariah. The usual solution in these types of situations. "Fine. I agree to wed him. Ware."

Aunt Lottie choked on a biscuit. "I beg your pardon?"

Tamsin swallowed. "If it will spare Aurora. I don't like him in the least. He's reputed to be quite odd, which was proven at our first meeting. Arrogant and far too obsessed with moths. Overly large. I can't imagine what his tailor must go through. But—"

Aunt Lottie peered at her. "Good lord. You're serious." She laughed so hard, great tears spilled down her cheeks as she slapped the cushion of the settee with one hand. "No, Tamsin, nothing of the sort."

"But when a young lady is compromised—"

"You were not compromised. Ware has not offered for you. There is no need for either of you to suffer needlessly. Lady Curchon would rather receive the cut direct by the queen herself than have you wed the Duke of Ware. Not to mention Ware's mother would have your head on a pike. The dowager duchess would *never* accept a girl with your pedigree into the family. I recall when Maxwell, that was Ware's middle brother, had an indiscretion with the daughter of a baron when he was barely out of Eton. Swept under the rug though the girl was thoroughly ruined. But her family was of little import and her dowry nonexistent."

"What a bunch of bloody snobs." Tamsin stood. "So, I'm not good enough for him."

"In a manner of speaking."

"He grows more awful with every moment."

"No liberties were taken. He plucked a moth off your knee."

He kissed the inside of my thigh.

Tamsin could have imagined the light brush of his lips; after all, she'd been in shock at being accosted in the gardens. "No," she said with a nod. "There were no liberties taken. So, if I am not to become a pariah or be forced to wed him, what is left?"

Aunt Lottie placed a hand on her arm. "You are not the first young lady to be caught in a questionable situation with a gentleman which does not culminate in marriage. We are fortunate this incident occurred at the end of the Season. The memories of society are prone to grow thin over the summer if the gossip ends. Lady Longwood has complicated matters."

"We can have her kidnapped and placed on a boat for India." Tamsin strode to the sideboard. Whiskey was in order. "I'll volunteer to bludgeon and toss her in a sack." She poured herself a healthy dollop of the amber liquid and took a sip, allowing the heat to sit on her tongue. "My concern is for Aurora, not myself."

"You will pretend a vague...attachment to Ware, and he to you. For a time. More friendship than anything of a romantic nature."

Tamsin regarded her in shock. "A *what?*"

"A vague attachment. Association. Acquaintance. Call it what you will. Doing so will help make the situation appear less sordid. You are—distantly related. Ware considers Odessa his cousin and she is married to your brother. It is not impossible that you and Ware could have struck up a friendship of sorts. Perhaps you found you had much in common. Pretending an attachment to Ware, even for a short time, gives the illusion that you weren't merely dallying with him in the garden. Or attempting to seduce him. Lady Longwood will have a difficult time convincing society otherwise, especially since you will be under Ware's protection and Lady Curchon's."

"Splendid." She had done nothing but sit on a bench in the garden and look where it had gotten her.

"Perhaps you might espouse that you have an inclination towards things of a scientific nature," Aunt Lottie continued. "You were naturally drawn to Ware because of this shared interest."

Tamsin coughed on her whiskey. "No one in their right mind will believe that I have formed a friendship with Ware, let alone that I am fascinated by insects."

"They will if you play your part." Aunt Lottie threw up her hands. "This will not be difficult, Tamsin. Ware will escort you about for intellectual pursuits. No one will expect him to take you to the theater or the opera, for instance."

"Why not?" Tamsin asked. "That seems acceptable."

"Well because Ware—is probably the least romantically inclined male in London. His brothers and father were all rakes of one sort or another, as I've mentioned. Ware seems to have gone in the opposite direction. At any rate, after a few weeks of such tedious, boring displays of a vague attachment from both of you, the gossips will fall silent in disappointment as they depart town. You will both retire to the country. Over the summer months, Lady Curchon will put out that her nephew's attachment to you faded away. Most will assume your friendship ended because it could go no further. The duchess would never approve. You see, very simple."

"You're mad. So is Lady Curchon." The entire idea was idiotic.

"This *will* work. And it is far better than I hoped for. I have been worried for you and Aurora. I didn't want to have to go to Jordan and explain this situation to him. It is an equitable solution for all concerned. Goodness, in my youth I had to pretend to care for a certain gentleman for several months before the Season ended and I was finally free."

No surprise. Aunt Lottie had quite a checkered past. "I'll assume liberties were taken in that instance."

"Possibly." Aunt Lottie shrugged. "Aurora will be spared, Tamsin."

"Yes, but I will not. I'll have to be in Ware's company." She paused. "He called me a rodent."

"I believe," Aunt Lottie said carefully, "that Ware said you *sounded* like a rodent. He is difficult, but also brilliant and well-respected in scientific circles. He studied at Oxford as a naturalist before determining that his area of focus should be insects. It is a poor twist of fate that had him inheriting the title. He *is* a duke, Tamsin."

She turned and sipped on her whiskey. It was a fair offer. She wouldn't be labeled a harlot; Aurora would be spared. Lady Longwood had no choice but to be silent or else risk offending Ware.

"Only a few weeks," Aunt Lottie assured her. "A carriage ride or two. A walk in the park. As I said, the museum. You could attend a lecture at that society he belongs to. Vague amusements which could be interpreted as either friendship or courtship. That will make it easier once we return to London. You can pretend that while he's broken your heart, Ware still regards you with fondness and keeps you under his protection."

Tamsin snorted. "Oh, good grief. This sounds like one of those lurid romances Aurora so adores."

The rebellious part of her wanted to ignore the offer. Toss aside Lady Curchon's thoughtfully nuanced plan. It wasn't as if she wished to marry Ware, but knowing even Aunt Lottie considered her to be so far beneath wedding the duke was rather humiliating. No one considered her a lady, which given her previous behavior wasn't unwarranted. But—

"Lady Curchon has agreed to sponsor Aurora's Season." Aunt Lottie interrupted Tamsin's thoughts. "That is surely worth your participation in this ruse." Her fingers drummed against one thigh. "I do not understand your hesitation; you have far more to lose than Ware."

"You're correct." Tamsin didn't think that entirely true. If Lady Longwood continued to spread, no matter how discreetly, word of the incident in the garden, Ware *might* be forced into something more than a ruse with Tamsin. That was what was behind Lady Curchon's generous offer.

Tamsin sucked a mouthful of whiskey between her teeth, savoring the taste. Did it matter what Lady Curchon's motives were? Or Ware's? Aurora would have a brilliant debut in society and such a sponsorship would go a long way in silencing any sort of talk about the Sinclairs. That was really all that mattered to Tamsin.

"I suppose," she murmured. "A few more weeks in London won't be terrible."

CHAPTER FOUR

"YOUR GRACE. HOW unexpected."

Tamsin swept into the drawing room, hands clasped before her, prepared to be as amiable as possible given she'd only received news of his arrival mere minutes ago. Several days had passed with no word from Ware or Lady Curchon as to when or how this charade would begin.

And after what she'd overheard yesterday, the need for such a ruse had become abundantly clear.

Aurora had begged for a new novel and Tamsin agreed to a trip to the book seller. After some consideration, she had decided it might be helpful for the sake of this charade if she knew something of what Ware studied. Emerson House wasn't exactly bursting with tomes on insects. So after sending Aurora off in the direction of the romantic tripe she favored, Tamsin headed in the opposite direction, browsing and selecting several volumes that might prove useful.

As she made her way back to collect Aurora, two well-dressed ladies passed by.

Their eyes roamed over Tamsin with calculated disdain. One whispered to the other, sharp tongue and claws ready to inflict damage should they so choose.

Tamsin shifted slightly so that they could both catch a glimpse of the books clutched against her chest. One was a catalog of insects in England by a man named John Curtis who belonged to the same insect-loving society in London as Ware. The second, a volume specifically on moths and butterflies, was written by two French men whose names Tamsin didn't even attempt to pronounce. Nor did she speak a word of the language.

Her intent was to ask the clerk if the book was available in English.

Their eyes flicked down to the books in Tamsin's arms. One raised a brow in disbelief. Another whisper. Then they both disappeared down another aisle, their pointed opinions on Tamsin thankfully muted.

She wasn't sure what she would do had they insulted her outright. Something reckless and stupid, no doubt. But the two women had served a purpose with their disdain. Tamsin needed Ware if her reputation was to survive the onslaught of Lady Longwood.

The marching about of a large person in the drawing room brought Tamsin's attention back to the present. She supposed she shouldn't have been surprised, given Ware's arrogance, that he would arrive to call on her without first sending a note.

Insect-loving scholar that he was, Ware was *still* a duke.

"I'm not sure why you think me unexpected, Lady Tamsin." His eyes, like a tarnished silver plate, narrowed as they took her in. "I've been instructed to call upon you and here I am." Bergamot and something earthy filled the air around him. The smell of wet leaves and damp soil.

He didn't look quite so large in Lady Curchon's garden.

Nor as imposing. True, she'd first assumed him to be some mad beast and wasn't quite ready to withdraw that opinion. The sheer breadth of his chest and shoulders must force his tailor to be mindful with fabric. Not to mention those giant, booted feet. Both covered with a hint of mud. His cravat appeared to have been tied by a child. A button was missing from his waistcoat. And there appeared to be a small twig attached to his shoulder.

"Shouldn't you offer me tea?" He marched about the drawing

room dropping bits of dirt onto the rug. "A scone perhaps?"

Tamsin was about to tell Ware to go hang, but bit her tongue, remembering the two discerning matrons at the book seller's.

"Of course, Your Grace," she returned politely. "Perhaps a scone or a handful of tiny villagers as well for you to snack on," she murmured under her breath before ringing for Holly, the Sinclair butler.

Ware stopped his tromping about. "Is that some sort of a jest, Lady Tamsin?"

Drat. He'd heard her. "Not at all, Your Grace," she demurred.

A disgruntled sound left him. "I'm not here to discuss your new bonnet. Or the weather," Ware informed her. "Or something equally tedious."

"What an enormous relief." She tried to keep the sarcasm from her words and failed. "Needless conversation is unnecessary. You've a twig on your shoulder, by the way."

Ware brushed off the twig with a flick of one finger. "I was...busy earlier and recently reminded of my appointment here today."

There was also a leaf stuck to one massive thigh and what looked like the fur of some animal around one ankle.

"Something to do with insects, I suppose. Either that," she gestured to state of his clothing, "or you were wandering the woods burying a body perhaps."

Ware stopped pacing around like a caged tiger and stared down at her. The very edge of his mouth twitched. "*Insecta*, Lady Tamsin. And I doubt I would ever care about someone enough to murder them and hide the body."

"How comforting," she replied without blinking.

"I will assume all the pertinent facts have been shared with you as to how we will proceed," Ware growled. "I assure you, I am no more pleased by this turn of events than you are. Stop staring at me."

"Apologies, Your Grace. It is only that I have never seen another human being quite so large." Or so careless in their appearance. "Your tailor is to be applauded. Do you suppose you are descended from Viking stock?"

"I find you unpleasant," he bit out.

"The feeling is mutual." Tamsin gave him a brilliant smile.

"I only wanted the *colostygia pectinataria*."

"And I merely wished to cool myself in the night air and avoid Lady Longwood. It is unfortunate neither of us succeeded."

Where was Holly with the tea cart? Tamsin could do with an interruption just now.

The line of his jaw grew taut. "Were you there purposefully?" His voice lowered to a rumble. "That is what Lady Curchon believes. That you were lying in wait."

"I beg your pardon, Your Grace?" Her hands immediately curled into fists. It was one thing to be insulted by two strangers at the book seller, another to be accused of deceit in her own home.

"Well, you were sitting alone, legs spread out. Skirts hiked up. Were you waiting for me to happen upon you or did I interrupt a previous assignation? I'm curious."

"Of course," she said, lifting her chin. "I intentionally put the moth on my knee to entice you. I also had a bag of caterpillars stashed beneath the bench in case you didn't fancy the moth."

Ware raised a coal black brow. "By the way, my lady. Punching me," he nodded to the fists at her sides, "will not help matters."

"But it might make me feel quite a bit better."

"As it did after you broke my brother's nose?"

"I don't *like* you," she hissed.

"Yes, we've already agreed. Where is Miss Maplehurst?"

"You are—" The remainder of Tamsin's scathing tirade was stopped by the appearance of Aunt Lottie.

"Your Grace, how lovely of you to call," Aunt Lottie said smoothly, glancing between Tamsin and Ware. "I've been expecting you."

Ware shot Tamsin a triumphant look.

"You might have informed me, Aunt Lottie." Tamsin forced her hands to relax.

Holly arrived at the door with tea and an assortment of pastries. His eyes widened at the sight of Ware before he carefully set down the tray. He nodded to Tamsin, casting another glance at Ware, and retreated, closing the door behind him.

Aunt Lottie waited until the click of the door sounded before speaking again. "I could hear you arguing down the hall. Thankfully, Lady Aurora is in the garden with a book, but the servants were probably listening." She gave them both a stern look. "I beg you to keep your voices down. No one, *including* me, is pleased with this situation. If you must, think of Aurora," she instructed Tamsin. "And you, Your Grace, consider your reputation. Or if that doesn't work, imagine society deeming you your father's son."

Ware's cheeks pinked at the remark. He immediately reached into his coat and retrieved a small notebook. Taking out a pencil, he scowled at Tamsin before scribbling something. Shutting the little book, he put it and the pencil back into his coat.

"What are you doing?" Tamsin had an unwelcome feeling that whatever Ware committed to paper had something to do with her.

"Research notes." He purposefully turned his chin from Tamsin. "I have set forth the agenda for the illusion my aunt has set forth, Miss Maplehurst. The length will be approximately three weeks, possibly a month. Lady Curchon has assured me that will be adequate."

"A life sentence," Tamsin muttered.

"I can hear you." The duke glared at her.

"You were meant to," she replied.

"No more than two carriage rides through the park." Ware's large forefinger shot up. "One stroll through the park, though we may do two strolls and one carriage ride. One afternoon visiting the museum." Another finger. "One lecture at the Entomological Society." He gave Tamsin a sideways look. "Do not embarrass me."

Tamsin bit back her retort. Maybe she would punch him in the nose before all his insect-loving friends.

"During the walk through the park, we can be observed looking for specimens—"

"I have no intention of sticking a pin through anything," Tamsin said defiantly. "Unless it is you."

The side of Ware's mouth twitched once more. "There will be no pin sticking, my lady."

"A pity."

"An intolerable dinner given by Lady Curchon, the date of which is undetermined at present," Ware continued in a clipped tone, ignoring her. "Near the end of this farce, I think. That should be enough to dispel the gossip or at least give the appearance there is nothing sordid about our acquaintance. Lady Tamsin will retire to country, as will I." He snuck a look at Tamsin. "Though not together."

"Certainly not," Tamsin snapped.

"During our time away from town," Ware ignored her outburst, "Lady Curchon will put out that *alas*, our attachment did not blossom into something more, but our familial association and friendship remains. We are all spared." Silver flashed at Tamsin. "Had you only remained still—"

"Your Grace," Aunt Lottie interjected. "I've written to Odessa, and she is aware of the situation. We have chosen to keep the situation from Lord Emerson and Lady Aurora for now." She looked at Tamsin. "I expect that Andrew will hear some of the gossip while he's in Bath. But he is discreet. Your brother will ask you first about the situation."

"A carriage ride first then." Ware said, grabbing a scone from the plate before him. "I'll retrieve you two days hence. While we are driving through the park, be sure to look at me with adoration," he instructed in a condescending tone.

Aunt Lottie's brows rose in the air. "Adoration, Your Grace?"

"Well..." Ware sat back, eyes glinting like mirrors at Tamsin with no small amount of amusement. "We *are* supposed to have an attachment, aren't we?"

CHAPTER FIVE

THE FOLLOWING MORNING, Tamsin once more rushed into the drawing room after being informed that Ware, who wasn't supposed to appear until tomorrow as they agreed, had instead decided to bless her with his presence *today*.

"Your Grace." Tamsin took a deep breath, resolved not to be rattled by him.

"Finally. I've been waiting a quarter of an hour for you."

"I apologize to have kept you waiting, Your Grace," Tamsin said in as polite a tone as she could muster. "Forgive me, but our carriage ride was scheduled for tomorrow. Miss Maplehurst is not available today. She has taken Aurora shopping. I have no chaperone."

Ware shrugged. "The carriage top will be down. You are well past the age of a chaperone at any rate." Ware glanced at the clock above the fireplace, frowning. "Ancient, in fact," he said.

Tamsin's lips tightened. "How kind of you to say."

Ware came a step closer, bringing with him that intoxicating smell of bergamot and forest. For such an unpleasant person, he smelled quite delicious. "The lecture is in less than one hour. We'll ride through the park after the lecture."

"Lecture?"

"Stephens is speaking on beetles today. He's written a book. *The Manual of Beetles*. And there are specimens to view. I don't want to miss it."

Tamsin imagined a room filled with dozens of dead insects stuck with pins surrounded by dusty, unpleasant gentlemen such as Ware. "Sounds delightful."

"I do hope you won't faint, Lady Tamsin. I'll be compelled to carry you out, which will cause talk and not help our cause."

"I never faint." She lifted her chin. "I'll just grab my bonnet."

He marched out ahead of her to the carriage, not waiting to see if she followed, only pausing when he reached the bottom step. A footman appeared to assist them into Ware's carriage, and again Tamsin was struck by how much larger Ware happened to be than everyone else. He towered over the poor footman. How could he possibly be comfortable in a carriage made for someone of normal height?

Ware drummed his massive fingers along the side of the carriage as he waited for her, not bothering to hide his impatience. "Beetles, Lady Tamsin." The silver of his eyes caught along her bodice briefly. "They won't wait forever."

"I daresay they will, Your Grace. Aren't the beetles dead?" Tamsin inquired as she settled herself in the carriage.

A grunt was her only response as Ware sat across from her, rocking the vehicle as the driver snapped the reins. His legs stretched across the aisle sideways, but still he had to bend his knees a bit.

"Are you certain you don't possess a Viking ancestor?"

Ware rolled his eyes, pulled out his notebook, and proceeded to ignore her.

At least the day was sunny and warm, a rarity in London. Glorious. Even if she had to spend it in Ware's company. The sides of her bonnet, a useless accessory in Tamsin's opinion, kept her face shaded when all she wanted to do was lift her cheeks to the sun. But it did keep her hidden from Ware, who when he wasn't ignoring her, studied Tamsin with cool intensity.

Mr. Stephens had written Tamsin's recently purchased book on beetles, though she didn't tell Ware she'd been reading up on insects. The books she'd found were dreadfully dull. Tamsin hadn't gotten past the first page of Stephens's beetle book before she nodded off. Which was to be expected. She only wanted to sound somewhat knowledgeable. Not become an entomologist.

"Is there a reason you decided to bring me to the lecture? I assumed our first outing was to be a carriage ride?"

A touch of pink colored Ware's cheeks.

It was the second time she'd seen him blush. The sight reminded her of a boy who'd been caught eating all the biscuits on the tea tray. Disarming in a man of Ware's stature.

"We have a vague attachment based on shared interests of an intellectual nature. A lecture is perfect."

"Do you really think the gossips will be haunting the streets at your insect society—"

"The Entomological Society."

Tamsin waved her hand. "Yes. I can't imagine Lady Longwood, if she is even still in London, would attend such an event."

"We will be taking the long way back from the Entomological Society. Through the park. Bound to be loads of vultures hanging from the trees there, don't you think?"

Tamsin looked out onto the passing street. "You're going to count today as *two* of our outings, aren't you? A carriage ride *and* a lecture. You didn't forget the day. You planned this."

His cheeks pinked once more, but his eyes dipped to Tamsin's bosom, lingering for a moment before withdrawing. "Possibly."

⇒⇒⇒⇐⇐⇐

OF COURSE, HAYDEN hadn't mixed up his days. He never forgot a date. Or an appointment. Mother thought him the most thoughtful of sons because he had never once missed her birthday, even when everyone else had.

Hayden turned his head from Tamsin to view the passing street.

He merely wanted to see her.

Stunning, was the first thought in his mind upon seeing Tamsin at Emerson House earlier that week. He'd been struck speechless. Which in turn annoyed him. Forcing himself to stomp about her drawing room, Hayden hurled insults and accused her of trying to entrap him as a way to ward himself from her. Otherwise, he'd be reduced to gaping at her like some lovestruck swain.

Why couldn't he find her unappealing? Lady Penelope was regarded as a great beauty, yet Hayden hadn't felt an ounce of attraction for her.

Not like Tamsin.

So, he decided the wise thing to do would be to condense their interactions lest he behave inappropriately. Today would count as one outing and one carriage ride as she'd guessed.

Tamsin was not only lovely to look at, but intelligent.

He glared at her from across the carriage.

She smiled sweetly back at him.

Hayden's lips had been on her inner thigh. He could still feel the heat of her skin beneath the silk on his mouth. He *had* taken liberties, of the sort no one expected Hayden to ever be capable of.

As the carriage rolled to the Entomological Society, Hayden thought of taking Tamsin's feet, discarding her slippers, and slowly sliding the stockings off her legs. He would lift her skirts and put his mouth—

He had to bite his lip to keep from groaning out loud. The fabric of his trousers tightened.

Danaus plexippus.

Reciting the Latin names for various insects often helped clear his mind.

Actias luna.

Acraea andromacha.

Hayden kept on reciting names until what felt like hours later, the carriage finally stopped before the Entomological Society. If he survived today in Tamsin's company without making an idiot of himself, Hayden would count it as a miracle.

CHAPTER SIX

T AMSIN STRUGGLED TO keep her eyes open as Ware's carriage rolled through the park, but the unmitigated boredom of the afternoon and the warmth of the day conspired to keep her only half alert. Walking out to the carriage, Tamsin had only been partially awake. Honestly, she'd *tried* to enjoy the beetles.

"I don't believe anyone noticed, Your Grace."

A snort of derision was her answer. Ware had barely spoken to her since leaving the Entomological Society, which had been as dull and dusty as Tamsin envisioned. Worse even. There was a cure for insomnia and Tamsin had found it. Beetle lectures.

Ware was quite put out with her.

"I only closed my eyes for a moment." In truth, Tamsin had dozed off midway through Stephens's presentation. He possessed a mind-numbing monotone which dulled the senses. She'd only awoken when Ware nudged her in the ribs with his elbow. He might have left a bruise.

"You didn't have to poke me so hard."

"You were snoring."

"I wasn't."

Ware gave her a scathing look. "Like a horse grabbing for oats in his stall."

Well, that wasn't very flattering. Tamsin knew a thing or two about horses and didn't care to be compared to one. Still, she did feel badly about dozing off.

"I thought the Entomological Society to be fascinating," she ventured.

Imagine, an entire building populated with an assortment of mini-Wares. Every gentleman in attendance possessed a scholarly way of speaking and basked in the superiority of their own intelligence. They tossed about Latin as if it was a secret language only to be used in those hallowed halls, never calling a butterfly…a bloody butterfly.

Ware led her about, his giant hand firmly wrapped around her elbow. He made an introduction or two, but no one seemed overly concerned with making her acquaintance. Tamsin had been terrified the subject of moths would be broached. Beetles. Crickets. But no one so much as asked if she liked insects. She counted three other women in attendance, all older and far more bookish in appearance than Tamsin, though she wore a dress of plain indigo with an exceptionally high neckline which was absent of any adornment.

She decided to embrace being a bluestocking, if only for short time.

The entire ride to the lecture, Tamsin questioned Lady Curchon's wisdom in visiting the Entomological Society. But once they arrived at the tidy brick building, she understood. The society was near several busy streets. The carriage top was down. She and Ware were visible to dozens of discerning eyes as they made their way to the Entomological Society. Ambitious harlots of the sort Tamsin was accused of being didn't flock to lectures on beetles.

Once inside, Ware's attention had barely strayed from the glass cases of specimens lining the walls. He ceased to acknowledge her presence beside him, his attention taken by the surroundings. Tamsin was no more than a leaf stuck to his coat. Or a twig.

Ware escorted her to a chair before the podium, ensuring she was settled. The drone of Mr. Stephens discussing beetles and the warmth of the room had Tamsin's eyes floating closed in mere minutes. She wiggled, trying to get comfortable on the chair. Her head drifted closer to Ware's shoulder, which was surprisingly hard with muscle. Solid. Like a grouchy pillow. He smelled of earth and leaves, bergamot, and soap.

Tamsin looked out at the park rolling by. Who cared how Ware smelled? It was only shaving soap, though it didn't look as if he bothered with shaving every day. And he really should. That coupled with the state of his clothing left Tamsin to consider that Ware's valet was terrible and should be fired at once.

"I apologize again." No one paid the least attention to her at the Entomological Society. She could have crawled into Ware's lap and all eyes would have been on Stephens and his miraculous work with beetles. Tamsin might have straddled those wide, heavy thighs and not one person would have noticed.

Ware shifted; the fabric of his trousers pulled, revealing the layers of sinew beneath.

Tamsin hurriedly looked away, her pulse beating a rhythm in her neck. She was *not* ogling Ware, merely observing him. He was an oddly curious person.

Taking a deep breath of air, she filled her nostrils with the scent of the river and rotted vegetation. Mind clear once more, Tamsin dared another glance in his direction. Ware had pulled out the notebook he carried and was furiously scribbling away. Her eyes ran over his coat. At first glance, one might consider Ware...*lumpy*. But now Tamsin suspected he carried a great deal of curious things on his person. If an interesting insect alit on the coach, she was sure Ware would immediately produce a tiny glass vial, as he had at Lady Curchon's.

The notebook was splayed open in one big palm. A pencil between his fingers. He would look up for a moment, then lower his head, the lead moving swiftly across the page. Ware was completely absorbed in whatever had caught his attention to the exclusion of all else. Her hair could catch on fire. Or her skirts. A flock of birds might attack the carriage. But Ware would keep scribbling away.

Tamsin found it irritating. She didn't like to be ignored.

"What is so important?" She nodded to the tiny book in his hand. "You seem to scratch at those pages incessantly. Is it for notes? You didn't take any during the lecture."

"How would you know? You were asleep," he said without looking up.

Tamsin looked up at the sky seeking divine intervention.

"I've apologized, Your Grace. Several times. Beetles are much more tedious than I was prepared for." She sat back and waited for him to comment. Or at least look up from the notebook. When he continued to behave as if she wasn't there, Tamsin exhaled. Loudly.

"Drawings of various insects," he rumbled, the sound plucking at her skin. "I also note scientific oddities as I encounter them."

"Scientific oddities?" That sounded somewhat more interesting than beetles.

Ware raised his eyes, catching hers for an instant.

He really had *lovely* eyes for such a bear of a man. Lashes, black as coal and lush, hovering over those harshly cut cheekbones. Tamsin wouldn't have called Ware handsome exactly. His mouth was far too wide. Features almost too masculine and far from perfect—except for the nose. Striking was what Tamsin would have said of Ware. Once you caught sight of him, *really* saw him, it was difficult to look at anything else. Though his personality left much to be desired.

I do not find Ware attractive, she reminded herself. Only somewhat interesting.

"Unusual things. Or unnatural," he stated.

"What sort of unusual things?"

The pencil paused. "Is this an interrogation of some sort?"

"I am making pleasant conversation, Your Grace. If we must endure a handful of carriage rides—"

"Possibly one more." He regarded her with determination. "One

51

carriage ride has already been satisfied by today's little adventure." His large shoulders gave a shrug. "Though if I must bring you back to the park for a stroll, I suppose we'll have to take the carriage there."

"That doesn't count as a carriage ride. Now back to these oddities. Can you explain further? I think it would be helpful for me to understand if anyone were to ask. For the sake of the illusion we are creating."

"No one will ask." The notebook slapped shut. "But very well, I once took Odessa to see a two-headed snake. Twins that did not separate. *That* is a scientific oddity. In addition to my research, I find such things of great interest."

"I have twin brothers," Tamsin said. "Though they are not identical. Much like the *arctia caja*" she informed him, trying to keep the satisfaction out of her tone. "No two are exactly alike. The spots on their wings are all different." She pursed her lips. "Tiger moths."

Ware did not look the least impressed. "I'm aware of the common name of *arctia caja*, my lady." The low rasp rolled over her skin. "I am a naturalist and a student of entomology. Your Latin pronunciation is terrible, by the way. Now," he gave a careless wave of one big hand, "I can ascertain no purpose in regaling me with a handful of details any schoolboy could glean from a book, Lady Tamsin."

Tamsin deflated and fell back against the seat. "I was trying to take an interest so we might converse when we are together."

"Well, stop it. We've only the museum, a walk in the park, *possibly* one more carriage ride, and a grand finale of a dinner party to attend. You can spout off your little facts over the soup course."

Tamsin wished she had something to throw at him.

"Have you always been so difficult? I fail to see the harm in being agreeable towards each other. This situation, I might remind you, is not of my making."

"You fussed."

"What else should I have done? You were beneath my skirts. Your mouth—"

"You have a vivid imagination," Ware interrupted, his cheeks turning the color of a rosebud. "And no matter how much Latin you spout, it is unlikely anyone would ever mistake you for a student of entomology or even a bluestocking. I beg you, stop speaking." He reopened the notebook he held. "You're making my temples ache with your chattering."

Ware had a tell. The pinking of his cheeks. Tamsin *hadn't* imagined the brush of his lips along her thigh, no matter how he might wish to deny it. She should have been outraged, but instead, the thought he'd pressed his mouth along her skin was strangely arousing.

"Fine." She tilted her chin lest he see the blush rising on her own cheeks. "Go back to your scribbles. That tiny pencil looks ridiculous in your giant hands, by the way."

Ware raised his chin, eyes gleaming like the underside of the moon, perhaps. Or the shine of pewter. The breeze ruffled through his thick hair, giving him a wild, somewhat dangerous appearance. Not at all like an overly intelligent scholar.

"I watched you break his nose." His voice roughened. "Thompson. I heard the crunch. I was seated in our carriage enjoying my ice. Can't recall the flavor."

"You were there?" Tamsin stuttered. "At Gunter's?"

"I was."

The act which had led to her family's dismissal from London. To Dunnings and all that they had endured. The sides of her face pulled taut, as did the rest of her body at the knowledge that her reckless, rash behavior had been witnessed by him.

"I enjoyed the show." Ware's tone softened. "Thompson deserved the punch, in my opinion. He cried like an infant the entire ride home." He rotated the pencil between his thumb and finger, watching her without a hint of condemnation. "And the pencil doesn't look ridiculous in my hand." His head lowered back to the page before him.

Tamsin looked out across the park once more, pressing a palm to her midsection and considering his words.

Two young ladies, arms linked, laughed with each other as they strolled down the path while their maids trailed behind. One of the girls paused in her steps and pointed to Ware's carriage before whispering to her companion.

Tamsin kept perfectly still. This was the entire point of today's outing.

A gentleman on horseback tipped his hat to a richly clad woman in a carriage rolling in the other direction. He studied Tamsin discreetly from beneath the brim of his hat.

Tamsin was accustomed to being stared at, but that was not to say she enjoyed the attention. First, she'd been gawked at because of her parents, and then because of breaking a lordling's nose. Among other, less-well-known missteps. She would never be like those girls walking about the park, or the stunning woman in her lavender riding habit passing Ware's carriage. But Aurora could be.

That was the only reason Tamsin sat in this carriage with the Duke of Ware.

As for the duke's reasons for agreeing to escort her about? Aunt Lottie had been blunt about Ware's father and brothers when Tamsin asked. The three had been on a pleasure barge, surrounded by courtesans, when it sunk in the Thames. Others had survived, but not the previous duke or his two sons. Thompson and Maxwell had been too deep in their cups and a courtesan they were sharing. Neither of Ware's brothers could swim. But the duke had been restrained below with rope by his latest mistress. If the previous Duke of Ware knew how to swim, he hadn't had a chance to show his skill.

The gossip had enveloped London for months.

Tamsin understood better than anyone what it was like to have your family's scandal continuously batter you. She didn't fault Ware for choosing to engage in this ridiculous charade if it kept him from being compared to the other males in his family. Or worse, marry so far beneath him. It would be nice if he acknowledged the olive branch Tamsin extended, but honestly, they did not have to be friends. Not being enemies was enough.

Her head fell back against the squabs, mind drifting along with the sway of the carriage. Life had been harder at Dunnings, but in some respects, easier. No gossip. No Lady Longwood. No constant fear that her behavior wasn't suitable. Acres of petticoats and a corset now restrained Tamsin as much as society's demands. She would never be molded into something proper and respectable. But Tamsin could keep her family's name from once more being colored by unwelcome talk and censure. Aurora could have the future she deserved.

Tamsin snuck a peek at Ware. An almost wistful look softened his harsh features as he wrote in his notebook. Adoration, she thought. Probably over a new species of moth. Or maybe a beetle. She tried to picture Ware, massive form tiptoeing about the tall grass, just waiting for some spectacular insect to pop out so that he could study it.

The thought brought a smile to Tamsin's lips as she drifted off.

UNACCEPTABLE.

Hayden had spent the time since leaving the Entomological Society not making notes on the lecture but studying the spot just below Tamsin's ear. A tiny, sensitive place he longed to touch with the very tip of his tongue. Perhaps graze with his teeth.

Intolerable.

Hunger had been his constant companion today, but not for food, for Tamsin Sinclair.

His fingers grasped the pencil tighter, which did not look silly in his fingers, no matter what she claimed. Tamsin had only said so to annoy him.

Upon leading her inside the hallowed hall of the Entomological Society earlier, Hayden had been greeted with unexpected interest. His fellow entomologists were far too well-bred to allow the surprise at Tamsin's appearance to show on their faces, but not quick enough to hide their admiration of her person. Gossip about him and Tamsin *was* circulating about London, so their curiosity didn't surprise Hayden. But neither did he like it.

Pulling her closer into the shelter of his larger form, Hayden eyed his peers as if they were a pack of wolves and he in possession of the only sheep. Which was an apt analogy. There were only three female members of the Entomological Society and none of them were remotely attractive.

Tamsin had fluttered about, peering at the display cases while pretending great interest in the contents. Brows wrinkled in an appropriately studious manner, she nodded as he pointed out various types of beetles to her all the while whispering beneath her breath.

"Disgusting. Why does it have horns? Is this what you were digging for the other day?"

She drifted from his side only once to study a display of butterflies, frowning at the sight before piercing him with an accusing look.

When Tamsin had dozed off during the lecture, exhausted, he supposed, from having been exposed to so many insects, her head had fallen to nestle on his shoulder. Hayden barely took a breath, fearing he might wake her. Jasmine had rolled into his nose, drowning out the musty smell of the lecture hall. The feel of her soft feminine curves had Hayden mentally stripping the clothes from Tamsin's body during the entire lecture. Desire for her had curled between his thighs, making it difficult to concentrate.

A pity. Hayden rather liked beetles and Stephens.

Someone near him had coughed. A curious look was thrown his way. Resolved to avoid further attention, Hayden proceeded to poke Tamsin in the ribs with his elbow to force her awake. He hadn't had to fake his annoyance at her.

A tiny snort erupted from the beautiful woman across the carriage from him before she settled once more against the squabs with a contented sigh.

Saturnia pavonia.

Tyria jacobaeae.

When Tamsin had casually mentioned tiger moths earlier in a blatant effort to impress him, Hayden's cock had thickened to a battering ram in his trousers. The only thing that would possibly unhinge him more was if Tamsin decided to attack him with her fists again.

Inhaling slowly, Hayden counted to ten, instructing his cock to stand down. Reciting Latin wasn't helping in the least. The scent of the river filled his nostrils. The horses. Dirt. Grass.

Warm jasmine.

Damn it to hell.

Hayden didn't *want* to hunger for Lady Tamsin Sinclair, but his cock seemed to be ignoring the command. He was attempting to be honorable, something no other male in his family had ever been. He'd agreed to this stupid farce, hadn't he? Put aside his research to squire her about?

Kissed the inside of her thigh while trapped beneath her skirts.

As a lad of seventeen, watching a gorgeous, brave young girl break his brother's nose, Hayden had been *undone* by Tamsin Sinclair. That was the honest truth. Worse, he was *still* undone by her. The wise thing would have been to never agree to this mad scheme of his aunt's, but what else could he do? One male in Hayden's family had ruined Tamsin's reputation a decade ago. She didn't deserve to have it happen again. Nor did Hayden want the escapades of his sire and brothers to resurface to be picked apart by the gossips.

Another sound came from Tamsin, a sigh this time, as if she was in a lover's arms. Her lips drew together in a pout.

Lush. Plump. The shade of a rosebud. Perfect. Just like the rest of her.

His cock twitched in her direction once more.

Dammit.

Hayden looked down at the pages of his notebook. For the first time in his life, the pages weren't filled with insects or keen observations. Instead, tiny sketches of Tamsin decorated the paper. Not so much as the scribble of a fly or a caterpillar. No moths at all. Her delicate features looked up at him from the page, almost daring him to continue.

He wasn't a half bad artist. But that wasn't the point.

The sight of all those Tamsins had panic flooding his chest. He hadn't even realized he'd drawn so many versions of her. Slamming the notebook shut, he looked out over the park.

Hayden had purposefully tethered his emotions a long time ago, the result of his father's disdain and two brothers who bullied him until he became large enough to fight back. Mocked for his quiet nature, larger form, and scholarly manner, Hayden found it much easier to simply withdraw. His father's habit of tupping anything in a skirt hadn't helped. He didn't know how many bastards the previous duke had sired, but Hayden did not mean to follow in his footsteps or have anyone assume his nature to be like that of the other Redford men.

For years, Odessa had been Hayden's only friend. It wasn't until he'd arrived at Oxford, secure in the knowledge of being the Duke of Ware's forgotten third son, that Hayden finally found a place for himself. But that was before. Now *he* was the duke.

A constant conundrum. He associated the title with his father, a man Hayden still loathed.

A chestnut curl teased at Tamsin's cheek until her nose wrinkled and she stirred. Her back arched sensually as she blinked. Her neck fell back, giving Hayden a glimpse at the hollow of her throat.

His tongue pressed against his teeth, wanting to lick at her skin.

Taste her. Had he been one of his brothers, Hayden would already have tossed up her skirts. A bolt of sensation zigzagged over his thighs while he pleaded with it to cease.

"Your Grace." Her eyes, a delicious, hazy combination of brown and green, widened at him. Beautiful. Mysterious. A tiny smile tugged at that incredible mouth. "I fear your company," she said with heavy sarcasm, "was so engrossing I fell asleep."

Every insult she flung at Hayden merely aroused him.

She had no bloody idea.

He dragged his attention back to the notebook, afraid to look at Tamsin a moment longer. It would be worth a broken nose just to have a taste of her.

Good lord, what is wrong with me?

Disgusted, Hayden deliberately turned the page of his notebook to a sketch of a beetle.

"My ears are throbbing from the sound of your snoring," he growled at Tamsin. "Try to stay awake."

CHAPTER SEVEN

WARE HAD DECLINED to visit Tamsin for several days, which was problematic considering the time limit for this farce had been set at approximately three weeks. She assumed he was still upset because she dozed off repeatedly while in his company, but that said more about Ware's conversation skills than anything else.

Thankfully, Tamsin's appearance at the Entomological Society had been deemed a success by Lady Curchon. *Beneficial* was the word she'd used to describe the excursion to the beetle lecture. Lady Longwood's vicious whispers about Tamsin declaring her an immoral ambitious creature bent on seduction were now mixed with pointed curiosity. Lady Tamsin had been seen attending a scientific lecture with the Duke of Ware. Such an event didn't speak of a passing indiscretion or seduction. Certainly nothing sordid.

That campaign to quiet the gossips was beginning to bear fruit.

Still, Aunt Lottie resolved to send Ware a note if he didn't arrive by the end of the week, successful beetle lecture or not.

Tamsin smoothed down her skirts. A reminder to the duke would no longer be necessary.

Ware was even now stomping about the drawing room, once more arriving without warning, demanding Tamsin's presence. Immediately.

Honestly, was it so difficult to at least alert her of his intent to call?

Tamsin, annoyed at Ware, asked Holly to bring the duke tea and advise him she'd be down momentarily then waited a full half hour to appear.

It sounded as if a caged bull was in the drawing room.

Tamsin strode inside, her hands clasped politely before her.

"Your Grace." She did not apologize for keeping him waiting, nor question why it had taken him so long to call upon her again. Or, most importantly, why he couldn't simply send her a bloody note informing Tamsin of his imminent arrival.

"Finally," Ware thundered, mop of black hair spiraling about his temples and into his eyes. He glowered at her through the tangled strands, looming over Tamsin with no small amount of menace.

"You did not inform me prior to your arrival, Your Grace. A messenger advising me of the time would have been appropriate."

He scowled.

She pulled on her gloves, ignoring his murderous gaze. "Where are we off to today?"

"The museum."

Tamsin nodded. "Wonderful." She enjoyed the museum, particularly the artifacts from Egypt and Greece. Better than moths and beetles at the very least, though the Egyptians did have scarabs which *were* beetles. She knew that much at least. "Will we be taking in the cat mummies?"

Ware appeared *slightly* less rumpled than normal today. His waistcoat wasn't missing any buttons, but his cravat was still mangled-looking. And he absolutely had been out of doors again before suddenly recalling Tamsin existed as the flower petal clinging to the edge of one elbow indicated. And there was another puff of animal hair around his ankles.

Was he chasing rabbits? Mice?

"No mummified felines." His crisp, clipped baritone echoed in the drawing room. "We'll be visiting the entomology collections." The coal black of his lashes dipped across the tops of his cheekbones as he looked down on Tamsin and took her arm.

There was nothing overtly sexual in his perusal, but Tamsin had the impression he'd tilted his head so he could get a better view of her bosom. And the touch of his hand sent unexpected warmth crawling up her shoulder.

"How odd to find that you and the duchess have something in common," he drawled. "Who would have supposed."

"Your Grace?"

"My mother admires the cat mummies and felines in general. Every ducal residence is filled with the creatures."

Tamsin looked down at the leg of Ware's trousers. That explained the animal hair.

"We had a cat at Dunnings named Wellington," she informed him. "A mouser of great skill." Dunnings had entire herds of mice eating at the walls. At night, she could hear them gnawing away at what was left of the wood and plaster while Aurora slept like the dead beside her. A mouse fell out of the ceiling one winter and landed in her brother's oatmeal. Malcolm, true to form, barely raised a brow.

Ware gave her a skeptical look. "You named your cat after one of England's greatest heroes?"

"He was quite the mouser." The big tomcat had left scores of dead rodents in his wake. "Wellington was a hero in his own right and deserved a name reflective of his skill."

The hard line of his mouth lifted just slightly. "The dowager duchess became enamored of Egyptian culture when I was a child, ordering statues, pottery, and other trinkets from an antiquities dealer." His voice softened. "Took me to an unwrapping party for a mummy once. The line was drawn, however, at housing mummies at Orchard Park," he continued, unaware that the corner of his coat had found its way into the folds of Tamsin's skirts.

"Orchard Park?" She tried to ignore the edge of his coat pushing along her thigh, the sensation far more intimate than the touch of his hand along her elbow.

"My seat. In the country. At any rate, once the duchess learned that cats were revered in Egyptian society as gods, it gave her the excuse she needed to populate every ducal residence with scores of them. The fact that the previous duke, my father, detested cats had nothing to do with her actions, I'm sure." He glanced at the portrait of Tamsin's parents above the fireplace. "The duke and duchess were not happy with each other."

"Over the cats?" Tamsin asked, though she doubted that had been the only reason.

"Over anything." Ware turned back to her. "Especially me."

The light streaming in from the drawing room window left streaks across the slash of Ware's cheeks, muting his eyes to pewter. This was the longest string of words he had ever spoken to her since their unfortunate meeting at Lady Curchon's, or at least the most he'd said without injecting an insult.

It *almost* made her forgive him for showing up unannounced, his unpleasant manner, and his obsession with insects.

"May we *make* time then for the cat mummies?" Tamsin asked hopefully.

Ware shrugged and led her out of the drawing room to his waiting carriage. He'd apparently used up the entirety of his conversation skills because he said not another word to Tamsin on the way to the museum.

Upon their arrival, Ware took her arm once more as she exited the carriage.

Unexpected heat slid from Tamsin's elbow up to her shoulder, the sensation unfurling between her breasts and vibrating along the skin of her stomach as if someone was humming a tune along her ribs.

She tripped as they climbed the steps.

Ware caught her deftly with an annoyed grunt. "Don't break your neck. Though it would make you a tragic, heartbreaking figure in

London, I suppose. Might save me the further trouble of escorting you about. I could return to my research that much sooner."

Tamsin kicked Ware's ankle in annoyance. It was like striking her toe against a piece of stone.

"Uncivilized." He made a *tsking* sound.

She tried to hit him once more with the toe of her half-boot but missed.

"Childish," he murmured, dragging her along.

Ware proceeded to promenade Tamsin about the marble floors, ensuring everyone at the museum saw them. He paused at various intervals to inspect the exhibit of fossils while dozens of curious looks were sent in their direction.

Tamsin thought the fossils *were* interesting. Like etchings in stone. Lovely, in their own way. Since returning to London, Tamsin and Aurora had wandered these halls, but never spent much time admiring the fossils.

Ware explained a fossil was merely a word for the preserved remains of a plant or animal and were found all over the world. He stopped before an insect trapped in a ball of tree sap.

Tamsin peered closer at the poor creature frozen and now on display forever.

"*Coleoptera* are often found in tree sap," he murmured to her, breath ruffling an errant curl of her hair.

Moths, Tamsin's mind silently whispered, proud she'd recognized the word.

The outline of a fern, tendrils set into the stone, was next. Then something that resembled a crab, which Ware informed her was a *trilobite*. She rolled the word around in her mouth for a bit, liking the sound. After another half hour of fossils, which Tamsin decided were interesting enough to require a return trip to the museum, Ware pulled her in the direction of the entomology exhibit.

Tamsin's eyes widened at the enormous display, housed in its own hall. Dozens upon dozens of insects of every kind, all carefully pinned and placed beneath glass. She shivered. There was something morbid about all those little bodies lined up so perfectly.

"My, this is—"

"Spectacular." Ware strode inside to stand directly before a series of small boxes all with glass tops. Inside each was a moth. "Petiver collected these. He was an apothecary. Can you imagine?"

Tamsin eyed the grotesque display of dried dragonflies, butterflies, and moths. "No, I don't believe I can." She pulled out the small notebook she'd recently purchased from her reticule. Opening to a page, she started writing while studying the display, though her scribblings had nothing to do with the exhibit.

"That's rather absurd," Ware scoffed.

"I thought it a nice touch. Me, imitating the great Duke of Ware. I'm not quite as intelligent, of course. Or as arrogant."

A rumble came from his broad chest.

"But I wish to record my opinions." Honestly, there really wasn't much she could say about dried insects that would be of any significance. She paused, tapping the pencil against her cheek.

I find the idea of some poor butterfly trapped beneath glass for an eternity to be unpleasant. I can sympathize, you see, for I often feel as if I am confined in a similar fashion for London to study.

Ware must have descended from Vikings. He is a head taller than any other gentleman here. Larger than Holly. I can see him covered in furs and tossing about an axe.

Does he even have a valet? The poor man must have to climb atop a stool to shave him, which explains the obvious.

Ware smells wonderful. Like a forest in autumn. But I won't ever tell him so.

He leaned over her, and Tamsin snapped the notebook shut, unsettled by the direction her thoughts had taken. "Apologies, Your Grace. My notes are for me alone."

"I should like to know your opinion on the display." He leaned in, breath once more fanning her cheek. "Or whatever it is you think of such importance."

"Observations of the day." It was an honest answer.

A scowl pulled at his lips, not happy with her response. At least Tamsin thought it a scowl. Ware didn't seem to have a great many facial expressions outside of annoyance. There was one that looked something like amusement, but Tamsin couldn't be sure.

"This collection," he stood over another group of cases, "is my favorite."

"Moths," Tamsin said. "I would never have guessed How did you come upon this…" She waved at the row of cases trying to think of an appropriate word. "Passion? I find it a strange way to occupy your time, Your Grace. Pinning defenseless moths to a board."

Something moved about in the depths of his eyes, flashing at her like quicksilver. "Perhaps I'll pin *you* one day, Lady Tamsin," he murmured.

The sound of Ware's voice vibrated along Tamsin's skin, raising every hair along her arms before taking up residence in her midsection and nipping at the spot between her thighs.

"Sounds vastly uncomfortable," she returned smoothly, reminding herself they were observing insects, not engaged in careless flirtation.

"I don't think it would be uncomfortable." Ware's gaze dropped to Tamsin's bosom, trailing across the tops of her breasts before retreating once more into his usual aloof expression.

Tamsin tried to keep her focus on the dragonfly pinned beneath the glass. She did not want to consider that Ware had just discreetly admired her bosom or that his remark did not seem scholarly in nature. Surely, she was mistaken. Tamsin was not a moth or a cricket.

They walked further into the hall. Ware paused before each of the glass cases to study the contents. Every so often he would bring out his notebook and write a few words before returning it to his pocket.

Tamsin left his side to wander about on her own. She pretended to inspect the insects, though she thought that one moth stabbed with a pin looked very much like another. There were a few people scattered about the gallery, so she made every effort to appear enchanted with the small, dried bodies. The fossils had been vastly more entertaining.

Finally, after nearly an hour of pretense, she stood before Ware and gently touched his arm, lest anyone was watching.

"I'm going to see the cat mummies, Your Grace," she murmured. "You may find me there when you are finished."

"I'm afraid we don't have time for that today." He shook his head, grabbing her arm before Tamsin could make her escape. "No cat mummies." Reaching into the folds of his coat, Ware produced a pocket watch and held it up to her. "We've wasted enough time as it is. I've work to do this afternoon. I believe my penance for today is at an end, Lady Tamsin."

"But—" She glanced down hall which clearly stated the Egyptian Antiquities resided within. "I shall only be a moment. Better yet, Your Grace, I'll take a hack when I'm finished." She smiled up at him.

"No, you won't. I recall the last time anyone allowed you to go about London unescorted."

Tamsin frowned. Why must he be so difficult? "If you are referring to the incident at Gunter's, that was hardly the last time I went out alone. I do so on a regular basis. If you'll recall, I am past the age of chaperone. You referred to me as ancient."

"We are engaged in a delicate affair, Lady Tamsin." He steered her out the door, hurrying her down the steps to his waiting carriage before pausing. "It would not do for you to go wandering about."

"I wouldn't be wandering about," Tamsin insisted. "I would be looking at the cat mummies."

"Not alone."

"Ware." Without thinking, Tamsin turned and placed her palm flat on his chest. "Allow me to visit the mummies." She gasped at her own boldness, but did not withdraw her hand. "I'm not asking you to leave me alone at Covent Garden. This is the museum."

The wind stirred the edges of his hair, tossing the mess about into his eyes. The noise around them grew muted and quiet as she looked up at Ware, feeling the heated muscles beneath her hand interspersed with the bulges and lumps of whatever he kept in his coat pockets. The air between them grew thicker. Tighter.

He bent so close Tamsin could feel his breath in her hair. For one brief moment, she imagined he meant to kiss her. The light brush of his mouth touched the curve of her ear, sending a ripple down her spine.

"No," he rasped in that low, delicious rumble. Spinning Tamsin about, he pushed her inside the carriage and shut the door. "Take Lady Tamsin to Emerson House directly," he said to the driver. "No stopping or I'll have your head. Deliver her up the front steps yourself if you must."

"Ware," she snapped at him through the window before throwing up her hands and falling back against the squabs. Bergamot was still caught in her nostrils; the heat of his chest still lingered on the tips of her fingers. Her heart beat out an unsteady rhythm.

Annoyance. That was what this feeling was. Nothing more.

Her fingers still pressed against the window, curled into her palm.

"You can't punch my nose at this distance," Ware said with a nod as the carriage rolled forward. "I'll take the hack for my own safety. Good day, Lady Tamsin."

⇾⇾⇾❉⇽⇽⇽

THE MOMENT HIS carriage left with Tamsin tucked securely inside, the tension in Hayden's body ebbed away. But the hunger, this insane craving for her, did not. He'd spent the last several days at a distance from Tamsin hoping that avoiding her presence would help temper his attraction to her. It was insidious the way she had burrowed inside him. Like the larvae of *dermatobia homis*, the dreaded botfly. Curling beneath his skin, itching at Hayden with every step.

He growled, causing the gentleman walking near him to step hastily aside.

Strutting about wielding her own bloody notebook and pencil. Deliberately enticing him with the curve of her hips as she leaned over to peer at a specimen. Not to mention her magnificent bosom, which only a blind man could fail to notice.

She is a botfly.

He stared straight ahead while he walked, but all Hayden could see was Tamsin's gloved hand, so tiny and graceful, pressing on his chest while begging to be taken to the bloody cat mummies. His heart and cock had begun pounding in unison, intoxicated by the scent of jasmine coming from her skin. Hayden's first irrational thought upon escorting her back to the carriage was to pull her inside and—

Hayden kicked a pebble all the way down the street.

This entire charade was built to ensure that Hayden's reputation, his honor, would not be questioned. Or be compared to the other males of his family. That was an important distinction for Hayden.

He barely enjoyed the entomology exhibit today, all too aware of her smaller form next to his. Each time he leaned over to peer at something beneath a wall of glass, Hayden caught a glimpse of Tamsin's reflection beside him. Beautiful face filled with determination to appear absorbed in both Hayden and a bunch of dead insects, which despite her efforts to the contrary, he guessed she couldn't give a fig about.

A stroll in the park. A dinner party. I will neglect the final carriage ride.

Doubts were quickly beginning to form over the veracity of Lady Longwood's claims given he and Tamsin had appeared publicly, but in such a way so that no one could determine the depth of their attachment or even whether it was romantic in nature. Hayden wasn't calling upon Emerson House with dozens of roses and whispering poetry in Tamsin's ear. Nor were they spied together in questionable circumstances. No impropriety had been observed. The most shocking thing was that Tamsin Sinclair was on the verge of being considered...a bluestocking.

"Yes, because I'm so dreadfully dull," he said under his breath as he rounded the street.

Lady Curchon was busy telling everyone within hearing that her nephew and Lady Tamsin had formed an indeterminate acquaintance. One based on shared intellectual pursuits. Any romantic feelings, if they were even present, would not survive the summer months.

Not one person disagreed.

Lady Longwood, tail tucked between her legs, departed London on her way to the country. She continued to declare Tamsin a harlot, but remained silent on what may have occurred in Lady Curchon's garden. Lady Longwood was many things, but not a fool. She'd been outmaneuvered.

The upcoming dinner party Hayden's aunt planned would only reinforce the story she was busy spouting to anyone who would listen. Only twenty guests or so would be in attendance, but those guests were all departing London soon for a seemingly endless schedule of house parties over the next few weeks. They would whisper about Ware and Tamsin, but more as a curiosity than anything else, refuting Lady Longwood's claims.

The charade would come to an end. Tamsin wouldn't be considered a trollop. Lady Aurora's come-out would be a success, especially with Lady Curchon acting as sponsor. Hayden would not be considered his father's son, nor would he be compelled to wed a female such as Tamsin Sinclair, who was far beneath him. England would be saved.

Yes, but Tamsin... beneath him.

The idea was followed by vision of chestnut hair spilling around the curves of her body. Green sparkling like emeralds in the depths of her hazel eyes as she looked up at him, pouting with that delicious mouth. Perhaps her delicate fingers plucking away at his trousers.

Hayden hastily smoothed down his coat. Thoughts of Tamsin always preceded the thickening of his cock, and it was becoming problematic. Wilkes, the latest valet in a string of half a dozen, had made the mistake of walking into Hayden's bedroom yesterday morning, *unannounced*.

Not so much as a bloody knock.

Red-faced and stammering, Wilkes had fled the scene, dropping the shaving soap and towels. Seeing your employer's hand stroking his cock as you pulled back the bed curtains had been enough for Hayden's most recent valet to give his not unexpected resignation.

Hayden gave a snort. "He should have knocked."

At any rate, Wilkes had been a shy, mousy man, lacking in the height department and only mediocre at his duties. Why was it impossible to find a valet who didn't have to use a stool to shave Hayden? Every man interested in the position of valet to the Duke of Ware was little more than a gnome.

Hobbs, the Duke of Ware's elderly butler, was already searching for a replacement.

What Hayden needed more than a valet was for these continuous erotic thoughts of Tamsin to cease. Disappear. She was no dazzling temptress, but a *botfly*. She had wings and went about annoying everyone.

Especially him.

CHAPTER EIGHT

TAMSIN TOOK A shaky breath as Lady Curchon's stately home appeared outside the carriage window. She'd hoped never to come here again. But the much-dreaded dinner party had finally arrived, an event at which Tamsin and Ware would be paraded about while the other guests speculated on their vague attachment. Her manners would be observed as well as her ability to engage in polite conversation. She would be forced to drink ratafia and not wince.

And there was also the matter of Ware.

After being banished by Ware at the museum, Tamsin had fumed and cursed the entire way back to Emerson House. His driver ignored her repeated pleas to drop her at the corner so she could return and view the cat mummies. Depositing Tamsin at the steps of Emerson House as if she were some sort of package, the driver gave her an apologetic bow and departed.

Tamsin was left with nothing but her annoyance and that slightly awkward, riveting space of time when the world stood still between her and Ware.

A tiny, inexplicable wave of longing had settled over her as she climbed the steps to Emerson house.

Now, days later, Tamsin still felt the beat of his heart beneath her palm. The tiny bulge Tamsin had traced idly with her forefinger—all the while thinking he might kiss her and wanting him to—that could only have been one of the vials he used to collect specimens. She had wanted to be enfolded in all of Ware's solid warmth. Inhaled by him. Inexplicably.

It isn't real. Not any of it.

"You are not on your way to an execution, Tamsin. Only dinner." Aunt Lottie interrupted her thoughts. "Pray, try to show some enthusiasm if for nothing else but the food. Lady Curchon employs an excellent cook."

"I fear my appetite is nonexistent."

"We are nearly finished with this little play. The rumors about you and Ware, so virulent mere weeks ago, are nothing more than whispers now." A smug smile pulled at Aunt Lottie's lips. "This charade has produced an abundance of unexpected dividends. I overheard someone the other day refer to you as unexpectedly intelligent."

Tamsin rolled her eyes. "How lovely."

"Lady Longwood is now considered to be something of a sot—"

"A sot?"

"Well, yes." Aunt Lottie's smile widened. "Too much wine makes one see things which aren't there." She winked. "Her daughter, Lady Fentwell, is also said to have been stumbling about Lady Curchon's that night having overindulged in ratafia."

"I wonder who would start such a rumor?" Tamsin said blandly.

"Who can say? But it has raised serious questions about the validity of any tale concocted by Lady Longwood. Her dislike of you is well-known and is now being viewed as mere sour grapes on her part. You are not your mother's daughter, it appears, but a bluestocking."

"I've certainly viewed enough dead insects to last me a lifetime," Tamsin agreed. "I do find it unfair that I was automatically assumed to be the seductress. Ware might be a scholar, but he is still a man."

Aunt Lottie made a puffing sound. "He is wed to his research. His studies. Why do you think Lady Curchon agonizes so much over finding him a suitable wife? Ware has never shown a romantic inclination or even flirted with a woman. As different from his brothers and father as night and day."

The opinion was incorrect. Tamsin did not imagine the press of his lips along her thigh while searching for his stupid moth, nor along the curve of her ear at the museum. There was also the matter of Ware admiring her bosom. "Maybe not as different as you imagine."

"He is no rake," the older woman continued. "Not one indiscretion has been ascribed to him. I'm not sure he's ever been involved with a female unless she was also an insect."

Again, Tamsin disagreed, but she didn't voice her objection to Aunt Lottie. She had far more important things at present to consider. Namely, leaving the safety of the carriage. Perhaps she could leap out, lift her skirts, and make a run for it.

"You wouldn't get very far in those slippers," Aunt Lottie said, guessing at her thoughts. "Should you consider fleeing."

"What if I use the wrong fork?" Tamsin asked in a mournful tone.

The incorrect use of a knife, spoon, or fork was a recurring fear of hers, why Tamsin had no idea. There were dozens of other social norms she could just as easily forget, but silverware represented a true trial. Mama had taught them all proper table manners, of course, but the vast array of utensils used for various courses had been lost to Tamsin during her time at Dunnings.

"Watch everyone else," Aunt Lottie suggested. "You survived Dunnings, you can endure an overly pretentious dinner presided over by Lord and Lady Curchon."

Tamsin bit back her reply, knowing that to argue with her elderly companion would do no good. After tonight's dinner, there would only be a stroll in the park to complete Lady Curchon's grand plan. There would be no more tolerating Ware.

The knowledge left an ache inside her.

Once inside, Tamsin and Aunt Lottie were greeted politely by Lady Curchon's butler and shown to the drawing room. They were not terribly late, but even so, the room was already full of guests. No one wanted to miss the show, she supposed. Heads snapped in her direction, gazes assessing her with a great deal of curiosity but no visible disdain.

Tamsin's shoulders, tight and ready to do battle, relaxed.

Lady Curchon, resplendent in cream and blue silk, swept forward. She took in every detail of Tamsin's gown, lingering over the modest neckline edged in a froth of lace and tiny silk flowers before nodding in approval. "Your gown is lovely, Lady Tamsin."

Meaning Tamsin in no way resembled a courtesan.

"Thank you, my lady." She bobbed politely.

"How did you enjoy the lecture at the Entomological Society?" Lady Curchon asked, raising her voice an octave for the benefit of those listening, which was nearly everyone in the drawing room.

"Stimulating," Tamsin answered. "Mr. Stephens is quite eloquent. I enjoyed his presentation very much."

The eyes of her hostess widened in surprise, a hint of laughter clinging to her lips. "I'm sure the duke was pleased you enjoyed it."

"Indeed, I am." The rich, raspy sound of Ware behind her forced a hum along the back of Tamsin's neck to trickle down her spine. It was a rather delicious sensation. "Lady Tamsin." Ware took her hand.

"Your Grace." She lowered politely, inhaling bergamot and something grassy as if she were in a meadow. Straightening, she examined Ware's trousers and coat but saw no evidence of the leaves, twigs, or dirt that usually decorated his person.

Ware did not immediately release her fingers; instead, she felt the press of his thumb along her palm.

"Stephens and his descriptions were so vivid Lady Tamsin even closed her eyes, imagining all he related." There was a glimmer of amusement in Ware's eyes. His thumb trailed over her palm once more before slowly drawing his hand from hers.

Tamsin inhaled, trying to formulate a tart response, but she was far too distracted by the humming along her skin. The press of his thumb did strange things to her insides.

"I spent a great deal of time," she cleared her throat, "envisioning each specimen as he described it. Much easier to do with my eyes closed, Your Grace."

The corner of his mouth lifted. "So I surmised. Walk with me, Lady Tamsin."

Ware didn't wait for Tamsin to agree, just took her by the arm and steered her away.

"For a gentleman who decries his title, you certainly carry the arrogance of a duke," she observed with no small amount of sarcasm.

"As of late, I've made some peace with the ducalness I've inherited."

"I don't believe that is actually a word, Your Grace. Ducalness."

"I attended Oxford. You did not," was his response as he pulled Tamsin to the edge of the drawing room. The walls in this corner belled out slightly to form a narrow hall which served as a small gallery. There were the usual portraits of past Lord Curchons and the like along with a painting of a storm breaking across the ocean.

Ware stopped before a gilt-framed watercolor of a butterfly.

"What do you think, Lady Tamsin?" The question carried through the drawing room.

The other guests immediately shifted, turning to get a better view of the gallery and Tamsin.

"I think I would prefer," she murmured, "not to be on display as if I am some sort of a circus act."

Ware perused her with his usual annoyance. "I meant of the painting. I would like your impression."

Tamsin took in the gilt-framed butterfly. She knew even less about insects than art, though she did like butterflies. Her interests were more along the lines of history and the occasional penny dreadful. Tilting her head, she studied the painting. The artist had not been talented. The outline of the butterfly was poorly executed and drawn with what looked to be a trembling hand.

"Pleasing colors," she answered loudly, for the benefit of those listening.

"The artist forgot the antennae." Ware's big shoulder dipped toward her. His breath, warm and mint-scented, trailed over curve of her neck. "There should be *two*. But you're aware of that, aren't you, my lady? Given your studies?"

Such mockery. Tamsin didn't think she deserved it. At least she had made an effort to try and understand his hobby.

"And missing a leg," came Tamsin's tart reply, not taking her eyes off the painting. "Clearly, the artist, in addition to their obvious lack of talent, was blind. Or completely unobservant."

Ware nodded in agreement. "Clearly." He regarded her from beneath the thick fringe of his lashes, silver flashing across her overly modest neckline.

"Ware doesn't have an interest in such things."

Aunt Lottie's assessment of Ware's character was utter rubbish. Another ruse, one much more successful than the one Tamsin was currently engaged in. She meant to prove it.

Drawing in a slow, *calculated* lungful of air, Tamsin made sure to expand her chest. As she suspected, the gown's demure cut was no match for her generous bosom, even with a froth of lace and silk flowers.

A low hissing sound came from Ware.

"Is something amiss, Your Grace?" Tamsin gave him an innocent look.

"Not in the least. I am only surprised at your brazen manner in trying to gain my admiration."

"Admiration? But, Your Grace, I'm told the great Duke of Ware has no interest in such things," Tamsin scoffed. "Stop ogling me." Her fingers curled of their own accord into fists at her sides.

"Unclench your fists," he countered. One large, gloved finger lowered cautiously, dipping to trace the outline of her knuckles.

Tamsin held her breath at the slight touch.

"There isn't any reason to consider punching me in the nose," Ware said quietly, finger still dancing over the top of her hand.

"I wasn't—"

"Don't bother to deny that's what you're thinking, my lady. Your arms are not so long, but—I should not like to take chances with my only elegant feature. My family is renowned in England for their probiscises." He tilted his chin to her, the slight lift on one side of his mouth now more resembling a smile.

"Probiscises?" Tamsin's brow wrinkled as the warmth of his finger fell away.

"Noses. I happen to like mine."

"I do too. Like your nose."

Also, the sharp cut of his cheekbones. The too-wide mouth. The way being beside him gave Tamsin the feeling of being behind an immense impenetrable wall, one that protected her from the rest of Lady Curchon's dinner party.

"Thank you."

"You're welcome."

Embarrassed by her odd confession—after all, what sort of young lady went about complimenting dukes on their noses?—Tamsin stared down at the hem of Ware's coat. When he shifted beside her, the bulge of a muscle in his thighs pulled at the seam of his trousers. Rather indecently.

Another ripple of warmth pressed along her midsection. What would it be like to be bedded by Ware? Have all that—*heaviness* pressing deliciously into you? Those large, muscled thighs pinning her to the bed—

"Perhaps I'll pin you one day, Lady Tamsin."

She swallowed and lifted her chin, struggling to focus on the atrocious butterfly painting.

"You'll accompany me to the park tomorrow," Ware finally said. "A stroll along the river. One last outing and then this charade will be over. I've decided against the additional carriage ride. It's unnecessary. Lady Aurora will have a wonderful come-out." His eyes flicked over her. "Unless you do something else ridiculous."

He really was a beast. Unbelievable that a few moments ago she'd been considering—

Could I kick him without anyone else noticing?

Tamsin snuck a peek at the other guests in the drawing room. Most were watching her and Ware, albeit discreetly.

Probably not.

"Look at me with mild adoration." The superior tone held a hint of mockery. "It will add much to our charade."

"I fail to see why I must adore you and not the other way around. I haven't so much as gotten a box of sweets from you. The least you could do is send me flowers. Doesn't seem fair."

"Life isn't fair." There was heat banked in his gaze, along with something undefinable before he looked away. "I'm a duke, Lady Tamsin. We are always adored even when we don't deserve it, which is a great deal of the time. And as you have surmised, I'm incapable of worshipping anything save a moth perhaps. You'll be happy to know I'm moving on to *coleoptera* very soon. Beetles," he clarified.

"I purchased a book by Curtis. I'm aware of *coleoptera*," she reminded him. "Also, I endured a dry lecture on the topic."

"Yes, but you fell asleep. Try not to pronounce anything in Latin tonight and save us both the embarrassment of me having to correct you," he said mildly. "And regard me with worship."

Tamsin opened her mouth to rebuke him but stopped at the teasing glint in his eyes. She hadn't thought him capable. Another delectable twisting of her insides followed.

"Did you know, Your Grace, that I am now regarded as something of a bluestocking? Your disparagement of my Latin is beside the point." She gave a deliberate, lung-expanding sigh, once more allowing her breasts to force themselves against her neckline. "Every dull, tedious scholar in England will now be in pursuit of me. I'll wager not one of them will care if I mispronounce a word in Latin now and again."

"I don't doubt it," Ware growled, pointedly ignoring her display of bosom. "Tomorrow we will collect specimens during our stroll through the park. A necessity, as I'm behind on my work due to escorting you about—"

"A total of three times, including tonight, Your Grace." When he tried to object, she continued. "You combined the carriage ride with the lecture. And it isn't as if you had to expend a great deal of energy or time on me. Everything we've done has been something you were likely to do on your own. You merely dragged me along for effect. Had I expired at the museum, for instance, you would have stepped over me on your way to a dried caterpillar."

Ware kept his focus on the painting. "I would have paused to check the pulse beating in your throat."

There was nothing improper in his words. Exactly. He wasn't even looking at her but at the stupid painting. It was more the inherent sensuality to his speech, something that you couldn't fail to notice once he dropped the annoyed superiority from his tone. If Ware read the book on beetles to her at this moment, in that seductive tone—an image of her and Ware popped unbidden into Tamsin's mind. Naked, intertwined, rolling about on a bed of leaves.

Stop this instant.

"Perhaps such a stroll, like the additional carriage ride, is unnecessary," Tamsin drew in a shaky breath. Her growing attraction to Ware was...unsettling and becoming worse by the moment. None of this was real, she reminded herself. Not the flirtatious banter or his perceived regard for her. "We can be finished with this tonight and be free of each other."

"Tomorrow morning, my lady, is when we will collect our specimens. One last outing to prove the truth of our attachment. Morning is a splendid time to be observed. Lady Harrington, a notorious gossip, often rides early in the park. She is hosting a house party at her estate in Surrey in three weeks. Nearly everyone at this dinner party has been invited. Lady Curchon insists on our stroll tomorrow, then you need not see me again unless it is unavoidable. Now take my arm."

Tamsin did so, ignoring the jolt along her arm as she touched him.

Lady Curchon awaited them. "Did you enjoy the painting?" she said to Tamsin. "Lovely, isn't it?"

"Beautiful." Tamsin agreed, dropping Ware's arm as if it were a hot poker. "A wonderful use of color."

A genuine smile crossed Lady Curchon's lips. "Ware painted that for my birthday many years ago. He was barely eight or nine as I recall. It has hung in my drawing room ever since."

Ware inclined his head. "I was rewarded with a great deal of cake. Lady Tamsin is being polite. She was kind enough to point out I'd missed a leg on the butterfly. Such keen observations," his words were louder than before for the benefit of the rest of the room, "are essential when engaged in fieldwork. Our collection of specimens tomorrow will prove fruitful, I have no doubt."

Tamsin pasted a polite smile on her lips. Ware had drawn the butterfly as a *child*. "Thank you, Your Grace. I look forward to our excursion."

Lady Curchon nodded, obviously pleased.

Ware, looking bored now that he'd done his part, reached into the folds of his coat to produce his notebook and the stub of a pencil. Slowly moving towards the drawing room door, he appeared oblivious to everything and everyone else.

Lady Curchon's shoulders lifted carelessly, regarding her guests with an apologetic smile. "Research," she said. "My gardens apparently contain a plethora of moths. His Grace will return in time for dinner."

Lady Curchon moved away from Tamsin, nudging her in the direction of Aunt Lottie who stood some distance away.

"Don't be distressed," Aunt Lottie said in a low tone. "He does that. Goes off. Writes in his notebook. He's been doing it since he was a child."

"Hmm." Tamsin watched as Ware's form became visible outside the drawing room window as he wandered about Lady Curchon's garden, finally disappearing behind a large shrub.

Taking up the glass of ratafia she was offered, Tamsin mused that pulling out a notebook under the guise of research was also an excellent way to avoid conversation or engage with others socially.

If you were the Duke of Ware.

CHAPTER NINE

T AMSIN SETTLED INTO her seat in Lady Curchon's opulent dining room, determined to pay Ware, who was seated next to her, little attention. Bad enough to be on display tonight without having to tolerate the duke's odd manner towards her which vacillated between annoyance and flirtation. Possibly at the same time.

I do not care.

What mattered, indeed the only thing that concerned her, was that Aurora's debut would be splendid and her future not once more ruined by her impetuous older sister.

Ware shifted beside her, his large, imposing form taking up every inch of space between their seats. Tamsin tried to turn, only to find Ware's shoulder wedged against hers.

"Stop fidgeting," he said blandly without looking at her.

"We should not be so near each other, Your Grace. Each time you raise your fork, your elbow will be driven—"

"Into your bosom. Yes, I quite agree. *If* I was right-handed. Which I am not. Surely, you've noticed given your keen powers of observation."

Tamsin, to her everlasting shame, had not. How had she missed that Ware wrote with his left hand? She'd seen him scribble in his notebook any number of times. "Of course. My brother Drew is left-handed."

"How wonderful for him." Ware made a sound before shifting his body further to the left. "Better?"

"Thank you." She turned her attention abruptly, determined to not speak further but engage her dinner companion to her right. Lord Banning had been introduced to Tamsin in the drawing room after Ware disappeared into the gardens. Bannning was an earl. Older. Still handsome despite the lines of dissipation creasing his face.

"My lord." She gave Banning a polite smile, unsure how to proceed. Polite dinner conversation was not her forte.

Tamsin hadn't eaten a meal with anyone but her family, as odd as that might seem. Her parents hadn't entertained often prior to her father's death. Obviously at Dunnings, there hadn't been a great deal of decorum observed. And since the return to London, the only guests at the earl's table had been Aunt Lottie or Mr. Patchahoo, the Sinclair solicitor. Nothing at all like the long, decorated table with Lord Curchon at the head, next to the duke, and Lady Curchon at the other end.

"Lady Tamsin." Banning's head tilted slightly so that he could better cast glances at her ridiculously modest neckline while simultaneously licking his lips.

Ugh.

Tamsin resented being equated with a lamp chop on such short acquaintance and found herself leaning in Ware's direction for protection, though she'd only just decided to avoid him.

"Are you suddenly infested with fleas?" Ware said under his breath. "Because your twitching about would give credence to such an assumption. Or are you attempting to sit in my lap?" One of his fingers trailed absently along the edge of her skirt.

"Stop doing that," Tamsin whispered. The gesture was oddly possessive and completely unwarranted. "It is cruel and unnecessary."

Ware's brows drew together in genuine confusion. "I did not mean it as such."

"Is your behavior revenge for the beetle lecture?" she whispered under her breath. "I've apologized to you for falling asleep." Her fingers curled around the fork beside her plate.

Ware glanced down. "You can't possibly stab me without drawing attention," he said softly. "Think how pleased Lady Chilcott," he discreetly nodded to an older woman directly across the table, "would be to relate the entire scene to Lady Longwood who already tells any who will listen that you are no more than a savage in a skirt."

"You should see me in breeches," Tamsin shot back.

Ware's cheeks pinked in that telltale blush.

"Lady Chilcott and Lady Longwood are close friends. Which I assume accounts for her presence across the table from you. She'll report that we seemed close, but not overly intimate. Our relationship friendly. Imagine Lady Longwood's frustration at not being able to define you as an ambitious woman of questionable morals intent on my seduction. Because, as you understand it, I am not interested in such things."

Tamsin blinked, willing her gaze away from his.

"I agree, Your Grace." She smiled sweetly, her words carrying so that poor Lady Chilcott didn't need to lean over her plate to hear. "If we are to find the male *saturnia pavonia*, an early morning excursion might be the best time to visit the park, particularly the area populated by fallen tree trunks."

Lady Chilcott shrewdly appraised Tamsin while sipping her wine.

She picked up her own glass, determined to brave this evening despite Ware and the snooty Lady Chilcott. Her nose wrinkled at the liquid in her glass. Ratafia once more.

Ware made a twirling motion with one hand.

A footman magically appeared, bowing before the duke.

"Lady Tamsin doesn't care for the ratafia. Frankly, I don't think anyone does. Lord Curchon's wine is French and incredibly expensive. Bring her that."

The footman nearly bent in half once more. "Yes, Your Grace."

Lord Curchon, seated on the other side of Ware, lifted his own glass. "Terribly expensive, Lady Tamsin. I can't imagine you won't enjoy it."

"Ratafia is detestable," Ware said quietly. "Terrible. My aunt believes young ladies too uncomplicated to enjoy anything requiring a decent palate. I disagree. I think you *entirely* complicated, Lady Tamsin."

A spark took root beneath her skin, tendrils fanning out across her chest. He *was* flirting with her. She supposed for Lady Chilcott's benefit, though the old harpy couldn't possibly hear him.

"And I think you a bit long in the tooth to be considered a *young* lady." Ware's eyes were the same color as the knife and fork beside Tamsin's plate, shifting subtly in the light of the chandelier above the table.

"Your insults are the price I must pay for our association." Though Tamsin didn't feel as if he were disparaging her. Not with the warmth humming along her skin. "A high cost, I think."

"There is a price for *everything*, Lady Tamsin." A hint of wistfulness crossed his striking features. "Something I am only beginning to realize."

Ware was terribly handsome just then, peering down at Tamsin through the dark tangle of hair falling over his brow and cheeks. Magnificent in a way that had her heart beating louder in her chest.

She turned her attention from Ware to her plate, barely nodding thanks to the footman who filled her glass with Lord Curchon's expensive wine.

"Lady Tamsin," Banning's toothy words sounded from beside her.

She'd been so focused on Ware, Tamsin had forgotten entirely about Banning.

"I was so pleased to finally make your acquaintance. How are you enjoying London? I understand you are only recently returned."

Tamsin's shoulders immediately drew together, tensing at Banning's oily tone. The earl was of an age to have witnessed the scandal her parents had created. "I find the city much as I remember."

Banning rotated his body in Tamsin's direction, knee purposefully sinking improperly into the folds of her skirts. She couldn't move away without causing a scene, something Tamsin was certain Banning realized. His wine-soaked breath buffeted her shoulder as he spoke. "I ride in the park quite often, but have yet to see you, my lady. I know you sit," he paused, "a *horse* exceedingly well."

"Because I ride astride, my lord." Tamsin forced herself not to cringe. She glanced at Ware from beneath her lashes, but there would be no help from that quarter. He was deep in conversation with his uncle, Lord Curchon.

"Ah yes. A superior way to ride, no doubt." He winked. "I quite agree. I suppose that is what allowed you to win so many wagers."

Banning knew she'd raced against the local gentry at Dunnings, which was frankly, not the worst thing she'd ever done.

"But I wonder if you can be induced to ride purely for pleasure." Another sly, toothy smile pulled at his lips. "As your mother once did."

Tamsin's chin snapped forward, fists curling in her lap.

What gall Banning possessed. It was rare Tamsin received an improper proposal and an insult of her mother in the same breath. And never at a dinner party.

Lady Chilcott gave her a thin smile from across the table.

"We can stroll about Lady Curchon's garden." Banning leaned closer. "I'll be the moth beneath your skirts. I promise I'll be easier and much more amusing to trap than him."

He discreetly nodded at Ware.

Tamsin attempted to compose herself, though she was mortified at the turn of the conversation. Angry too that Banning thought he had some right to say such things to her. Her inclination was to utter a loud and scathing defamation of his manhood to the entire table, but she restrained herself. Staring into her glass of wine, Tamsin considered spilling it into her lap so she would have an excuse to leave the table. When Tamsin lifted her chin once more it was to see Lady Banning down the length of the table, regarding her with distaste.

Her entire jaw tightened, tilting in a mutinous manner. It was rather exhausting being judged at every turn. Morally bankrupt simply because your mother had once been a scandal and you happened to resemble her. Just now, seated at this fine table, Tamsin found it intolerable.

"Lord Banning." Ware leaned over his plate. "I didn't mean to eavesdrop." His dark brows drew together in an inquisitive manner. "If you are interested in searching for moths, I believe I can be of assistance."

Banning, taken aback by Ware's interruption, nonetheless answered smoothly. "A comment, no more." The earl waved a hand before taking another sip of his wine. "*Riding* was actually the topic of our discussion. It is my understanding Lady Tamsin excels at such an activity. I thought I might join her in the park one day. With your permission, of course, Your Grace," he added as an afterthought.

There was *nothing* respectful in the way Banning spoke to Ware.

"Riding in the park? Good grief," the duke said, shocked.

Banning bestowed Ware with a patronizing look. "I understand you do not care to ride, Your Grace. I thought to offer my services as escort to Lady Tamsin."

Ware's eyes hardened until they resembled shards of glass, though Banning failed to notice.

"How kind of you, Banning. Lady Tamsin, is of course, free to do as she pleases." The edge of Ware's foot pressed into her slipper, urging Tamsin to remain silent, though he didn't once look at her. "I don't ride, as you've kindly reminded me, but prefer to walk. Though at present, I've refrained from doing so in the park. Because of the *papilio antimachus.*"

"The papi—" Banning's pronunciation was worse than her own.

"*Papilio antimachus.*"

"I apologize, Your Grace. I'm not familiar." Banning pasted a bored, polite look on his sagging features. "I know very little about moths."

"Which is why I found it so curious you wished to hunt for them with Lady Tamsin." Ware waved his hand before Banning could respond. "*Papilio antimachus* is not a moth, you understand, but a butterfly." Ware reached into his pocket and drew out his notebook. "I've made sketches, if you'd care to see."

"I'm afraid I wouldn't appreciate your artistry, Your Grace," Banning replied, failing to keep the derision from his words.

"You really should take a look." Ware gave a nonchalant shrug, though Tamsin could see the tense set of his shoulders.

Ware wasn't being pleasant. Or polite. He was *angry*.

"Especially since you ride in the park," Ware continued in the same friendly tone. "The *papilio antimachus* is a *poisonous* butterfly." He placed the notebook back inside his coat.

"Butterflies are not poisonous," Banning took another sip of his wine, leaning back so that the soup course could be placed before him. "Not in England. Even I know that much, Your Grace."

Tamsin startled at the fleeting warmth of Ware's fingers along her skirts once more. But his attention remained on Banning.

"I must disagree," Ware said in a solemn tone. "And I would know, wouldn't I? Having studied a multitude of scientific matters at Oxford." He shrugged. "But so few lords make it past Eton or Harrow." He gave a soft laugh. "Which did you attend, Banning?"

Banning's glass paused inches from his lips. "Neither, Your Grace."

Tamsin wanted to smile but did not. Ware had subtly insulted Banning's intelligence and the earl wasn't quite sure how to respond. He no longer looked so vastly superior as he had moments ago.

"The *papilio antimachus* are native to Africa," Ware continued in a dry tone. "The *continent*."

Banning took another large swallow of his wine.

"Brought here on a ship. Accidentally, mind you. I can only surmise that one of them escaped the hold on someone's coat and that person then rode through Hyde Park. Now the *papilio antimachus* are multiplying at a rapid pace and have settled in."

"Forgive me, Your Grace, I realize such things are of great interest to you. But I must confess butterflies are not a topic which draws my attention." Banning picked up his soup spoon, assuming he had ended the discussion. He shot a put-upon look across the table to Lady Chilcott, as if it was the worst possible luck having to listen to the eccentric Duke of Ware.

"The *papilio antimachus* bites, my lord. One butterfly has enough venom to put down a hippopotamus. They are swarming in the park." Ware gave a roll of his shoulders. "You ride daily. I thought you might wish to know." He took a spoonful of his own soup.

"You're joking." Banning turned to regard Ware. "Poisonous butterflies in the park." A laugh came from him as he shook his head at Lady Chilcott who sipped her own soup slowly, listening to the conversation.

"I rarely joke, my lord. And never about *insecta.*" Ware's features remained scholarly and earnest.

"I've read nothing in the papers." Banning insisted. "Surely—"

"Inquire with Curchon." Ware lowered his voice. "I plucked *papilio anitmachus* off his shoulder just the other day after he and Lady Curchon took a stroll near the Serpentine. Attached itself to his coat and went unnoticed the entire carriage ride home. If it had bitten him or my aunt," Ware inhaled sharply, "well, we would not be attending such a lovely dinner, would we?"

Banning glanced at Curchon then back at Ware.

"Inquire *discreetly*, Banning. I don't wish to cause a panic."

"How did you retrieve it?" The earl's entire tone had changed at the mention of Curchon.

"I used a bit of laudanum on a handkerchief to put the *papilio anitmachus* into a deep sleep so that I could extract it. Couldn't risk being bitten. I then immediately turned the specimen over to the Entomological Society for further study." Ware glanced at his uncle. "Lord Curchon has consulted with the Home Office at length. I'm not yet certain what has been decided. But I expect the authorities to cordon off the path along the river any day due to the infestation. I'm surprised they haven't done so yet. But the queen didn't wish to cause alarm, I expect."

Banning paled. "Perhaps you might show me what these butterflies look like, Your Grace."

"Now that the soup has arrived?" Ware's brows lifted in surprise. "My aunt would not be pleased. Later perhaps."

Banning studied Ware, still uncertain whether or not to believe him but unwilling to take the risk. "What should one do if one of these creatures is encountered?"

"Run, my lord," Ware stated simply. "If the *papilio anitmachus* is capable of killing a hippopotamus, you wouldn't stand a chance."

"You said the path along the Serpentine, Your Grace?" Banning asked.

But Ware ignored him, pretending great concentration on his bowl of soup.

Banning sat back in frustration, glancing at Ware every so often as the soup was taken away, his mind completely on murderous butterflies and not attempting to trap Tamsin in the gardens after dinner.

She calmly picked up her glass and took a sip of the wine, doubting there was any such insect haunting the park; deadly butterflies were more likely to be found in the pages of a penny dreadful or one of the criminal broadsides her sister-in-law Odessa so adored.

Ware had deftly vanquished Banning before the earl even understood he'd done so.

Tamsin adjusted her skirts, using the opportunity to whisper, "I'll assume there aren't hordes of butterflies intent on the assassination of condescending earls inhabiting the park."

"Anything is possible, Lady Tamsin," Ware answered. "And I believe the word is lecherous, not condescending."

Ware *had* heard everything. "He'll inquire with your uncle."

"I hope so. I asked him to do so discreetly, but that isn't a strength of Banning's. Discretion. Every gentleman who joins my uncle for a brandy after dinner will hear him spouting off about poisonous butterflies. I'll find it vastly amusing. As will Lord Curchon."

Ware turned back to his uncle to continue their conversation, speaking in a low voice, though Tamsin didn't think it had anything to do with Banning. There was an intensity to Ware's features which the earl at Tamsin's side didn't merit.

He came to my rescue.

Tamsin most often did the rescuing. She'd never felt like a young lady in distress in need of protection. Thanks to her brothers, she knew how to throw a punch and fire a pistol. She rode better than most men. Jordan had always been the responsible one. The glue holding them all together. Tamsin was the warrior. Unafraid to challenge or do battle on behalf of her family, especially Aurora. There had been little thought to her own protection.

She stared at the trout on her plate, trying to sort out her mixed emotions, and reached for her fork.

"Not that one," Ware growled softly so only she could hear. "The smallest."

Tamsin's fingers slid over to the correct fork, sparing a glance at Lady Chilcott who watched her like a hawk. Every misstep of Tamsin's would be related to Lady Longwood and scores of others.

"Thank you," she whispered. "And for Banning. I—"

"I can't have you displaying poor manners. The mispronunciation of Latin is bad enough."

Picking up the fish fork, Tamsin considered that if anyone deserved a good stabbing, it was Ware, though she was grateful for his defense. She sucked in a breath, making sure her breasts were forced to the very edge of her neckline, lace be damned.

A noise came from Ware before he hissed, "Well played, Lady Tamsin."

CHAPTER TEN

Lady Tamsin Sinclair was possibly the most stunning, hostile, stubborn woman Hayden had ever known. And she wore breeches while riding. The mere thought of her marching about in tight leather breeches outlining those delicious legs he'd once touched made him dizzy.

He'd been in that enjoyable state, thinking of Tamsin in breeches, when he overheard Banning.

Hayden did consider drowning the earl in a bowl of the artichoke soup, which was excellent. In addition to Tamsin's profound effects on the specific parts of his anatomy, she also aroused every protective instinct Hayden didn't know he possessed. Savage instincts, which made him want to tear Banning's limbs from his body. The earl had gotten off lucky with just the embarrassment he was bound to face later. Blatantly proposing an assignation. At the dinner table. In front of Hayden and God knows who else overheard.

Lady Chilcott to be sure.

Certainly, Lady Banning didn't mind her husband's wandering eye. She regarded the earl with the look of a woman who had long ago decided it would be better to be a widow. Banning's peccadilloes were no great secret in London. He'd once been a crony of Hayden's father and cut from the same cloth. Meaning he shared the previous duke's opinion of his odd third son.

Hayden couldn't honestly fault Banning's assumption that Hayden was overly intelligent, obsessed with insects, and had little interest in taking his place in society. And Hayden had done little to alter anyone's opinion because it meant he was left alone.

But that didn't mean Hayden had to tolerate Banning's disrespect.

"You are a duke. Take your place. You can no longer be that odd little boy."

Mother's words right before she launched herself into her waiting carriage, headed for an extended stay on the Continent. She was right. Hayden had known it for some time. Hiding from the world behind the shield of his studies and the Entomological Society was no longer feasible now that his father and brothers were gone.

Especially because Hayden's world now included Tamsin Sinclair.

Jasmine hovered in the air beside him. A chestnut curl dangled just at the top of her cheek, and she batted it away. Hayden longed to bury his nose in the nape of her neck. Nibble at that skin. Every rustle of her skirts tempted him. The curve of her breast, hidden beneath a mountain of lace, had Hayden's fingers shaking as he held his fork. When Banning leered and made his ugly comments, Hayden had wanted to pull her into the shelter of his arms. Slay her dragons, so to speak. Or in this case, one lecherous earl.

Flirting with Tamsin wasn't working. He'd tried earlier, in the drawing room. But all Hayden had succeeded in doing was annoy her. And now that he wanted—

Well, he wasn't actually sure, only that Tamsin was at the center.

When the meal finally ended and the gentlemen departed, making for their brandies and cheroots, Hayden had come to the disappointing conclusion that he didn't know *how* to express himself to Tamsin, or even if he should. She found him to be condescending, gruff, and unpleasant. An overly large gentleman who lumbered about looking for insects.

Hayden slowly came to his feet, casting one last glance at Tamsin as she trailed the other ladies to the drawing room.

Could he really say goodbye to her tomorrow?

Do I want to?

The only thing that lightened Hayden's mood as the gentlemen crowded together was, ironically, Banning. The earl, true to form, made a complete idiot out of himself over the butterflies. Hayden opened his notebook, pretending complete absorption in his notes so as not to collapse into a fit of laughter. Banning would be mocked for the remainder of the evening. Possibly longer.

A milder rebuke than some of the others the earl would face in the next few weeks. Hayden's title wielded quite a bit of influence, something he was still getting accustomed to. Banning would not trouble Tamsin again.

Slipping outside to the quiet of the gardens, Hayden found a bench and sat, content to watch the moths flit about and listen to the frogs begin their songs. He'd resisted the truth of what he was for a very long time. But Hayden could no longer continue to do so.

"I don't have to be *you*," Hayden whispered into the night air, hoping his father could hear him. "Or Thompson. Or Maxwell. But I *will* be the Duke of Ware."

CHAPTER ELEVEN

"**H**URRY ALONG." WARE halted abruptly and glared at Tamsin. He stuck out his elbow, meaning for her to take his arm.

Whatever had brought about his flirtatious manner towards her at Lady Curchon's dinner party last night seemed absent today. If anything, Ware appeared distracted and out of sorts. In other words, he was back to his usual disagreeable self.

Which was fine. Truly. After today, she might not see him again for some time. Or ever.

An ache started in her chest, but Tamsin pushed it away.

This was for Aurora. Had only *ever* been for Aurora. Even *if* Ware had formed an attachment to her, and she wasn't sure she would welcome such an entanglement, nothing could come of it.

"It's barely dawn, Your Grace. Surely we could have delayed our departure until I had breakfasted. Or enjoyed a cup of tea."

Tamsin was typically an early riser, but even she was shocked at the presence of Ware standing in the breakfast room waiting for her. Drew was upstairs but still abed, having not arrived home until the wee hours of the morning. Aurora and Aunt Lottie rarely left their rooms before mid-morning. Thankfully, only Holly bore witness to Ware stomping about demanding the presence of Lady Tamsin.

"Did I not inform you over dinner that this excursion would be an early one?" Ware tugged her along beside him.

"You did, Your Grace. But you failed to mention the exact time.

There is also my concern over the poisonous butterflies." Tamsin gave him an innocent look. "Won't they be compelled to attack?" She gave a terrified shiver.

"Amusing."

"You haven't told me how Banning took the news," she sniffed. "And I should like to know." Ware had neglected to return to the drawing room after dinner. Tamsin had felt abandoned, which was ridiculous, of course, because she and Ware weren't actually— *attached*. He'd been kind in vanquishing Banning but only for the sake of their charade. Just as he'd done in directing which fork she should use for the trout.

The entire dinner party was an affair best forgotten. Perhaps she would have behaved differently had Ware rejoined the other guests, especially when Lady Banning felt the need to voice her opinion of Tamsin to her directly.

Tamsin, in turn, *accidentally* stepped on Lady Banning's gown, tearing the silk at the hem.

Lady Banning hissed that Tamsin was *ill-bred*.

But after another horrid glass of ratafia, Tamsin recognized that Ware, who didn't care for social situations, probably could not tolerate another minute of society and awkward conversation. He'd fulfilled his part of their little play and there was no need to do more.

Just as Ware was doing today.

His eyes glinted at her in the early morning light. "Lord Banning didn't appreciate my jest as much as you might think. And there is no murderous population of butterflies residing in the park, as I'm sure you've surmised."

"Yes, but I'm not observant." She looked up at him in expectation. "As you reminded me."

"The *papilio antimachus* is indigenous to Africa," Ware stated in a superior tone. "And would never survive in the climate of England."

"Well, you said anything is possible."

Ware tilted his head. "Yes, but not that."

"What a relief." Tamsin clasped her hands. "I was quite terrified."

A noise left him. Something between grunt and snarl.

"I beg you to take smaller steps." Her skirts were already wet from dew-soaked grass because Ware seemed intent on ignoring the perfectly good path to their left, deciding instead to walk along the edge of a wooded area.

Another puff of irritation left him. "Your legs are far too short."

"Perhaps it is that yours are too long."

Ware looked down at her, real amusement shining from him, which nearly made up for the annoyed tone. The brush of dark hair along his jaw was heavier than usual. And though he didn't seem completely rumpled, his cravat was poorly tied once more.

"Are you between valets again, Your Grace?"

"As it happens, I am. Lost another last night." Sunlight danced over Ware's sharply cut features, pulling out the blue-black glints in his hair and reflecting the silver of his eyes. He reminded her of a rough-cut mountainside, all slopes and jutting rock.

Pulling her into the thick wooded area to her right, she wondered where exactly Ware was taking her. Not a soul was about. Certainly no one who could claim to have seen them collecting specimens. Perhaps Ware meant to dispose of her and hide her body in a tree trunk. Tamsin could see him explaining her disappearance to Aunt Lottie.

She annoyed me so terribly much and her Latin was terrible.

Tamsin cleared her throat and nodded at the small clearing before them. "Plenty of *insecta* in there, I'll warrant."

"Stop bandying about the term. Just say *insect*. Latin coming from your mouth sounds nonsensical."

Tamsin thought that unfair. She'd practiced after all. "It satisfied Lady Chilcott."

"Lady Chilcott is a nitwit." Ware continued to pull her along.

"Come, I want to show you something before all the riders and carriages arrive and frighten them away." He took Tamsin down a small rise where a spray of wildflowers bloomed.

"Do you see?" He stood behind Tamsin and leaned over her shoulder, warm and solid, smelling of bergamot. He pointed to a cluster of daisies.

As if at his command, a cloud of blue drifted up from the flowers and circled before descending once more.

"Oh," Tamsin breathed.

Tiny wings fluttered about in the air as the butterflies moved in and out of the grass and daisies.

"I've seen them before," she said, awestruck by the sight. "But never so many at once. What is their proper name? In Latin?" The butterflies were so beautiful with the morning sun gilding their wings.

"*Polyommatus icarus.*"

"*Polyommatus icarus,*" she whispered, watching the butterflies float in the air. A sudden yearning for her mother, one that never truly left, pulled at her heart. "Blues. That's what my mother called them."

A vision of Mama, hair streaming behind her, laughing as Malcolm and Drew, still toddlers, chased her about the gardens at River Crest flashed before Tamsin. "She said butterflies were a sign of new beginnings. When my father—pursued her, he gifted Mama with an enormous bouquet of wildflowers. A butterfly flew out of the bouquet and landed on his coat."

Mama had often said it was a sign that she was meant to love the Earl of Emerson.

Sometimes, Papa would just stand and watch her, his love for the woman all of London considered no better than a common doxy stamped in every line of his body. Jordan looked at Odessa in the same way, as if she were the most fascinating creature he'd ever beheld. Tamsin had wanted such a thing for herself once.

"I never saw the Blues," Tamsin stuttered, her throat suddenly thick. "After we—*left* for Dunnings."

Another vision of her mother, this one of her withered and pale against the sheets, dying a slow death, had the moisture gathering in Tamsin's eyes. That was when she had started challenging the sons of the local gentry to races, so that there would be money to summon a doctor. But it was already too late.

It was my fault she died at Dunnings.

Jordan and the rest of her siblings didn't blame her. Mama hadn't blamed her. But Tamsin knew, in her heart, that if *only* she hadn't punched Sokesby that day, maybe Bentley would have reconsidered banishing the Sinclairs from London.

Maybe—

She dropped Ware's arm and took a step away from him, clearing her throat several times to keep the tears at bay. The last thing she wished to do was start weeping in front of Ware.

"Apologies, Your Grace. I was caught up in the past." She gave him her cocky smile. "But I'm ready now."

"I did not mean to distress you." A small wrinkle took up residence between his dark brows. "Truly."

"You didn't." Tamsin assured him, willing away the pain of Mama's death and her own guilt. "I was only considering that while Dunnings has a great deal of coal, the estate lacks a cloud of butterflies. Thank you for showing them to me, Your Grace."

The light, unexpected touch of Ware's fingers pressed into the base of Tamsin's spine, bringing with it a wave of comfort and that slow, insistent hum she felt whenever Ware was close.

"I have only ever seen so many of them early in the morning when I come to walk. After all those beetles, I wanted you to see how beautiful insects can be."

There was a beat of her heart. Then another. "You meant to surprise me. Thank you, Your Grace."

That deceiving bit of color entered his cheeks once more. A sign he was discomfited by her remark. "And according to Mr. Epps, your brother's future wealth will one day rival my own. So perhaps it is fortuitous that there are no *polyommatus icarus* at Dunnings."

Tamsin wondered at Ware's revelation. How could he possibly know Mr. Epps? Tamsin hadn't even met him. But before she could ask, Ware started down the edge of the woods, passing through the field of Blues still hovering about the daisies. He had his hands out, fingertips stretched as if inviting the butterflies to land on him.

Her heart stuttered once more at the sight of his immense form surrounded by daisies and a field of Blues. Tamsin shut her eyes at how beautiful Ware was to her.

This isn't real. Not for him. And it must not be for me.

"Come along," he said over one shoulder. "Don't dawdle. I see Lady Harrington riding with her groom." He nodded to the other side of the pond. "Who is also her lover."

She hurried to catch up to him in time to see Ware pick up a small tree branch about the width of Tamsin's wrist.

"I'll beat the grass around us."

"What? Why?"

"If there are moths or any other flying insect about, they will be disturbed and soar upward." The annoyance was back. "You can catch them with this." He pulled out what looked like a miniature broom handle from a pocket hidden in his coat. There was a net at one end.

"What else do you have in your coat? At this point I wouldn't be surprised if you brought out an entire chicken." Tamsin had to skip to keep pace with his longer strides.

"Look at me with admiration for my intelligence," he grumbled, though Tamsin saw just a hint of a smile touching the wide mouth.

Lifting her skirts, she marched after him. "I hardly think this necessary, Your Grace. The admiration. Neither Lady Harrington nor her lover will be able to see us clearly from such a distance."

"She has excellent eyesight." Ware swung the stick about, nearly hitting Tamsin as she gamely jumped and tried to catch whatever was flying out of the grass.

Grasshoppers, she thought as one jumped on her skirts. Another hopped across her arm. The insects were leaping at her and then bouncing away. Laughter burst from her as she twirled about, catching nothing at all in the net. "I look absurd."

Ware stopped beating the grass and straightened. No command or cutting remark rolled from his lips; instead, his bold features softened with what looked like longing before he abruptly turned away and headed towards one of the trees.

"Ware?"

Raising a hand, he waved Tamsin over to a fallen tree. Holding up a finger to his lips, instructing her to be silent, he pointed to an area of the roughened bark.

She crept closer, net held at the ready, trying not to giggle. Was this really what Ware did all day?

"Just here," he whispered.

Tamsin came closer, scrutinizing the gnarled bark, but saw nothing unusual. She stepped forward another inch, lowering the net.

Ware frowned at her.

"My arm is tired," she murmured. "Lady Harrington can't even see us and there isn't—" A slight, almost imperceptible ripple moved against the gnarled bark. A delicate wing lifted, one nearly the same color as the tree trunk. She got on her knees in the grass, fascinated as the tiny moth stretched its wings, revealing more of itself.

Ware lowered, folding his large body silently into the grass beside her.

What an interesting morning this had been thus far. First the sight of the Blues and now this fragile moth. Tamsin sensed Ware didn't share such intimacy with everyone. Or possibly anyone.

"Ware," she turned. "What sort of m—"

The rest of her question was cut off as Ware's mouth brushed gently over hers.

A soft gasp left Tamsin, one of surprise and pleasure in equal parts. The press of Ware's lips fully over hers sent a trembling sensation down the length of her back.

Ware devoured Tamsin in an instant; there was no other word for it. As if he'd been starving his entire life and only now was given a bite of food. He cupped the side of her face with one big hand, pulling at the curls dangling near her cheeks. Tongue sliding along the seam of her lips, he urged her to open for him as his other arm wound firmly around Tamsin's waist.

The hum inside her, the tantalizing vibration felt only in Ware's presence, intensified. Her heart pounded fiercely as the hum slid down across her stomach to take up residence between her thighs.

Tamsin's knees buckled and she fell back against the tree, praying the moth had flown away and wasn't being crushed beneath her. She welcomed the onslaught of Ware, craved it, realizing she'd wanted this for so long.

Ware's teeth nipped seductively at her bottom lip before his tongue wound seductively around hers.

Oh goodness.

Tamsin had expected that at the very least Ware knew something about kissing, but—this masterful control of her mouth and body proved he was no stranger to passion. Or things of a carnal nature despite his reputed disinterest.

It was shocking and wholly unexpected. Also, bloody marvelous.

Madness. Mindless intoxication. The desire between them erupted so fiercely, Tamsin thought she might burn to ash.

Her fingers curled into his coat, clutching at him with desperation, feeling the bumps beneath the fabric. He must have a half-dozen pockets in his coat, all filled with notebooks, glass vials, and other tools any proper entomologist must carry.

"Tamsin." The rough version of her name resonated along her

skin.

She slid further down the tree trunk, uncaring that the fabric of her dress would likely shred. Half-lying in the grass, somewhat propped up against the tree, Ware's big hands trailed over her waist and stomach as if she were some sort of miracle before palming one breast.

For a scholarly sort, he certainly knew exactly what to do with his hands and other parts of his anatomy. No one would ever assume— well, that was the true ruse, wasn't it?

Ware would *never* wed a girl of Tamsin's reputation.

There was only *one* reason why a duke took liberties with a woman deemed unacceptable, one too far beneath him to ever consider wedding. Society was only too eager to spread such tales. In fact, she'd spent the last few weeks determined to escape such a fate for her sister's sake. Ware was no different than his father or his brothers. Indeed, he had much in common with Lord Banning, except Ware hid his nature better.

In a panic, she tried to pull away from him, the disappointment filling her heart nearly breaking it.

Ware didn't budge. In fact, his hand was inching up beneath her skirts, fingers trailing along her stockings.

So Tamsin did what she always had when faced with unwelcome advances by a gentleman.

She balled her fist and punched Ware solidly and firmly in the stomach.

CHAPTER TWELVE

T HE SENSATION OF Tamsin's small fist sinking into his abdomen
   didn't hurt; Hayden barely felt it. But the pressure was enough to
release her.

She pressed herself further into the tree trunk, shrinking back from
Hayden as if he meant to attack her. Honestly, he didn't blame her.

Willing his breathing to return to normal and his cock to stand
down, Hayden tried to think of anything but the overwhelming desire
he had for Tamsin Sinclair. A desire so powerful he'd nearly taken her
against a tree in the park.

"I didn't mean—" Shame filled him for treating Tamsin like—he
had only meant to show her the moth. Hayden had never felt more
like his father. Or his brothers. Looking across the grass to the path
some distance away, Hayden saw Lady Harrington, but her back was
to them.

"Tamsin." His throat felt thick, her name unwieldy in his mouth.
"I—" The words refused to leave his mouth, unprepared to admit to
this gorgeous creature how very much he wanted her. Had always
wanted her.

She brandished the net at him like a sword, a distressed look on her
lovely features. Her breasts pushed against her bodice with each angry
breath.

Something inside Hayden had *unraveled* watching Tamsin's wonder at the *polyommatus icarus*. Helen of Troy, chin lifted to the morning

sun. He had never seen anything so beautiful in all his life. Hayden's heart, never reliable, thudded painfully to life in his chest at the sight. But when she hopped about with grasshoppers flying all over her skirts, giggling and holding up that stupid net, well, Hayden was *forever* lost to Tamsin.

Because in that moment, the *only* thing that mattered to Hayden had been Tamsin Sinclair. Every insect in the world could have disappeared and he wouldn't have cared.

There was *nothing* vague about his attachment to her. Only Hayden didn't know how to tell Tamsin. He was terrible at expressing himself.

"At least Banning was honest in his intent."

Hayden inhaled slowly, allowing the insult to sink in. Is that what she thought of him? But of course she did. "Tamsin."

"And I find you far worse than your brothers. Using my gratitude to make me malleable." A wounded sound came from her. Her leg jerked out, kicking him in the shin with the toe of her half-boot. "I don't even like you."

"Ouch. Stop that." He hopped out of range, feeling the sting of her disdain and his own anger at being compared to Thompson and Banning. But that wasn't what cut him to the quick.

I don't even like you.

"That is unfair," he returned. "Your comparison."

"Don't try to dissuade me of my well-formed opinion." She held up a hand and took a shaky breath. "This unwelcome association is at an end." The tiny net was tossed at his feet. "And as much as I appreciate your efforts on behalf of my sister, it does not bestow upon you the right to take liberties with my person even if you are a bloody duke."

"Is that your assumption?" The words sliced along his throat, tearing at his mouth. How little Tamsin thought of him. Another truth he hadn't yet realized.

A slender hand thumped her chest. "I cannot afford to allow my sister's come-out to be ruined so that you may satisfy your curiosity, Your Grace."

"My curiosity?" Hayden knew well what she implied.

"You have been abominable to me since our *first* meeting. I suppose you assumed after your efforts of the previous evening that I would be charmed." She made a noise in her throat and dismissed him with a wave of her hand. "Well, I am not."

Was she referring to Hayden's pathetic attempts at flirtation during Lady Curchon's dinner?

"I suppose you preferred Lord Banning's proposal?" Hayden spat out before he could think better of it. He wasn't sure how he'd imagined things this morning, but—well it was not *this*.

"I've nothing more to say," she threw over her shoulder.

"I do," he snapped at her. "The carriage is in the other direction."

She stopped. Spun in a half circle and took off in the opposite direction to his waiting carriage.

Hayden, furious, strode off after her, easily catching up to Tamsin just as her hand landed on the handle of the carriage. He placed his palm flat against the door, unwilling to allow her to just climb inside until she listened to him.

Taking a deep breath, he reined in his own temper. "I think you have misunderstood my intent, Tamsin. I wanted you to see the moth and—"

"Just stop," she cut him off. The bits of green in her eyes sparkled with wounded anger. "If you *ever* touch me again, Your Grace," she said in a low, brittle tone, "I *will* break your precious nose."

"We should—there is a reason—a feeling," he finally managed to get out.

"There is *nothing* between us," she shouted at him. "Nothing."

Hayden lifted Tamsin into the carriage, ignoring the way she attempted to swat him away. "I disagree," he growled.

"*Nothing*, Your Grace. I am not interested in what you offered me moments ago. And there is little you can do to change my mind."

Tamsin did not want him, that much was abundantly clear. His hands dropped to his sides, not willing to touch her a moment longer. Rejection was a familiar sensation, but that didn't make it any less painful. No wonder he preferred insects to people. Crickets did not reject you. Or butterflies. Moths. Beetles.

Hayden took a pointed step back from the carriage. The strings around his heart, so recently unraveled, rewound themselves, this time much tighter than before. He didn't blame Tamsin. Hayden was aware that he was odd. Strange. Incredibly unpleasant. Difficult to care for.

"Why did you agree to this?" Her question was fraught with so much peril for Hayden.

Because I was foolish. Because I was undone by you the moment you punched Thompson in the nose.

"For my own sake." The lie slid easily from his lips. There was nothing left now but salvaging what was left of his pride. "I *did* put my mouth on you in the garden in a lapse of control. Pity that little nitwit was hiding beneath a tree with her husband and overheard. But it wasn't as if I could wed you. My aunt found an unusual, but ultimately splendid, solution." He shrugged.

My God. He'd never sounded so much like his sire. Every word was filled with arrogance and chilly disdain.

There is nothing between us.

Hayden would ensure that there was not. Could not be. His entire chest felt like someone had sliced him open with a sword.

"Then there was the matter of Lady Penelope Worth," he added. "*She* was my mother's choice, and my aunt's, for Duchess of Ware. But not mine. After word of our vague attachment spread, Lady Penelope blessedly set her cap for someone else."

Tamsin inhaled at the words, her fingers tightening on the wood of the carriage.

"Now I will remain blissfully undisturbed until at least the start of the Season. It only cost a few weeks of my time."

"How convenient for you, Your Grace."

"Convenient? Hardly, my lady. I liken you to a pebble in my shoe, one I can now cheerfully kick away."

Tamsin reddened. Her beautiful mouth, still swollen from his kiss, thinned into a tight, grim line. He was fortunate she didn't have a weapon.

"This has all been *somewhat* amusing, but I have work to do. And as you said, this unwelcome association is at an end." A terrible chill had settled over his shoulders, as if Hayden had stepped into a snowstorm. "Take Lady Tamsin home," he instructed the driver. "I believe I'll stay a while longer."

A ragged breath came from her. A stricken sound that Hayden decided to ignore. "Ware," she choked angrily from behind him. "I'm not done talking to you."

"Unfortunate, as I am done speaking to you."

Hayden walked swiftly back the way they'd come. Not once did he look back.

CHAPTER THIRTEEN

AURORA BOUNCED ABOUT in the seat of the Earl of Emerson's coach, thrilled to finally be returning to River Crest. Jordan's vehicle, a glorious contraption that smelled of rich leather, had been waiting when they exited the train. Tamsin had immediately fallen back against the squabs, exhausted from the journey which had consisted of an endless stream of stops and gave Tamsin far too much time to consider the Duke of Ware.

The parting with Ware should not have pained her. Their association was one based on avoiding any further connection between them. Was it really such a surprise that Ware found her acceptable for a dalliance but not marriage? His reputation remained intact. Hers had dramatically improved. Lady Longwood had been silenced. For now. Aurora had been spared a gossip-filled debut. London now had a far different opinion of Tamsin Sinclair, for which she supposed she might be more grateful.

Excepting Lady Curchon, of course. Her opinion of Tamsin had not improved.

"I do wish Drew was here. And Malcom," Aurora said, interrupting Tamsin's thoughts.

Drew's trunks had been brought down and loaded, but then just as unceremoniously unloaded. She'd seen Holly hand Drew a letter only moments before informing Tamsin that a business matter had come up, one which would delay his trip to River Crest. Strange considering her brother's "business" mostly consisted of playing cards and tupping widows. Drew promised to be along in a day or two, but Tamsin wasn't so sure.

"I'm sure Drew will arrive by the end of the week." She took Aurora's hand, allowing none of her feelings to show as the coach climbed a small rise. "And Malcolm promises to return home before your come-out. Hopefully, we will all be together for Christmas. Look."

Tamsin pointed out the window as the estate of the Earl of Emerson came into view. How long had it been since she was home? Over a decade. The house on Bruton was lovely, of course, but River Crest had been where the Lord Emerson and his second family had spent most of their time and where Tamsin had grown up. After Bentley's unexpected death, the entire family, excepting Malcolm because he was on the Continent, had gone to London before coming here, to support Jordan as he assumed the title and accepted the marriage being foisted upon him.

Yes, but that resolved itself in the best possible way.

"What do you think, Aurora, is River Crest as you recall?"

"Yes." Her sister nodded solemnly.

Aurora had been little more than a child when Bentley banished the family to Dunnings. It was doubtful she remembered anything of the estate, which made Tamsin unaccountably sad. This had been their home, so much more than the London house. But perhaps that wasn't the case for Aurora. She adored life in town, as did Drew. Staying in London while Jordan and Odessa retired to River Crest had been as much for Aurora as to give the newlywed couple time alone.

Now, finally, her father's estate, her home, spilled out before Tamsin like a long lost jewel.

As the coach rolled down the drive, Tamsin took in the countryside. Land, a great deal of it, empty of crops and absent of tenants, could be seen from the coach window. Bentley's doing. He'd bled

River Crest for years to support his extravagant lifestyle in London. It made Tamsin detest her half-brother all over again. Several cottages dotted the landscape to her right, all with smoke rising from their chimneys.

Smoke was a good sign in this instance.

"I'm eager to see Emerson's pigs," Aunt Lottie mused. "Odessa writes he's quite proud of them. And she has been busy putting the house to rights and hiring staff. Well, there's little else to do here, I suppose. Certainly no time to read the London papers."

Aunt Lottie's gentle reminder that Tamsin need not be concerned news of her involvement with Ware would have reached Jordan. Odessa knew, of course. Drew most assuredly did, though he would say nothing. But Aurora was still left unaware, which everyone agreed would be for the best, especially since Lady Curchon had agreed to sponsor Aurora. Support she would rescind if Tamsin didn't keep her distance from Ware.

Lady Curchon, resplendent in a traveling outfit of violet and lace, had called yesterday at Emerson House. She was on her way out of town but wished to extend her congratulations that their little scheme had worked.

Of course, she gave most of the accolades to her own brilliance.

After an agonizing half hour of conversation punctuated by tea and biscuits, Lady Curchon made clear she was already whispering the news that Ware's attachment to Tamsin, never truly romantic in nature, mind you, had already begun to wane. Those whispers were already being carried about the countryside. When the Season started up once more, no one would even remember the incident.

When Lady Curchon finally rose, insisting she must be on her way, she asked Tamsin to see her out, smiling all the while. Once the drawing room door was shut and they found themselves in the hall, Lady Curchon dropped all pretense.

"I feel I should be honest, Lady Tamsin, about the depth of our acquaintance." Lady Curchon paused. "Or rather, how it will continue from this point forward."

Tamsin came to a stop, heels making no sound on the tile beneath her slippers. She had expected Lady Curchon to retract her support of Aurora now that her nephew was in no danger of being forced to wed Tamsin or being compared to the previous Duke of Ware. It angered Tamsin, but only because Aurora deserved a spectacular debut. At least a scandal had been avoided.

"Allow me to be blunt."

"I doubt you can speak any other way, my lady."

Lady Curchon's eyes narrowed. "I don't give a fig for your reputation. I care even less for that of Lady Aurora's. I did not carefully curate this farce for your benefit."

Well, that was hardly a surprise. "I never assumed so."

"My nephew's reputation is impeccable and shall remain so. Do you understand, Lady Tamsin? I did not dodge one scandal," she scoffed, "only to become embroiled in another."

"I'm not sure—" Tamsin started as realization slowly dawned.

"Don't you dare pretend innocence." Lady Curchon's fingers curled like claws around Tamsin's wrist, nails pressing into her skin. "You are far more ambitious than I gave you credit for. I witnessed your manner towards Ware at my dinner party, and Lady Banning relayed to me your brazen behavior with her husband. I'm only surprised you didn't follow Ware out into the gardens in an effort to once more compromise him. I thought you innocent that night, but now I feel certain your behavior was carefully planned."

Tamsin had lifted her chin at Lady Curchon's baseless accusations. "You are incorrect. Regardless of what you may think, I would never do such a thing. Compromise Ware? You realize he isn't some young girl who has only just made her debut. Ware and I don't even like each other."

"How clever you must think yourself," Lady Curchon had spat.

"Very much like your mother who thought herself far better than she happened to be." She leaned forward. "Lady Harrington is an acquaintance of *mine*." There had been steel in her tone.

Tamsin had kept perfectly still, unable to defend herself, recalling Ware's kiss in the park. "My lady—"

"I salvaged your reputation. Your sister's debut is safe. And this is how you repay me." Lady Curchon shook her head. "You, Lady Tamsin, will keep your distance from the Duke of Ware. Though you doubtless fancy yourself an actress, I will have no repeat of any of your recent performances."

She stayed silent. Lady Curchon had made up her mind about Tamsin. Ware was far from being an innocent. How did his aunt not realize that Ware used his studies as an excuse to avoid society? He was not the naïve, unsophisticated scholar Lady Curchon liked to believe. At least, not all the time.

"Don't force me to withdraw my support for Lady Aurora. Or cast further doubt in your direction. Wouldn't it be a shame if Lord Curchon were to find fault with Lord Emerson's mining operation in Northumberland? Not when your family's fortunes are only now being restored."

As threats went, it was a good one. Jordan was only now rebuilding the Sinclair wealth which had been so decimated by Bentley. Aurora talked non-stop about her entrance into society. Tamsin could not once again ruin her family's future. "There is nothing whatsoever between Ware and me, my lady."

"Splendid. I expect that to continue," Lady Curchon said as she sailed out the door.

"Tamsin."

Yesterday's conversation with Lady Curchon had sent Tamsin directly to the sideboard for a much needed glass of whiskey.

"Tamsin?" Aurora nudged her. "Whatever is the matter? Aren't you happy to be home? You're frowning."

"I am deep in concentration considering how lovely it will be to ride around River Crest once more, properly attired and not on some horrid sidesaddle." She winked at her sister. It would do no good to keep thinking of Ware. Her worst fears had come to the forefront after he kissed her, even managing to tarnish the sight of the Blues.

"Riding as a lady isn't so terrible. I've become quite adept," Aurora said in a lofty tone. "It is only that you are stubborn, Tamsin. When asked to do one thing, you do the opposite."

Not a very flattering assessment of her character. "I am often correct."

Tamsin had spent the last few days congratulating herself that Ware was no longer part of her existence. She need not tolerate dried beetles or the stomping of giant feet. Nor be dragged about trying to ensnare a herd of grasshoppers.

"A brilliant skill." Aunt Lottie patted Aurora on the hand. "To have a ladylike seat upon a horse."

Tamsin smiled at the obvious affection between the two. The sponsorship of Lady Curchon for Aurora's debut had not been withdrawn. And it was within Tamsin's power to guarantee that the offer would not be withdrawn. Easy enough to avoid Ware. He was unlikely to come to River Crest. Tamsin would go to London for Aurora's debut, but she was reasonably sure she could elude Ware. After all, he wouldn't be seeking her out.

A field of daisies came into view as they drew closer to River Crest and a vision of Ware standing among them, the Blues floating over his arms, had Tamsin shutting her eyes. That moment had stayed embedded within Tamsin, often followed by the memory of his lips claiming hers. A hollow sensation took root in her midsection, as if someone had scooped out a portion of her stomach with a spoon.

The kiss had felt real. She had wanted it to be real.

No matter Ware's motivations, Tamsin had clung to him. Returned the kiss pressed against her lips. She had wanted him. It was only upon remembering the circumstances of their association that Tamsin had broken away.

The coach rolled to a stop before the front door just as a legion of servants streamed out to greet the travelers, lining up in a neat row.

Aurora jumped out, followed by Aunt Lottie and finally Tamsin.

As Tamsin stood and looked up at her family home, she had to blink back tears. One of her biggest fears at Dunnings had been that she would never see River Crest again. Memories flooded her. Of her parents. Jordan chasing her around the gardens. Punching one of the village boys when he'd been too free with his hands.

A sigh left her. She had always been uncivilized.

A bright blue butterfly sailed past Tamsin's nose, floating about in the air before disappearing into a spray of struggling foxgloves. The sight didn't bring forth thoughts of her mother. Not this time.

Polyommatus icarus, the voice inside her head whispered in Ware's gruff tone.

It was foolish to miss someone, especially Ware, merely because of one splendid kiss.

Not splendid. *Magnificent.* Her body hummed every time she relived being nearly tupped against a tree by that massive moth lover.

The hollow feeling returned once more, spiraling out in her midsection.

Regret, Tamsin thought. Because she'd—said horrible things in the park and he had returned her sentiment in kind. Ware did not have an attachment to Tamsin, but hers for him was firmly and resolutely in place. No matter Lady Curchon's threats.

Odessa appeared at the door, flushed and smiling, her hands stretched out to the three of them as they came forward. Wrapping her arms tightly around Aunt Lottie, Odessa moved to widen her embrace, pulling Aurora and then Tamsin towards her.

"There you are." There was a thickness to her words. Tamsin's sister-in-law pulled back and wiped a tear from one eye. "I've missed you all. Jordan has only recently returned from Northumberland and the pigs are not much for conversation."

"I disagree. I enjoyed their witty banter at Dunnings," Aurora said in a solemn tone. "We chatted often."

"Different pigs," Tamsin reminded her.

"At any rate," Odessa said with a pointed look, "*these* pigs don't care quite as much for your brother, which disappoints him greatly. His status as earl does not impress them. Especially the sow. I've asked him to leave such things to Mr. Halwhipple."

"Mr. Halwhipple?" Aurora asked.

"The *actual* pig farmer. He has bred prized hogs for at least a decade. I believe he is conspiring with the pigs to depose of Jordan. A conspiracy of sorts." Odessa waved them forward. "Goodness, that sounds fit for a penny dreadful, doesn't it? Mad pigs conspiring against their owner. Perhaps they attack and eat—"

"Odessa." Aunt Lottie gave her a warning look.

"Sorry." She winked at Tamsin.

"A splendid story for a penny dreadful, Odessa," Tamsin agreed. "Perhaps you should give up on your wax creations and attempt writing terrifying stories instead."

"Hmm. That is a thought. Jordan would be happy at an absence of wax heads." She grinned. "I've been practicing, you see. Trying to learn the correct technique, but I fear I'm not any good."

Odessa had a passion for the world's oddities, which had morphed into an unquenchable thirst for lurid tales, stories of executions and criminals, ghosts, haunted cemeteries, and the like. Her interest in the macabre had led Odessa to the gruesome wax effigies created by Madame Tussaud who had an exhibit hall on Baker Street in London. Tamsin had visited and found it fascinating and incredibly lifelike. Terrifying, if she were being truthful. Jordan had encouraged his wife to try sculpting in wax herself, but the results had been mixed.

"In addition to my lack of artistic talent, I've no place to properly store the heads. The warmer days has them melting, which make them that much more gruesome. I left one in the kitchen the other day and Cook fainted. We did not get pie for dinner that night."

Now knowing Ware, Tamsin no longer wondered at the bond between him and Odessa. What terrifying children they must have been with Ware pinning insects and Odessa going on about murderers.

"Jordan has gone to make the rounds of our tenants but should be back shortly." Odessa rolled her eyes. "I do not think he trusts Halwhipple."

Raising pigs had been a hobby of Jordan's and a way to eke out a living at Dunnings. Malcolm joined the army. Andrew became a proficient gambler at a shockingly young age, earning enough to buy Tamsin a horse. Tamsin, in turn, used the horse to race anyone who had a purse. They'd all done their part, even Aurora who managed the small kitchen garden and learned to cook. Not well, mind you. There was only so much you could do with cabbage.

"Your rooms are ready." Odessa took them inside. "I—hope you find them comfortable. Aurora, I took the liberty of placing you in your old room. If you don't like what I've done, I can change you to another. Or redecorate."

"My old room?" Aurora said softly, looking up the stairs. "I don't even recall what colors Mama used anymore. Only that my window looked out over the pond."

"Pale blue," Odessa answered, "was the color I settled on. I hope you like it. I handpicked each piece of furniture." She waved a hand about. "Jordan tried to recall how everything looked. He drew me pictures and discussed color schemes. I've done my best to restore River Crest."

Bless Odessa. Bentley had sold everything at the estate when he drew short on funds. River Crest had been nothing but an empty shell when Jordan arrived. But now, the air smelled of fresh paint and plaster. New paintings hung on the walls, and luxurious rugs once more covered the floors. Tamsin could see a delicately carved table gracing the hall.

"Everything looks marvelous, Odessa." Tamsin took her hand and pulled her close. "Thank you," she whispered.

"You're welcome." Odessa pressed her cheek to Tamsin's.

"I'm exhausted from chaperoning these two. Do you mind if I have a lie down, dear? Wake me for tea." Aunt Lottie took Odessa's hand.

"Of course. This is Chapman." Odessa waved forward a slender man with ginger hair. The butler had been standing in the shadows, waiting to be summoned. He was nothing at all like Holly, who one could not miss if they tried. "He'll show you up."

Chapman bowed. "This way please." The butler motioned towards the stairs.

Aurora slowly made her way up, hand trailing along the wooden banister. "It is exactly how I remember." She smiled down at Odessa. "Or at least, what I do recall. Come, Aunt Lottie." She took the older woman's hand and followed Chapman.

After her sister and Aunt Lottie disappeared up the stairs, Odessa tilted her head, gesturing towards the drawing room. "You look in need of a refreshment. Probably something stronger than tea, I imagine." She started down the hall. "*Everything* is new. Bentley left little, and what was here lay beneath layers of dust or was broken. He sold nearly everything. Jordan was devastated to see the destruction his brother had wrought. I didn't want to say so in front of Aurora."

"I don't miss Bentley. He was a rotten brother. Do you have whiskey?" Tamsin said hopefully. "Please don't force me to drink ratafia."

"Never." Odessa strolled into the drawing room and went immediately to the sideboard. Pouring out two glasses of the amber liquid, she handed one to Tamsin. "I've acquired a taste," she said at Tamsin's look of surprise. "Your brother's influence, no doubt."

"No doubt."

Jordan and Odessa were such an odd pairing, but one Tamsin found incredibly beautiful. They were perfectly *imperfect* together. Madly in love.

The Blues floating about Ware in a field of daisies invaded her thoughts once more and she resolutely pushed him aside in favor of the whiskey. "Oh, this is quite good."

Odessa regarded her patiently, rolling her own glass between her palms.

"Do you stare at my brother in such a way?" Odessa's eyes were a unique color, a mix of blue and gray. Far too shrewd for Tamsin's liking. "It's disturbing, to say the least. I feel as if you are contemplating my demise or else considering a wax mask of my face."

"You would look splendid in wax." Odessa's lips curved up. "I'll practice on you later. But I think we should discuss Ware before Jordan arrives and while Aurora is upstairs."

Tamsin peered into her whiskey, contemplating how much she should admit. Had Ware written Odessa?

"I'm afraid there isn't much I can say only that I don't find Ware as pleasant as you do."

"Oh." Odessa took a tiny sip from her glass. "I don't find my cousin pleasant in the least. He's a bear of a duke, isn't he?"

A tiny bit of heat pinched Tamsin's cheeks. "Lady Longwood should not have been in attendance that night. Nor following me into the gardens." She shrugged. "The last ball of the Season. Barely more than a little dance with a few musicians and refreshments."

"Lady Curchon has a rivalry with another snobbish lady of the *ton*. The two are in competition with each other and often host events on the same night. You can imagine the anguish it causes in London." Odessa's dislike for society was difficult to miss. "Though I suppose Lady Curchon has won this round. Her little dance, as you call it, was *officially* the last event of the Season. When I was Aurora's age, those were usually the only events I was invited to. Less risk of offending anyone with my presence. Lady Curchon and my mother were cousins and quite close when they were young."

"Much like you and Ware."

A small ache made itself known at the mention of name.

"Somewhat, though Ware and I aren't related by blood. Cousin Alice is Ware's aunt by marriage; Lord Curchon is the Duchess of Ware's brother. When I was a child, Cousin Alice visited my mother and often brought her nephew. Ware was an odd child, almost as strange as me. His father, the duke, had little affection for him, which is why the duchess often sent him to be with Lord and Lady Curchon. I'm sure Cousin Alice didn't expect that Ware and I would become so close; if she had, she never would have brought him. Cousin Alice does not claim me as a relation. And she's cautioned Ware for years not to announce any connection between us."

"Too late." Tamsin sat back. "He claimed you as cousin to Lady Longwood."

"Oh, dear." Odessa took another tiny sip of the whiskey. "I don't imagine Cousin Alice was pleased."

"Not in the least."

"She imagines herself to be Ware's protector," Odessa said. "And when he was young and his brothers tormented him, it was she who comforted Ware. Defended him. Encouraged his scientific nature. The duchess—had her hands full with Thompson and Maxwell. Not to mention the duke. I'm sure my aunt has told you the stories about them."

Aunt Lottie had told her some things. That Ware and Odessa weren't actually related but had been close as children. The character of the previous duke and Ware's brothers. But very little about Ware's mother.

"The duchess did not protect Ware?" A flicker of anger for the child Ware had been filled Tamsin's heart. Beast or not.

"Ware was always his mother's favorite." Odessa gave her a pointed look. "And thus, the duke took great pains to torment his youngest son as much as possible. The duchess entrusted her youngest child to Lady Curchon. It is why Cousin Alice is so proprietary over Ware."

Tamsin had witnessed Lady Curchon's protection of Ware firsthand.

"I'm speaking out of turn. Forgive me." Odessa leaned forward. "Aunt Lottie informed me that you and Ware were caught in Lady Curchon's garden. Together."

"We did not go to the gardens *together*. I was overly warm and unaccustomed to so many layers of underthings. At Dunnings," she gave Odessa a wry look, "my lone petticoat was so ancient one could read through it. A moth landed on my knee. Ware was in pursuit of the moth." She swallowed the last bit of the whiskey in the glass. "Not me."

"The moth landed on your *knee*?" Odessa asked. "Not on your skirts?"

"I—may have had my skirts raised. Because I was warm," she hastened to add. "And I thought I was alone. When he first came lumbering out of the shrubs, I assumed him to be some sort of grotesque monster, for which I blame you."

Odessa lifted a brow, gaze far too perceptive for Tamsin's liking.

"All your gruesome tales. Insisting there are creatures not of this earth inhabiting London." Tamsin shivered. "I may have overreacted. I attempted to punch him, which dropped my skirts over his enormous head and Ware became trapped." She held up a hand before Odessa could speak. "*Briefly.* I proceeded to box his ears. Pummeled him with my fists. Defending my honor, so to speak."

"You could do no less," Odessa agreed.

"At any rate, that is where Lady Longwood and her daughter found us. Insults were hurled at me. At you. Ware tromped back out of the shadows from where I'd vanquished him with my fists and became utterly ducal."

Ware had been magnificent instilling such fear in Lady Longwood. At the time, Tamsin hadn't appreciated the power he wielded.

"Terrifying, isn't it? Watching Ware transform before you when your initial impression is that of an overly intelligent, oblivious scholar. I'm guilty of assuming the same, though he has always been arrogant and commanding. But—when he threatened Angus White-hall—"

Odessa's estranged father. She never referred to him as her parent. Not anymore.

"That was the first time I ever saw Ware's father in him. He *was* the Duke of Ware, not my beloved cousin Hayden. And I was grateful for it." Odessa had a far off look in her eyes. "I think—that is really who he is." Her gaze returned to Tamsin. "I don't mean to say that he is not also an entomologist. Or a scholar. But I have lately concluded Hayden uses insects as subterfuge. No one at a ball wants to discuss moths, for instance."

Or at a dinner party. Tamsin had witnessed it firsthand.

"It's an excellent strategy to keep the world at bay. He isn't the most sociable creature."

"An interesting assessment." Tamsin was of the same opinion. And yet Ware had shown her the Blues. And the tiny moth. Kissed her.

"I understand, you see." Odessa took another small sip of her whiskey. "When one is declared unacceptable and others deem you beneath them, you go to great lengths to make yourself even more intolerable. Jordan taught me that. And it is a useful tool for creating distance. I assume it was Lady Curchon who came up with such convoluted subterfuge."

"Her scheme made an odd sort of sense. As much as I did enjoy the look on Lady Longwood's face when Ware revealed himself, doing so complicated things. Still, it was kind of Lady Curchon to protect my reputation," she finished.

"Kind?" Odessa gave a quiet bark of laughter. "You know there was no kindness towards you. She was trying to avoid a scandal and spare my cousin the indignity of possibly being forced to wed someone so far beneath him. No insult meant."

Tamsin raised her glass. "None taken. My unsuitability is no secret."

"Cousin Alice was saving her own neck. She probably got the idea from Aunt Lottie. My aunt engaged in a similar affair during her second or third Season and pretended an attachment to a gentleman until everyone departed London. The attachment, of course, faded over the summer months, as did the gossip, leaving Aunt Lottie scandal-free. It's quite genius, but the scenario only works if the couple isn't actually caught engaging in physical relations."

Tamsin thought of Ware's lips on the inside of her thigh. "The only thing I engaged in was fisticuffs."

"Terrible luck to have Lady Longwood present. Horrible old thing. Spewing her gossip. She would have used the scandal created to ruin Aurora's come-out. That's why you agreed, isn't it? Not for your sake, but your sister's."

"I'm not the one having a come-out."

"Speaking of which, Aunt Lottie tells me Cousin Alice offered to sponsor Aurora."

"She has." Tamsin nodded. "I am grateful."

"Again, I doubt there was an ounce of kindness in her offer. Cousin Alice likes to control the outcome of any situation. But, nevertheless, your reputation has not only been salvaged, but elevated. Aunt Lottie wrote me you are now considered something of a bluestocking."

"Better than a trollop."

"Agreed." Another sly glance was directed at Tamsin. "Perhaps he'll take you to another lecture when we return to London. Aunt Lottie wrote me about that as well."

Unlikely. Dear Cousin Alice has threatened to destroy us all if I so much as come within an inch of Ware.

"We argued fiercely at our last encounter," Tamsin informed her.

"I doubt I will be invited to admire insects in the future. At least with Ware."

"You argued?" Odessa sat back once more, blinking at Tamsin with those oddly discerning slate blue eyes. "But why? What could you possibly have argued about? Your association is vague at best, is it not?"

What was it Jordan always said about Odessa? She was *cunning*.

"More familial in nature." There had been nothing familial at all about that kiss in the park. "Ware is unpleasant. He said something rude, and we argued over it."

"You're oddly flushed, Tamsin." Odessa tilted her chin. "There is more than a hint of color in your cheeks. Are you well?"

"The drawing room is warm." Jordan was right. Odessa was far too clever. It was as if she could smell Ware's kiss on Tamsin.

"I suppose it is. If you'll excuse me, I believe I should check on Aunt Lottie." Odessa came to her feet. "I doubt her chaperoning duties exhausted her as she claims. Having once been her charge, I found my aunt to be lax in certain areas. Which is why Jordan and I will be in London when Aurora comes out. I'll see you a little later." Odessa touched her shoulder. "I'm so pleased we are all together."

"Me too."

Once Odessa's footsteps faded, Tamsin reached across the table to take up Odessa's glass which was still half-full. Good whiskey should not go to waste. Besides, she needed something to take her mind from Ware.

CHAPTER FOURTEEN

TAMSIN URGED HER mount faster, racing across the fields surrounding River Crest. After nearly a week of cloudy skies, the sun was out and the day absolutely glorious. Her shirt, pilfered from Jordan, was far too large and billowed out as she rode. The leather breeches she'd paid a junior groom for fit much better. As did the boots. Jordan bade Tamsin to have a few shirts made as well as breeches, along with a proper pair of boots. Money was no longer an issue and she shouldn't be tromping about in his leftover clothing or purchasing what she needed from his grooms. But be discreet, he'd pleaded.

Discreet wasn't often a word used in conjunction with Tamsin. She'd promised to try.

Bursting across a small stream, she came out on the main road leading to River Crest. She slowed the horse to a walk, lifting her face up to the sun. In London, she'd been ever mindful of wearing a bonnet to shield her complexion. Another rule she must follow. But in the country, Tamsin felt no such compulsion. There was no one to see but her family and the servants.

"Good job, Teach." She patted the horse's neck. It was a terrible name for a horse in Tamsin's opinion, but Odessa had named the gelding and several others in the stables after menacing pirates who all been executed in some dramatic, horrible fashion. In addition to Teach, named for Edward Teach, or Blackbeard as he was otherwise known, there was also Kidd and Black Bart.

Slowing Teach to a walk, Tamsin came around the bend in the road, narrowly avoiding a luxurious coach pulled by a set of perfectly matched bays. The coach was headed in the direction of River Crest, but Tamsin didn't recognize the coat of arms emblazoned across the doors. Not unusual. She had a poor memory for such things. Coats of arms. Insignias. Which fork to use for trout.

Thinking of proper forks for fish brought Ware to mind once more after spending most of her ride attempting to keep him away. Tamsin didn't want to think of him. If she and Ware happened to cross paths again, she would run in the other direction. Even if a warning shot hadn't been fired by Lady Curchon, Tamsin would still avoid him. No good could come of her continued association with a duke.

"At least," she said to Teach, "I received an introduction to the study of insects. I'm not sure how that will help me in future endeavors. But I can now identify several types of moths by their Latin names."

Odessa, after their initial discussion, hadn't asked anything else about Ware, for which Tamsin was grateful. Her feelings were strained enough without having to explain them to her sister-in-law. The important thing, *the only thing*, was that no scandal had erupted because she'd made the poor choice to cool off in the gardens and box the ears of a duke. Aurora's come-out would not be ruined by Lady Longwood. And Tamsin's reputation had improved, not greatly mind you, but enough.

"I did nothing wrong, but the world is exceptionally unfair to females," she said to Teach. "You're lucky to be a gelding." She looked down at the horse. "You probably don't think so, but trust me on this, Teach."

She turned down the drive to River Crest and stopped. The coach she'd passed mere moments ago now sat outside the stately manor. Who could possibly be visiting the Sinclairs? River Crest wasn't isolated exactly, but the location was a good distance from London.

And her family wasn't exactly popular. Patchahoo might be their only visitor. Or possibly Drew, but neither would arrive in such a lavish vehicle.

Tamsin pulled Teach to a stop.

A small wiggling sensation started in her stomach. Like a worm on a hook. Not dread, exactly. Or anticipation. But a mixture of both.

A footman hopped down from the coach and opened the door with a deep bow. He did not straighten immediately. As if royalty were inside or—

One incredibly oversized duke.

That unwanted delicious hum, like a dozen bees buzzing across her skin, stretched over Tamsin's limbs.

A large, booted foot stepped onto the gravel drive, followed by a second, as the Duke of Ware unfolded himself from the coach. There was really no other word for the way he slowly crawled out and straightened to his full height. Tamsin could almost hear his neck and the bones of his spine cracking.

Her heart beat unsteadily, flipping about in her chest. What was he doing here? Had he come to see her? Maybe Ware regretted the way they'd parted. She had declared there was nothing between them, but Tamsin didn't think that entirely true.

Another footman appeared and bowed deeply.

Ware pointed to the trunks atop the coach.

Trunks. Which inferred a much longer stay than a valise.

The sensation rolling over Tamsin's arms and thighs intensified. A tight curl descended to settle low in her belly.

The duke reached inside the coach and withdrew a large satchel, which he draped over one arm before gesturing to the footman further.

Lady Curchon had threatened Tamsin to avoid Ware at all costs, but she had obviously forgotten to give her nephew the same instructions. His arrival at River Crest was both unexpected and unsettling. And his stay wasn't going to be brief as the small pile of trunks indicated.

Her fingers tightened on the reins.

Chapman opened the front door with a bow and Odessa rushed down the steps to fling herself at Ware. Laughter floated on the air as she greeted him. His shaggy head bent towards hers.

The delicious sensation in Tamsin's belly tightened, and then disappeared completely, wiped away by embarrassment at her own foolishness. Ware wasn't here for *her*. He was here to see Odessa. Which he had every right to do. As unlikely as it might seem, he had come to River Crest. Hopefully, Lady Curchon agreed and wouldn't decide that Tamsin had anything to do with it.

Honestly, Tamsin wasn't even sure Ware had even recalled she'd be in residence.

HAYDEN BRIEFLY CONSIDERED that he'd gone mad. Quite a few dukes had lost their minds to his recollection, though he didn't think they'd done so over a woman. He might be the first. The knowledge that he would be under the same roof as Tamsin kept Hayden in a constant state of arousal and trepidation for the entire length of the journey to Emerson's estate. Hayden had no idea what he planned to accomplish by seeing Tamsin again. Her feelings for him had been made abundantly clear at their last meeting.

Turning slightly, he caught sight of a rider on the rise above River Crest, barely paying attention to the footmen scurrying about. The breeze had the rider's shirt billowing out like a sail around her slender form. He wished he could see the breeches she wore from this distance.

Oh. Yes. There is my madness.

Lady Tamsin Sinclair, Hayden reasoned, was akin to a storm expected to bring only rain but surprises you with strong winds, hail, and torrential downpours before ripping the roof from your home. A month without her had been far too long.

She did not raise her hand in greeting, though Hayden was sure Tamsin could see him. He was difficult to miss.

Not a promising start.

His aunt had called upon Hayden shortly before her departure from London. She had fussed over him, extolling the virtues of a handful of young ladies whom Hayden couldn't have cared less about. In great dramatic fashion, Aunt Alice declared how grateful she was to be rid of Tamsin Sinclair. Their little ruse had been a success, but the price had been to tolerate the girl. And there was the matter of sponsoring Lady Tamsin's sister for her debut.

His aunt had waited somewhat impatiently for Hayden to withdraw his earlier demand that she sponsor Lady Aurora.

He did not.

"I'm not so certain Lady Longwood's opinion of Lady Tamsin is incorrect. I'm convinced she was attempting to trap you into marriage. Very much like her mother, though much more ambitious."

Hayden loved Auntie Alice. She'd been his protector during a turbulent childhood. But that little speech filled him with so much dislike for her he nearly had his butler show her the door. His aunt didn't notice the change in Hayden's mood; instead, she told him not to worry. The tale that a duke's interest in Lady Tamsin, never great to begin with mind you, had waned was even now making the rounds. She'd seen to it.

Hayden wished Aunt Alice a pleasant stay in the country and hurried her out the door.

After her departure, he threw himself into finishing the research on moths. The treatise was nearly complete. He tried not to think of Tamsin while enjoying several thrilling lectures at the Entomological Society, one of which was on *blattodea*. But even during the spirited discussion on termites, Tamsin invaded his thoughts. He pictured her beside him, pretending to be interested and then dozing off in boredom. Scribbling away in her own tiny notebook. How she smelled of jasmine.

How much he missed her.

Once his research was finished, Hayden presented it to his colleagues at the Entomological Society, receiving scores of accolades for the careful curation of his collection, which would now be put on permanent display. An enormous achievement. He even joined his fellow entomologists for dinner after his presentation, something he had never done before, and indulged in a great deal of wine.

Which resulted in a flood of carnal thoughts all involving Tamsin naked carrying about the butterfly net.

Determined to keep himself busy, Hayden dined out frequently, when before he did not. He settled in at White's for drinks. Gambled a little, but found he didn't care for it. Thankfully, there were no stupid balls to attend during the summer months. He received invitations to *three* different house parties and came to the realization that as an unwed duke under the age of sixty, he would be highly sought after if only he put in a small effort.

He refused all three invitations.

Dinner at his club was one thing, but an entire household of individuals he had no desire to know better was another. What would he do besides sleep in a bed far too small for him and converse with giggling nitwits? Go on scavenger hunts with some silly young woman who would scream at the sight of a cricket? They would all fear offending him. No sarcastic remarks about his size or the absence of a valet would be forthcoming.

Boredom set in a few weeks after Tamsin's departure. He wasn't motivated to start any new projects. So, Hayden called in both his secretaries, his steward, *and* his solicitor demanding to be shown, well, *everything*. He studied each holding, investment, and estate of the

Duke of Ware until Hayden was confident he knew where every last pound of his vast fortune was located. Going forward, he instructed the collection of employees that he expected to be informed of his affairs on a weekly basis.

"But you have never taken an interest, Your Grace. Your work takes precedence. You are an entomologist." This from his solicitor, a gentleman who he was almost certain had mismanaged some of Hayden's affairs.

"And I am also the Duke of Ware."

He'd annunciated each word, glaring at his quivering solicitor, wishing he'd taken a firm hold of his affairs when Father had died.

The days dragged by. He considered returning to Orchard Park, but his ducal estate was more mausoleum than home since the death of his father and brothers. There was nothing but statues and cats roaming about. So, Hayden came to the conclusion that what he needed was to visit Odessa, reasoning that River Crest was an excellent place to start his next research project: beetles.

Halfway to Emerson's estate, Hayden acknowledged that while he bore his cousin Odessa a great deal of affection and there were certain to be a variety of *coleoptera* present at the estate—he *missed* the pebble in his shoe. Desperately.

I should never have called her such.

And Tamsin *bloody* Sinclair had kissed him back with far more passion than any disinterested woman could possibly muster. She'd also punched him. But not in the nose. Which gave Hayden a great deal of hope.

"Be careful with my trunk. My specimen cases are inside," he instructed the footman as Odessa wrapped him in an embrace, exclaiming over his unexpected visit.

"You'll be doing research then?" Odessa eyed him. "Are you done with moths?"

"I am. I presented my work to the Entomological Society where it was received with great praise. My collection is now on permanent display within its hallowed halls."

Hayden sometimes thought himself a moth. One that circled a blazing torch that was Tamsin, willing to singe his wings for only a moment in the light. Longing for the very thing that terrified him. He was a man of logic. Science. It wasn't that Hayden didn't believe in love, more the idea of it seemed far too fanciful.

He glanced back once more at the glorious creature on horseback while Odessa chattered away, instructing the footmen to place the trunks in a parlor at the back of the house Hayden could use as a study. Thank goodness Tamsin was a distance away else Hayden would be tempted to pull her from the horse and—

Would he have to court her? Go to Emerson and beg permission? He thought he might. The very idea had Hayden rolling his eyes in disgust. Shouldn't the beetle lecture and the museum count?

Hayden's previous attempts at charming Tamsin had ended in disaster. He had some experience with women, but his engagement had been strictly limited to things of a physical nature. His companions had enjoyed clever innuendo. Slightly improper remarks. Did Tamsin want compliments? Flowery prose?

Dear God.

"Why didn't you send a note, Hayden? Had I known you were coming, I would have been better prepared. I don't think I even have a bed that will fit you." Her brows drew together. "And you didn't bring a valet. Jordan doesn't have one either."

"I decided to surprise you. And I'm between valets at the moment."

"You've lost another?" Odessa hugged him again.

"I don't lose them. They leave. Of their own accord," he grumbled.

"I've missed you, Hayden. I've just read the most lurid tale of a murderous tavern owner in Wales and had no one to share it with."

"Not even Emerson?" He smiled down at her. Few people welcomed Odessa's obsession with the macabre. Hayden wasn't even sure he did at times.

"Jordan doesn't appreciate my stories as you do."

"What don't I appreciate?" Emerson, boots caked with mud, came around the side of the house looking more like the pig farmer he'd once been than an earl. "Odessa? Why are the footmen scurrying about? They are behaving as if we are expecting the queen—" He stopped short as he caught sight of Hayden. "Your Grace."

"Ware will do, Emerson." He and Emerson weren't well acquainted, but he supposed that would change. "Since you and Odessa wed so quickly—"

"A necessity, Your Grace." Emerson frowned, shoulders tightening in a way that reminded Hayden of Tamsin. Both she and her brother always appeared moments from jumping into a tavern fight.

"I decided a visit to my cousin was in order. I wish to ensure her happiness. Also, there is the matter of beetles."

"Beetles?" Emerson came forward, one roughened hand tugging gently at Odessa's skirts. A proprietary move of a male staking his claim on a female. Animals often did so in the wild. And Emerson was a bit of a savage.

"There is a species particular to this part of England," Hayden explained in a lofty tone. "Odessa wrote to me about them, knowing I was considering beetles for my next project."

Odessa, to her credit, played along, though she'd never exclaimed to him over beetles at River Crest. "Yes, Your Grace. When you told me of your interest, I felt I must mention the curious ones I've seen in the surrounding area."

"Done with moths then?" Emerson's fingers toyed absently with a lock of Odessa's hair. "I suppose as long as it isn't spiders, my home is yours, Your Grace."

Emerson, in addition to being somewhat rough, had a strange preoccupation with spiders, which were *not* insects. "Just Ware.

Wedding in haste and without me present was a terrible broach of manners, *considering*."

When Angus Whitehall, Odessa's vile father, tried to keep the news of coal at Dunnings from Emerson in a bid to keep the earl under his thumb, it had been Hayden who had intervened. Odessa knew, of course, but he and Emerson had never spoken of it.

Amusement crept into Emerson's features. "Unavoidable. I'm not known for my manners, Your Grace."

"Wait." Hayden took ahold of one of the footmen. "Inside the coach is a stack of pamphlets tied with string. Bring those in for Lady Emerson, if you please." He winked at Odessa. "The latest criminal broadsides and a half dozen other horrible stories in a slim volume I purchased from a strect vendor. Apparently, there is a creature haunting the depths of the Thames which snatches its victims from passing barges."

Odessa eyed the stack greedily. "Thank you."

"Yes," Emerson said in a resigned tone. "You have my thanks."

"I'm sure I do. I attempted reading one on the journey here, but the crimes detailed are so horrible, the descriptions so ghastly, I had to stop. You should sleep with one eye open at all times, Emerson."

"Oh, I do, Your Grace. Or I tie my wife to the bed." Emerson paused and pressed a kiss to Odessa's temple. "Helps to keep her out of mischief."

Odessa turned the color of a beet. She cleared her throat. Twice. Taking Hayden's arm, she pulled him inside, purposefully ignoring her husband.

"Come, Your Grace. Let us get you settled."

CHAPTER FIFTEEN

THE INVASION OF the Duke of Ware was now entering its third day.

Ware's massive presence was felt in every corner of the house, sucking all the air out of River Crest, like a giant mountain which suddenly appears in the midst of a meadow full of wildflowers, frightening the woodland creatures.

After a brief introduction in the drawing room performed by Odessa, one in which Tamsin had to pretend for Jordan and Aurora's sakes that she'd never met Ware, the duke excused himself to take up residence in the back parlor he'd commandeered for his own.

Ware did not appear for dinner that evening, stating work as the cause, for which Tamsin was grateful. He also remained absent at breakfast the following morning; instead, requesting a tray be delivered to the back parlor each morning along with coffee, followed by a small basket of food left outside the parlor door promptly at two o'clock each day. In the late afternoons, his large form could be seen skirting the edge of the lawn and vanishing into the surrounding trees, satchel over his shoulder and basket dangling from one arm as he went about the business of collecting his specimens.

Beetles, Odessa explained when Aunt Lottie asked why Ware wasn't at dinner the first night. The late afternoon and evening were perfect times for collection. Ware would join them when he was ready.

Tamsin had been fully prepared to avoid Ware and had gone to great lengths strategizing how to behave if she *did* see him. But her careful plans had been for naught because she had the sneaking suspicion that Ware was avoiding *her*.

Terribly annoying considering Tamsin had no idea whether to be happy or filled with dread at Ware's sudden appearance.

On this third day of Ware's invasion, Tamsin rode Teach for the better part of the morning, hoping to settle her thoughts. As she strode back from the stables in the direction of the house, the sound of Ware's raised voice stopped her. A large, bulky form moved back and forth in front of the window to her left, which Tamsin assumed was the location of Ware's parlor. She knew the room was at the back of the house, but had not taken the time to investigate further.

Because…she was avoiding him.

Ann, the downstairs maid, burst through a side door, weeping hysterically, clutching her apron. She sagged against the brick of the house, wiping at her cheeks with a trembling hand.

"Ann." Tamsin hurried over to her. "What is it? Are you hurt?" She scanned the girl for any sign of injury. A bruise. A cut. Anything which might have warranted such weeping.

"Oh, please," Ann sobbed. "Don't sack me, my lady. I am *so* sorry. How was I to know they weren't just—" Another wail left her. "Leavings? I didn't know it were His Grace's beetles. I thought—" She wiped at her cheeks once more. "There was a pile of dead things on the corner of the desk. I swept them into my bucket. How was I to know?"

"You couldn't possibly." Tamsin patted the girl's shoulder. "I would have done the same."

"He's so very angry, my lady. He *roared* at me." Ann sobbed. "I need my employment here. I—"

"Don't you worry," she assured Ann, squeezing the girl's shoulder as anger surged through Tamsin at Ware's treatment of the maid. "I'll speak to the duke."

Terrifying the maids. Stomping about. Making Cook go to the extra trouble of packing him a bloody basket so he could skip about and look for beetle larva. Invading River Crest unannounced, making them all rush about to make him happy.

The maid's eyes widened. "You mustn't, my lady. He's—

"I'm not afraid of the duke. Now dry your eyes and go about your duties, Ann. No one is getting sacked today." Tamsin gave the maid a determined nod and strode to the side door of the house, fingers curled into fists. The girl had made an honest mistake. He didn't have to terrify her. Half the staff already thought Ware was up to something nefarious what with his collection of pins, glass vials, tweezers, and the like. Not to mention one of the other maids had nearly fainted in horror at describing how Ware had stuck a pin straight through a winged beetle of some kind when she brought him breakfast.

An insistent pulse took up beneath her skin.

It was *not* anticipation at seeing Ware, Tamsin told herself, but anger at his threatening of the household staff.

She marched into the hall, stopping before the parlor, which was now Ware's study. Flinging the door open, she declared, "You will not continue to frighten our staff with your growling about and dead beetles."

The room appeared empty.

"Ware?"

A grunt reached her ears. Sounds came from behind a once lovely sofa covered in floral damask that now sported a torn cushion. Odessa's efforts to remake River Crest obviously hadn't reached this parlor yet.

Tamsin went down on her knees and peered beneath the sofa, gratified to see a shock of coal-black hair. Never mind the fluttering pulse in her throat.

"Your Grace."

A pair of tweezers was clutched between his large fingers. He appeared to be extracting something from between the floorboards. Silver glinted at Tamsin briefly before his eyes dropped once more to whatever was wedged between the floorboards. "What an unexpected pleasure," he grumbled.

Tamsin's heart thudded in a ridiculous way.

"You will not sack Ann," she stated. "As a maid, her duties are to clean up after our guests, even the uninvited ones, which in this case is you, Your Grace." A whiff of bergamot floated beneath the sofa to her nostrils, along with the scent of leaves and damp earth.

He smelled wonderful. Always. Like home and a warm fire.

Which only incensed her more. What right did he have to a pleasing smell when the rest of him was so unpleasant?

"Your maid disposed of an entire day's worth of carefully collected specimens," he answered, holding up the tweezers. Something small and black was caught between the pinchers. "Got you."

Tamsin assumed that Ware was speaking to whatever poor insect he held in the tweezers, but his gaze remained on her. His breath dislodged a small mound of dust and it rolled in Tamsin's direction. They stared at each other in silence for a space of time. Long enough for her to realize how much she'd missed him, unpleasant, pleasingly-scented giant or not.

Abruptly, Tamsin came to her feet, unnerved by that intimate silence. "Cease your harassment of our staff."

Ware rose from the other side of the sofa, looking far larger in this tiny room than he ever did out of doors. His coat had been discarded, shirtsleeves rolled up to display powerful forearms dusted with dark hair. Bits of bark clung to the tangle of black hair standing up in disarray around his ears.

Another rapid flutter of her heart. Pure irritation, Tamsin told herself. Ware simply annoyed her to such an extent she might have a fit of apoplexy.

Ware was staring at her mouth in much the same manner he studied a moth.

"I've harassed no one." He shrugged, raising his eyes to hers. "Save you, perhaps." Ware started around one side of the sofa and Tamsin went in the other direction, determined to keep the piece of furniture between them.

"You're more adversarial than usual, Lady Tamsin. Is something the matter?"

A great many things were *wrong*. Starting with the buds of her nipples drawing taut at his scent. Ware couldn't fail to notice. She wore only a cotton chemise beneath the thin fabric of the shirt, and her riding breeches, while loose, made every curve feel exposed beneath his regard.

She'd had only one lover in her life. Captain Talpin. He had claimed to love her. Adore her. But he had never once looked at Tamsin as Ware did. As if he might tear her apart with his teeth.

She shifted to the left and Ware followed, wide mouth curling in amusement.

"I did wonder when you would visit me, Lady Tamsin. Honestly, I'm disappointed it took you three days."

Sidling to the right, she said, "Why would I welcome your presence here given our last encounter? And I would like to add that there are *coleoptera* all over England—"

"Someone's been practicing their Latin." He circled the sofa once more, holding up the poor insect trapped by his tweezers.

"You do not have to collect beetles at River Crest. I'm quite sure beetles can be found all over England."

"True, but you are unlikely to be able to stop me from collecting them from your brother's estate." He peered at her, a lazy sort of half-smile pulling at his mouth. "I doubt you can throw a punch higher than my jaw, but we could wrestle instead." His eyes glinted dangerously. "If you win, I'll leave River Crest."

141

Tamsin's mouth popped open but no words came out; her mind was too busy considering Ware pinning her sensuously to the ground.

"Don't do that. Open your mouth and squeak in outrage. Makes you sound and look like a surprised rodent. Fine. We won't wrestle and I won't leave River Crest. Agreed?" His gaze fell to her mouth once more, as if remembering all the things he'd done to her lips, before dipping lower. "I like the breeches, by the way. Very becoming."

He took a step in Tamsin's direction. Then another. Set down the tweezers on a scarred table near the sofa. Ware's broad chest rose and fell as he looked down at her with curious intensity before his forefinger reached out to trace the line of her jaw.

A soft inhale was her only response.

"I owe you an apology, my lady." The words were soft. "For the park."

"You do?" she breathed. One touch from him and her body had erupted in sensation. The nearly painful tightening of her nipples pushed in his direction.

"I do not think you a pebble in my shoe. I misspoke. I was—out of sorts," he finished. "Will you accept my apology?"

Her eyes fluttered shut an instant. "I accept." She waited several moments, feeling his eyes on her though he did not touch her further, only running the pad of his finger along the curve of Tamsin's cheek.

Ware stepped deftly away from her; his hand fell away from her face, but slowly, taking time so that she felt every brush of his finger against her skin. And she allowed it. With no clutching of her fingers into fists and no scathing remarks uttered.

I want him to touch me. I have missed him so bloody much.

Tamsin's eyes opened as the words shouted in her mind. Ware was watching her from beneath the thick brush of his lashes. He didn't seem nearly as affected by this—*discussion* as she did.

"I—" Tamsin stammered.

"Yes?" Ware raised a brow.

She took a deep breath, willing the humming along her skin to disappear. "Our vague attachment, Your Grace, is at an end," she said with more determination than she felt. "There can be—"

"That is where you are mistaken, Lady Tamsin," he interrupted quietly. "Now, be on your way. I have things to do. I won't yell at the maids again." He took her elbow and rushed her towards the door.

"But—" Tamsin spun about, prepared to ask Ware what exactly he meant. Of course their attachment was over. It *had* to be over. Didn't it?

Ware shut the door in her face and threw the lock. Leaving her standing like an open-mouthed idiot in the hall.

CHAPTER SIXTEEN

HAYDEN REGARDED TAMSIN with amusement as she rushed into the dining room, an apology on her lips, only to clamp her lips shut at spotting him seated beside her brother. She shot him a look, one that spoke volumes about her opinion of him. Their discussion earlier today in the parlor had done little to improve things.

If she had any idea how arousing it had been for Hayden to have her march in to the parlor and demand he stop terrorizing her staff, Tamsin would never do so again. She saw herself as a warrior. A defender of those who could not do so themselves. Had she been born male, Tamsin would have made a brilliant Hussar, charging into the midst of battle with little concern for her own safety, only for that of those following her.

Perhaps that was where the fierce need to protect Tamsin came from, because she would not do so herself. Even if she decided to— dismiss Hayden once more, Tamsin would forever be under the protection of the Duke of Ware. He could not let her go about without a shield.

"Are you well?" Emerson said to Tamsin as he waved at his butler to start dinner. "You missed tea. The duke has decided to join us this evening."

"Your Grace." Tamsin bobbed politely, a wary look hovering in her eyes.

She was right to view him with some trepidation. Hayden had

nearly devoured her in the parlor earlier and was reduced to forcing her from the room. Tamsin's slender form had arched towards his. Sounds, delicious ones, had come from between her delectable lips when he touched her. He wasn't even sure she'd been aware.

Hayden hadn't been wrong about what lay between them. He just wasn't sure what to do about it.

"Lady Tamsin," he greeted her, watching the gentle sway of her hips. She was to be seated directly across from him, which was both thrilling and tortuous.

Hayden found her to be the most fascinating of creatures.

"I'm quite well," she answered Emerson, barely acknowledging Hayden. "I dozed off while reading. And I had a most challenging afternoon." Tamsin's finally caught his. "One of the maids was frightened by a large, hideous insect. Of course, I came to her rescue."

Hideous? Hayden shot her a bemused look. "How terrifying."

"Can you describe it?" Odessa asked. "Ware might be able to iden-tify such an insect."

"As I said, overly large." Tamsin tapped her cheek, considering how best to insult him, Hayden decided, without giving herself away. "Almost *grotesque* in size. Black. It buzzed about poor Ann for some time in annoyance, threatening to attack."

"Sounds unappealing," Aunt Lottie said, not looking up from her plate.

"Incredibly so. Don't you agree, Your Grace?" Tamsin bestowed a sweet, innocent smile on him.

"The appeal of insects would, I fear, be lost on you, Lady Tamsin." Hayden regarded her blandly from across the table.

"I doubt it." Her nose crinkled in irritation. "Do you know what sort of insect it was, Your Grace?"

"The sort that bites," he returned blithely, gaze lowering discreetly for a moment to her bosom. "And might leave a mark."

Hayden did love when Tamsin blushed.

Those were the last words he spoke directly to Tamsin for the entirety of the meal, purposefully. He wished to test his theory. Tamsin, Hayden had noted during their time in London, did not care to be ignored, especially by him. He intentionally engaged Emerson in a discussion of crop destroying insects. Weevils were the topic for nearly twenty minutes before Hayden switched to aphids. Not once did he glance in her direction.

Tamsin made disgruntled sounds over the soup course.

Hayden smiled to himself.

Odessa joined the conversation, having recently read an article on a worm which had burrowed inside a gentleman's ear and had to be dug out with the end of a blade.

Aurora listened intently for a time before asking Hayden about the worms that are found on cabbages, something she'd experienced firsthand at Dunnings. He took his time explaining to Aurora that the worm which attacked cabbages was actually a type of moth, pausing in his recitation to finally, discreetly look at Tamsin.

She was watching her sister, the love for Aurora stamped plainly on her features.

Had Lady Curchon told Tamsin the only way to salvage Aurora's debut was sail to America and dance naked on tables, Tamsin would have done so in an instant. She would do anything for her sister, even tolerate an eccentric duke for several weeks.

Tamsin inclined her head in his direction, a silent thank you for his being so patient and kind with Aurora. *That* meant a great deal to Tamsin.

"How long do you intend to stay at River Crest, Your Grace?" she asked, turning all eyes at the table in her direction. "I only meant, you said you were doing research. I—have a limited knowledge of such things, but I do know some insects are more prevalent at different times of the year. Won't the beetles disappear during the autumn months?"

What Tamsin really meant was *when will you leave?*

"As long as it takes, Lady Tamsin. Beetles, the sort I'm interested in, can present quite a challenge. Determined to escape until I," he paused, "pin them." Hayden had nothing to lose at Tamsin knowing he wanted her. He decided not to make it such a bloody surprise.

Her lips parted; the attraction between them, the one felt earlier in the parlor, sparked to life across the table. "Then I shall take the side of the beetle," she snapped. "Your Grace."

CHAPTER SEVENTEEN

Tamsin returned from riding in an unusually foul mood, most of which had to do with Ware still in residence at River Crest. A week had gone by since their strange encounter in the parlor, and though he still joined the family for dinner most evenings, Ware paid her little attention. Except for the occasional flash of hunger directed towards her, which Tamsin spent a great deal of time convincing herself was for the *food*.

It was a lie, of course. The attraction between them seemed to build and strengthen each day.

He still took his breakfast in the parlor, which made avoiding him in the morning that much easier. But Tamsin would still catch glimpses of his large form meandering through what remained of River Crest's once glorious gardens, leather satchel thrown over one broad shoulder as he went out in search of his beetles. His tangled mop of hair had grown longer; the strands now brushed along the edges of his poorly tied cravat. He'd taken to pulling back the heavy waves with a bit of leather. Once she'd seen him sporting a pink ribbon, likely filched from Odessa.

Life would be so much simpler if Ware would return to London.

Lady Curchon's words still rang true for Tamsin, and even if she didn't think Ware's aunt capable of ruining Aurora and Jordan completely, she could still wreak a great deal of damage. And Tamsin's heart saw the reality of the situation. She was a girl who'd lost her virtue to a sea captain, wore breeches, punched a large assortment of gentlemen, including Ware's brother, and drank whiskey. There was not any instance in which Tamsin would ever be good enough for a duke, not even one considered odd and eccentric. The list of reasons to not allow Ware any closer was lengthy. Even if—

A deep sigh of resignation halted her progress through the house.

Yes, she *was* an earl's daughter, but that was a matter of birth and not behavior. She garnered a great deal of attention from men, but none of it polite. Tamsin was well on her way to becoming a spinster, which frankly was not without its appeal. Her existence would be one of discreet lovers and quiet affairs.

Ware would make a terrible candidate for such a role even if he was under consideration—and he was not.

Laughter, Aurora's, echoed down the hall. The deep rumble of a man answered, though Tamsin couldn't make out the words. But there was no doubt it was Ware. Then the low, rolling baritone hummed, sounding as if someone were plucking at a cello. She recognized the tune as one she'd heard at Lady Curchon's.

Tamsin headed in the direction of the drawing room, stopping abruptly at the entrance.

Ware spun Aurora with graceful, practiced movements as he hummed, twirling her about the drawing room rug. The steps of the dance were complicated, far beyond Tamsin's meager ability. As she watched, Ware paused and adjusted Aurora's hands before resuming their dance.

The Duke of Ware could dance. Splendidly. As if he'd been born to it.

This was another side of Ware Tamsin had never seen. The one that didn't stick pins through moths but instead knew the intricate movements of a dance and could execute the steps to perfection.

Tamsin sucked in her breath. If she needed any further proof that she was completely unsuitable, it was before her.

He lifted his chin and caught sight of her, slowly twirling Aurora about like a top.

Aurora was glowing, beaming up at Ware with undisguised adoration.

Who would have thought him to be so charming?

"Lady Tamsin." He skimmed her form, lingering far too long over the curve of her hips in the breeches. Male admiration shone from him, but there was something else, a flick of possessiveness which had the pulse beating more fiercely in her throat.

She pushed her palms down her thighs. "I didn't know you could dance, Your Grace."

"It isn't a talent I consider useful." He smiled at Aurora. "Except in this instance."

An unexpected bolt of jealousy struck Tamsin.

"Tamsin." Aurora waved at her with a giggle. "The duke has been kind enough to help me improve my steps before my come-out. I will be dancing the entire Season."

She would. Tamsin would make certain of it.

"I do wish we had someone to play the piano for us. Odessa does not play. Nor Aunt Lottie." Another laugh. "You certainly did not take piano lessons at Dunnings."

"No." Tamsin gave her a weak smile. She'd been too busy trying to give Aurora some semblance of a childhood. Overcompensating for the guilt in the part she'd played in their banishment to Northumberland and their mother's death.

"The duke has been forced to hum in the absence of musicians. He's rather good at it."

"It is my pleasure." Ware bestowed another smile on Aurora.

When had he become so accommodating? So pleasant? So strikingly beautiful to Tamsin that she had to look away? He'd pulled back his hair once more and a crimson ribbon dangled where he'd secured the coal black strands.

"You should cut your hair, Your Grace," she said more harshly than she intended, "instead of resorting to such measures." Tamsin nodded at the ribbon.

"I'm between valets, as I've mentioned."

"I have some experience in cutting hair." Tamsin had already begun to detest that crimson ribbon. She recognized it as one of Aurora's, which disturbed her greatly.

Aurora coughed, sputtered, then gave up and allowed her merriment to erupt. "Oh, Your Grace. Do not allow my sister near you with shears. Jordan was nearly shorn bald when she offered to assist him."

"There isn't any fear of that happening, Lady Aurora. I'm more concerned Lady Tamsin's fingers might slip and take off a bit of my nose. I'll wait until I return to London."

"And when will that be, Your Grace?" Tamsin couldn't help asking. Her entire body was pulsing softly in his direction, though she willed it to stop.

Ware shrugged. "When it is merited."

"Your dancing is deplorable." Aurora came forward and took Tamsin's hand. "The duke has helped me immeasurably. He is a superior dancer. Far better than Monsieur Pierre. I'm sure he can help you as well." She looked at Ware. "Jordan dances poorly too, though I doubt you'd partner him. Would you mind, Your Grace?" Aurora tilted her head in Tamsin's direction. "I can play the piano. I've been taking lessons in London. You won't have to hum."

"I'm sure His Grace has work to do," Tamsin said with no small amount of panic, afraid to be clasped in Ware's arms. When he'd touched her in the parlor the other day, her knees had buckled, and she'd nearly embarrassed herself. "Don't you?"

His big shoulders gave a shrug. "I can show you the steps, Lady Tamsin. But I'm not sure you'll absorb them."

"I have a keen mind for a female, as I'm sure you'll agree."

Ware raised a brow at her.

"I *can* dance," she informed him. "I am merely out of practice, Your Grace." She held out her hands to either side. "Begin playing, Aurora, if you please."

TAMSIN WAS TERRIBLY easy to provoke.

Hayden's larger hand carefully took her smaller one. He'd discarded his gloves earlier after collecting his specimens when Lady Aurora waved him into the drawing room. And Tamsin wore no gloves. The feel of her naked fingers against his sent a slow, simmering boil along Hayden's skin and he had to refrain from pulling her up against his chest. Tamsin's beautiful curves were only inches from his chest, hidden from him by a scrap of a shirt and those damned tempting breeches.

A tremble went through her as he took her hand.

Tamsin was not unaffected by Hayden. She only didn't wish to admit to it.

Aurora began to play rather terribly, her pretty features pulled together in concentration. Whoever Emerson had engaged for piano lessons had been paid far too much.

He carefully turned Tamsin, swaying gently to the music. Or whatever one wished to call the noise Aurora summoned from the piano.

She was a terrible dancer. Tamsin's graceless floundering was far worse than Hayden could have ever imagined. Reminiscent of a fit where the poor soul has no command of their limbs. He counted out the steps, hoping that would induce her to follow or at least not ignore the subtle squeeze of his fingers as a sign for her to turn.

Hayden looked down at the curve of her cheek and the spray of chestnut curls at her temples; this naturally led him to peer down the front of the shirt she'd donned for riding. He could just make out the gentle slope of her breasts.

Aurora hit another wrong note.

Something would have to be done about the youngest Sinclair's abuse of the piano. Tragic, was the kindest way to refer to Aurora's playing. Invitations for her to showcase her talents during the Season must be adamantly refused. The only sort of gentleman Aurora's piano playing would attract was one hard of hearing.

Tamsin stumbled over his foot.

Hayden caught her, using it as an excuse to pull her closer. Those bloody breeches were going to be his undoing just as they had been the day Hayden lost his temper with the poor maid assigned to clean up after him. The parlor was at the very back of the house and its window overlooked the path to the stables. Every damned morning Tamsin paraded before Hayden in those breeches, strolling along the path, breasts swaying with her confident strides, the leather pulling at her hips. What would it be like to have Tamsin on her knees before him, hands on his thighs, mouth on his—

"Ouch." Tamsin kicked his shin. "Watch your giant feet, Your Grace."

"Apologies."

The maid, poor girl, had interrupted Hayden's increasingly erotic thoughts of Tamsin. She had come too close to the desk and wiped up the dead beetles, which he wasn't going to use in any case, nearly catching sight of the enormous tenting of Hayden's trousers.

Tamsin, oblivious to his wicked visions of her, was busy worrying her bottom lip, trying without success to match her step to his. Dancing together at a ball was out of the question. She was that terrible.

But Hayden didn't really care for balls.

"Stop staring at me like that," she insisted, kicking him again. A quiver went through her as Hayden's arm brushed against the side of her breast, along with a gentle halting of her breath.

"I am only dazzled by your skill, my lady."

"There is no need to mock me. I am trying." A mortified look crossed her features.

"I wouldn't dream of doing so." He twirled her expertly, counting out the steps in a whisper only she could hear.

Tamsin stumbled over his feet and hers.

"If you wish to dance properly, my lady," Hayden murmured, "you must allow me to lead."

Her chin jerked up. "That will never happen."

Tamsin would always be a constant bloody challenge.

"In the matter of the dance," he grumbled, attempting to sound annoyed when in fact he relished her defiance and mutinous behavior, "the gentleman leads. Surely that French fop Emerson hired taught you that much." He spun her about once more, moving his feet quickly so she wouldn't stomp on them. "I signal like this," he said, squeezing her hand.

Tamsin tripped again. There was a deflated look pulling at her shoulders.

Aurora's fingers paused on the piano.

Thank God. Hayden's ears were literally aching.

"Monsieur Pierre did indeed explain as much to her, Your Grace," Aurora said. "But Tamsin ignored him." The awkward tune echoed in the room once more.

"I did not," she protested. "I *tried* with Monsieur Pierre. But he was difficult to understand. That atrocious accent—"

"He is from Paris, Tamsin. I found his accent to be quite musical," Aurora said in a lofty tone. "You must make more of an effort. You promised to attend balls with me, and you will be required to dance."

"I must agree, Lady Tamsin," Hayden concurred, watching her jaw grow so taut he thought a tooth might snap. Her glorious mane of chestnut hair, pulled into a loose plait, bounced over her shoulder, the tail landing between her breasts.

Hayden moved her across the rug, leaning in just enough so he caught the hint of jasmine lingering in her hair. A fierce burst of arousal shot straight between his legs to wind down his thighs. He breathed her in, his nose nearly touching the curve of one delicate ear.

A small, lovely sound came from Tamsin. Her lips parted, the green sparkling in her eyes becoming more pronounced.

Aurora cleared her throat. "I've stopped playing."

Hayden's fingers drew over Tamsin's, releasing her. The tip of his forefinger traced over her knuckles before lingering over the top of her hand.

A velvety whisper came from between her lips. She blinked as if dazed before stepping away. A hint of rose colored her cheeks. "Thank you for the dance, Your Grace. I—there is something I must attend to. Don't keep the duke too long, Aurora."

"Tamsin," he murmured, wanting to clasp her hand once more.

"Please excuse me," she stuttered before marching out of the room, the soles of her boots ringing out as she hurried down the hall.

CHAPTER EIGHTEEN

T AMSIN HEFTED THE bottle of whiskey to her lips and took a deep swallow. What must she do to get him to leave River Crest? Her biggest concern was no longer Lady Curchon discovering Ware roaming about the estate. No, Tamsin was far more concerned what she might do if Ware didn't leave.

She took another swallow of the whiskey, feeling the burn descend and warm her belly. Monsieur Pierre's tutelage had led Tamsin to believe that dance lessons were not so…arousing in nature.

This entire situation with Ware was rapidly becoming…untenable. Unwelcome. Unsettling.

Virtually any *un* you could possibly imagine.

The charade between her and Ware had been in place to assure that there could be *no* further relationship between them.

And now there was…*well*—she flung one hand up in the air dramatically. *This.*

Foxed. She would get completely foxed. No matter that it was barely twelve o'clock. Jordan would pretend to be horrified that his sister was a sot, mostly for Odessa's sake. Odessa, for her part, wouldn't care unless whiskey somehow transformed Tamsin into some horrible creature bent on terrorizing the countryside, the sort Odessa liked to read about. Aurora, unfortunately, had seen far worse after growing up at Dunnings. Aunt Lottie would say nothing due to her own weakness for brandy.

He had *sniffed* her hair. Inhaled her scent. While dancing. It could not continue.

Ware has to leave. I must demand he do so.

She had been hiding in the garden for the last half hour after filching the bottle of whiskey from Jordan's study, intending to stay behind these half-dead roses until nightfall. But now, Tamsin came to her feet with determination. A certain moth-loving duke must be confronted.

Reentering the house, Tamsin made her way inside and down the hall to the parlor Ware had been using for his research. The door stood open.

The room was empty. Devoid of his large form.

Fine. I can wait.

Tamsin made her way to the battered sofa and plopped down, frowning as a spring dug into her backside. She wiggled about until she was comfortable, catching sight at something beside her on the faded damask. A random leg—belonging to *something.*

"Repugnant." She lifted the bottle to her lips and flicked the insect leg to the floor. Ware had unended all of River Crest with his presence. Dukes were such arrogant, entitled creatures no matter if their coats were full of bugs. Well, his invasion of River Crest was going to come to an end. Tamsin would see to it. No matter that Ware inhaled her scent as if she were the fine French wine Lord Curchon favored.

"Couldn't find a glass?"

Tamsin clutched the bottle to her chest. Ware was standing in the doorway, regarding her with an amused look. "Stop lurking about. Hiding and then popping out at inopportune times," she snapped at him.

"I feel as if we've had this discussion." He gave her a resigned look. "I am far too large to surprise anyone." A grin tugged at his wide mouth.

A ripple of awareness, magnified by the whiskey, settled over Tamsin's skin.

Ware was far too attractive when not being an annoyed grouch.

Tamsin looked down at the bottle before taking a deep breath and facing him once more. "I have come to inform you, Your Grace, of your imminent departure from River Crest."

"Are you throwing me out, Tamsin? I did offer to wrestle you for the honor as I recall, but you declined." He came further into the room, his presence causing her nerves to prickle.

"You cannot stay here any longer." Tamsin tipped the bottle up to her lips. "You really cannot."

"Waltzing about dressed like stable boy, no matter how appealing I happen to find it, does not give you license to order me about." Ware turned and shut the door behind him. "I like River Crest. Odessa adores having me here. Aurora needs more dance lessons. I may stay indefinitely."

"Did I not endure enough of you in London?" she stated bluntly.

"I think your tolerance has improved, or at least it will, given time." Ware made his way to a table near the window holding a decanter of unknown spirits and a lone glass. Picking the glass up, Ware came back to the sofa and sprawled against the end, stretching out his legs. He reached for the whiskey.

Tamsin held on, but Ware was stronger. A tug of war ensued, until she ended up wedged between his thighs, slightly mortified and far too comfortable.

"Foxed before dinner, Lady Tamsin," he murmured close to her ear. "How scandalous."

"I'm a Deadly Sin." She reluctantly handed him the bottle. "Haven't you heard? And I'm not foxed. At least not yet. Give me some time."

"Hold this." He pushed the glass at her while taking the bottle from her grasp. He shifted so that her back lay against his chest and reached over her, splashing out some whiskey. "Only one glass. We'll have to share."

"I don't wish to." She was far too comfortable lying atop his chest, her body trapped between his thighs. "This is improper." Especially since Tamsin could feel the hardness poking into her back.

"So it is." He took the glass from her fingers and swallowed half the whiskey before returning it to her. "My father, were he still living, would be vastly impressed with my behavior. Here I am drinking whiskey with a beautiful woman in the middle of the day."

She'd been called beautiful many times, but it sounded different coming from Ware.

"You didn't like him."

"No, but I still wanted his approval, if not his affection. I was the third son. Destined to be a disappointment but free of expectations. Thompson was the heir. Maxwell the spare. What bloody irony, don't you think?" A deprecating laugh came from Ware's chest. "He despaired that I adored nature and not the debauching of women. My brothers, fortunately, excelled at such skills."

"I know all about that." She took the glass from his fingers and took a swallow, frowning when he immediately took the glass back. "It is why we had to find an honorable yet creative solution to our predicament. You did not want to be like them. Or wed Lady Penelope."

"Lady Penelope matters far less than I led you to believe. But not being Thompson or Maxwell matters greatly to the duchess." He refilled the whiskey again before putting the bottle on the table beside the sofa. "But given the things she witnessed, I do not blame her for wanting at least one of her children to be honorable. Especially the one who was always considered too intellectual but naïve about the way the world works."

"I don't think you're naïve, Ware. I merely think such things aren't important to you. Society. Parliament. Estates. Perfectly tied cravats."

"I told you, I am between valets. They keep quitting."

Tamsin hid a smile. "You adore insects to the exclusion of all else."

"I disagree. My love of insects does not preclude my admiration for other…things. *You* for instance, Tamsin."

Tamsin's fingers wrapped around the glass and she took a large swallow. "Don't say such things." It was on the tip of her tongue to inform Ware that his beloved aunt would outdo Lady Longwood in the destruction of the Sinclairs if he—

Ware's arm tightened securely about her waist, pulling Tamsin back until she was flat against the warmth of his chest. His fingers trailed along her neck before tightening, thumb rubbing slowly over the pulse beating beneath her skin.

Tamsin gripped the glass tighter as Ware's other hand moved to stroke gently at the underside of her breast, his fingers teasing just beneath her nipple, circling, though never touching the small, sensitive peak.

I should stop him.

She sucked in another breath, her head falling back to Ware's shoulder. Tamsin had never been very good at doing the proper thing; that was how she ended up with Captain Talpin as her lover. But Ware—

Tamsin gasped at the ache of her body, how every brush of his fingers forced a delicate pulse between her thighs. He explored each curve and hollow of her breasts with great attention, pausing every so often to flick his tongue along the edge of her ear. His palm stretched over Tamsin's stomach, big fingers moving possessively before pressing along her ribs and falling lower to her hip.

The hand at her throat squeezed ever-so-gently. Ware turned her chin, his mouth falling over hers in a long, indulgent savoring, tongue wandering over the seam of her lips.

A moan erupted from her. Any thought other than what Ware was doing to her, with such skill, fled Tamsin's mind. She'd enjoyed Talpin. There had been moments of great pleasure between them. But nothing like this slow memorizing of her body, systematically determining what press of his finger or caress brought her the most pleasure.

Oh God. He's pinned me. Just like a bloody moth.

His hand moved over the rise of her mound, thumb stroking at the juncture of her thighs through the leather of her breeches. Back and forth, finding the exact spot Tamsin was most sensitive, the chafing of the leather against her flesh only enhancing the sensation.

She writhed back against him shamelessly, attempting to force him to exert more pressure. The plea was on her lips to beg him to slide his big hand inside the waist of her breeches and touch her damp flesh with his fingers. "Please."

The hold on her neck tightened briefly. "Be still."

Tamsin obeyed. She didn't want this to stop, though this was dangerous territory, for both of them.

Ware captured her mouth once more, pushing the heel of his palm between her thighs, rotating slowly until Tamsin panted, straining towards that blissful pleasure she'd only experienced once before. She realized as Ware expertly manipulated her body that Talpin hadn't been an incredibly talented lover. The duke had aroused her to a feverish pitch while they were still fully closed. She had her boots on.

His lips moved back to the curve of her ear, tongue and teeth delicately nipping at the edge.

"There *is* an attachment," he whispered, the vibration of his words stealing down the length of her body. "I will not hear you say differently. Ever again, Tamsin. Promise me."

She whimpered, willing to give him anything if he kept stroking her. "I promise."

Another press of his hand, the torturous insistent pressure of his thumb through the leather, drove her mad. Tamsin's mind, already half muddled by the whiskey, floated away from her as bliss tickled along her limbs.

"All I think of is you." The dark rumble circled her ear. "Spread out before me. Naked."

A great rolling wave of pleasure tightened deep inside Tamsin before unraveling and snapping across her body. His teeth sunk into her earlobe, and she cried out, the force of her climax making Tamsin writhe like a wild thing within the circle of Ware's arms.

HAYDEN WISHED HE could blame the whiskey, but he hadn't had enough to even make him remotely intoxicated. He wanted nothing more than to slowly peel the clothes from Tamsin's body, and explore every delicious naked inch of her, but Hayden restrained himself.

Looking down at her still pulsing body, Hayden surmised that making Tamsin climax by stroking her through the leather of her breeches didn't exactly make him a saint. Nor any better than Thompson or Maxwell. Or his father.

The fingers at her neck fell away and Tamsin gave a lovely, sated sigh. Winding his entire arm about her, he held her slender form against his chest, her weight a balm to Hayden's soul. He hoped this would settle things between them, but knowing Tamsin, it would not.

She leaned over to pick up the bottle, splashing out another mouthful of whiskey into the glass. Cradling the whiskey in her hands for a moment, Tamsin lifted the glass and took several swallows, but otherwise stayed silent. Her reaction told Hayden that she was no stranger to physical pleasure.

"Are you going to drink all of that yourself?"

Holding the glass aloft, she said, "No, Your Grace."

"Do not call me that when we are alone and especially not in the given situation." Hayden drank the rest of the whiskey and handed the glass back, which she promptly refilled once more and propped on her stomach.

"Don't say anything, Tamsin." If she dismissed him once more, given what had just occurred, Hayden wasn't sure what he would do.

"I won't." Her voice was soft. "We are—only enjoying some whiskey together."

They sat in silence for a length of time, passing the glass back and forth. Not speaking. The throbbing of his cock screamed at Hayden to simply turn and take her on this sofa now, with no witness but the small collection of insects on the desk. But he couldn't.

Tamsin finally said, "I'm not a maid, Ware." The words slurred just a bit. "I haven't been for some time."

He had assumed as much, given her manner. Hayden wasn't sure how he felt about Tamsin having had a lover, but he'd have to sort that out later. "I—"

"Now I wish you to remain silent." Tamsin drained the glass. "I know that fact makes me—exactly what Lady Longwood claims me to be. But I want you to know there was only the one lover, Ware. It isn't as if I lifted my skirts for every man in Spittal."

Spittal must be outside of Dunnings in Northumberland. Hayden made note of the name.

"I never thought you had," he replied. Tamsin was the furthest thing from a lightskirt. Such women generally didn't concern themselves with worrying over how a tarnished reputation would affect their families. Or go about tossing punches at men who were improper. But Tamsin did.

A hiccup escaped her. "You may release me now. I've had quite enough whiskey. And you." She made a pitiful attempt to sit up, not really trying.

"I will never release you," Hayden whispered to the top of her head. "And frankly your tolerance for whiskey drinking is spectacular. I'm impressed."

"Thank you." She gave a deep sigh, which ended in another hiccup, and turned so that she lay on her cheek atop his chest. "I'm very sleepy. But I feel marvelous." She looked up at him and patted his stomach. "I like a bit of padding. Makes you comfortable."

His heart gave a hard, blissful thud. A dizzy, lightheaded feeling came over Hayden as she curled into his chest. Her lack of virtue, he decided, was of no import. There was something much more valuable he wanted.

Tamsin's heart.

A moment later, a snore sounded against his chest.

"You are forever dozing off in my presence." Hayden pressed a kiss to her temple. "But, given your whiskey drinking, ordering about dukes, and attempting to dance, you are likely exhausted. I'm sorry I'm so terrible at courtship. You deserve so much better though you don't think so." He squeezed her tight.

Years of being told she was uncivilized or an ambitious trollop like her mother had slowly eroded Tamsin's view of herself. Lady Longwood's vicious attacks didn't help. Nor his aunt, Lady Curchon, decrying her as beneath him. To society, Hayden supposed Tamsin was unsuitable. But not to him.

That fierce protectiveness for her swelled up inside Hayden once more.

"*You* make sense to me, Tamsin."

Another snore as her slender fingers grasped at the folds of his shirt, disrupting his thoughts. Ignoring the throbbing between his thighs, which was rapidly becoming painful, he toyed with a curl at her temple, content to only hold her while she slept. When the clock chimed out the hour, he slowly came to his feet, careful not to wake Tamsin as he lifted her in his arms. The servants' stairs were just around the corner and Hayden knew which room was hers.

"Hayden," Tamsin said, voice muffled by his chest.

His heart stuttered at the sound of his name. "Shush. Go back to sleep." Hayden started to hum, the same tune he and Tamsin had danced to in the drawing room.

"You hum well," she whispered. "I can feel it on my skin."

He smiled as he carried her up the stairs. She weighed next to nothing in his arms. As light and fragile as any moth. But he liked Tamsin far better.

CHAPTER NINETEEN

TAMSIN LOOKED AT the plate before her, careful to keep her eyes averted from the gentleman seated down the length of her brother's table. Only a muted pounding still thundered in her temples, proof at least that she hadn't imagined the whiskey drinking. Or that Ware had made her climax, fully clothed.

He was much more skilled than an insect-loving duke had any reason to be.

Why must he be a duke?

Had Ware not been a duke, there might be a possibility for them to—

To what?

Even a well-to-do third son who studied insects would not possess a family who would cheerfully welcome Tamsin. Not with the gossip dragging at her skirts.

My reputation has improved.

Not that much.

She had obviously fallen asleep on the sofa with Ware because Tamsin had awoken only a short time ago with a start, fully clothed and lying across her bed. There was a sour taste in her mouth and the space between her thighs was still wet and aroused.

He carried me to my room.

Her eyes drifted to Aurora who was leaning over her plate, chattering away to Ware as if they were the dearest of friends. They probably were. Ware was sporting a pale green ribbon tonight in his dark hair, which she assumed also belonged to Aurora.

He looked ridiculous.

He's marvelous.

Tamsin looked down at her plate, uninterested in the delicious smells wafting into the dining room, though her stomach growled. The feeling for Ware was real. Not vague in the least. But that didn't make it any less impossible.

The mild affection she'd had for Derek Talpin, dashing ship's captain, wasn't close to her feeling for the man watching her as he sliced into his lamb. But at the time she'd become involved with Talpin, Tamsin assumed she would never see London again. Never make a proper match. Never assume her place in society as Lady Tamsin Sinclair. And she was feeling utterly rebellious. Her virtue had been of little import, and she'd wrongfully assumed Talpin meant to wed her eventually.

Except Talpin already had a wife.

Tamsin looked up to see Ware regarding her, his quicksilver eyes warm and fluid where they touched her skin.

"Is your headache better, Tamsin?" Odessa sliced off a bit of roasted lamb on her plate, regarding her with concern.

She pulled her attention from Ware. "Headache?"

"Didn't you return to your room after dancing with Aurora and Ware?" She inclined her head in the direction of the duke. "Ware mentioned at tea you'd retired with a headache brought on by Aurora's piano playing."

"Your Grace," Aurora said in mock outrage.

The tops of Ware's cheeks pinked just a bit. "I believe more lessons are required, my lady. Or perhaps you might take up the harp. In any case, Lady Tamsin appears to be recovered." His shaggy head turned to her, green ribbon falling over one shoulder. "You were as pale as the larva of a *callimorpha dominula.*"

Odessa sent her cousin a patient look.

"How flattering, Your Grace," Tamsin replied, chewing on the lamb which was far too rare for her tastes. "A young lady *dreams* of being compared to larvae."

The edges of his mouth tipped up.

The space between she and Ware drew close and narrow until it seemed no one else sat at the dining room table but them. Her heart counted out a series of beats as he regarded her with an intimacy he made no attempt to hide.

Aunt Lottie coughed.

Tamsin pushed her thighs together to stop the insistent pulse building between them and returned her attention to the plate before her. She listed each of Lady Curchon's terrible threats one at a time and forced herself to recall that her behavior forced Bentley's temper to snap and send them all to Dunnings. Mama died. Aurora never had a childhood. Those things were all the fault of her inability to—cease her impetuous behavior.

And she was in danger of being reckless again.

The remainder of dinner, Tamsin carefully kept her gaze averted from Ware. Odessa related a story from one of the criminal broadsides he'd brought her, much to everyone's horror. A woman who had secreted her lover in the attic of her home, unknown to her husband. When the woman traveled to the Continent, she neglected to unlock the attic door. The lover died of starvation, but not before attempting to escape through the walls of the house. Where a maid later found his body.

"What a horrible tale, Odessa." Aunt Lottie waved for another glass of wine. "Poor lad. Why would she lock him in the attic?"

"I suppose she didn't want him running about at night. The husband thought a rat had perished in the walls." Odessa wiggled her brows. "Gruesome, don't you think?"

"Completely," Jordan agreed with a roll of his eyes. "Ware, can't you regale us with insects? Moths? Anything to banish your cousin's bloodthirsty tales?"

Ware complied, launching into a detailed explanation of the mating habits of the speckled bush cricket, sufficiently boring them all so that Aunt Lottie had to be nudged when her chin dipped to her chest.

Once the meal was finally over, Aurora announced she would play for them all in the drawing room, but Tamsin pled a return of her earlier headache and announced she would retire for the evening. Truthfully, her temples did still pound from the whiskey she'd had earlier, but what she needed was time away from Ware and his presence at River Crest. Today's *experience* had left her feeling unsteady. She felt no shame over what had transpired with Ware, but neither was Tamsin pleased she'd once more allowed her emotions to override common sense.

Heading in the direction of the lawn, Tamsin silently took in what had once been magnificent gardens. All of it had fallen into ruins under Bentley's care. He'd fired all the gardeners when he stripped the estate of anything of value.

Tamsin turned at a patch of struggling roses to take the path towards a small rise at the very edge of the gardens. When she and her brothers had been children, they'd rolled down this tiny hill, often landing in a bed of peonies which had once stood at the bottom. The tall grass whispered about her skirts as she walked. Glow worms winked in and out, lighting up the garden like dozens of tiny stars. She was sure the glow worms had a fancy name in Latin. Ware would know.

Tamsin plopped down in the grass and wrapped her arms around her knees. She couldn't take up residence on this grassy knoll until Ware left River Crest, which meant facing him once more. Worse, part of her didn't want him to leave but instead begged Tamsin to cling to him. It was incredibly unsettling. She'd never—had an attachment to anyone. Not even Talpin. Not the sort she had for Ware.

A dark shadow came out of the gardens and paused before striding in her direction.

"I am not some horrid creature you've read about. Do not, I beg you, box my ears." The rich, melodic tone floated to her. "It is me. Ware."

"Highly amusing, Your Grace. Are you looking for moths?" Tamsin's heart beat stronger. Louder. The delicious hum, brought on only by him, started along her skin.

"Why? Do you have one on your knee?" he answered.

"Not at present, Your Grace. But if it is a moth you seek, you will have better luck anywhere but the gardens, which are full of half-dead plants and a fountain that no longer works. Gardens contain nothing Bentley could sell, and thus he allowed them to fall into disarray."

Ware settled beside her, big and warm. Far too close. "The hated half-brother."

Tamsin looked back at River Crest. "My father had just died. Suddenly. It was a shock to all of us and I—" An ugly sound came from her. "*I* had just broken the nose of the Duke of Sokesby. Odd that you are now the Duke of Sokesby, isn't it?"

"I often forget how many titles are attached to me. You blame yourself for being sent away." He shifted closer, brushing his shoulder along hers. "But it is my understanding Bentley never cared for any of you. I doubt anything you did, Tamsin, could have changed that."

Tamsin looked out at the dying gardens. "The nose breaking set Bentley off. He claimed that my actions resulted in enormous embarrassment to him and the title. I—threw a pastry at Lady Longwood."

"How was your aim?"

"Perfect," she whispered, recalling that horrible, terrible day. At the time, there had been a great deal of satisfaction at watching crumbs and jelly drip off Lady Longwood, but in actuality, that one act had made things that much worse. "A fight erupted shortly after.

Cakes and biscuits were thrown. We were escorted out to the waiting coach for our journey to Dunnings. The rest is a tragedy all of society knows well."

"The tragedy, Tamsin, is that you were brought back to London." The low vibration of his words rippled over the grass. "You don't belong there, do you?"

Hardly a flattering assessment, but true. She had tried so hard. "That is terribly unkind of you, Your Grace." Her hands curled into fists where they rested on her lap.

"You misunderstand, Tamsin," Ware growled softly. "I don't belong there either. Please stand down." He nodded at her hands, already closing into fists. "We have agreed that my nose is valuable and should not be altered in any way."

"I agreed to nothing," she breathed at the feel of his palm trailing down her back before glancing along her leg to take hold of her hand, forcing their fingers to lace.

"I meant only that you belong—here." He tilted his head back and looked up at the stars. "The country. Where you can ride and wear breeches and not have to worry overmuch on which fork is used for fish. It does not come naturally to you. I—have some experience in that area."

Tamsin tried to pull back her fingers.

"No," he said calmly, tightening his grip. "Do you see the glow worms, Tamsin?" Ware motioned with his chin to the sweep of grass spilling into the gardens. The tiny specks of light blinked like a barrage of twinkling stars around River Crest. "I've always found the name somewhat amusing. *Lampyridae noctiluca* are not worms at all but beetles."

"The latest objects of your adoration." Tamsin allowed herself a tiny smile.

"Not the only one." Ware's thumb stroked along the edge of her palm. "The females of the species emit a steady glow of light to attract the males. Much like young ladies at a ball, with their extravagant gowns and elaborate coiffures winking with jewels and feathers to draw the attention of the right gentleman."

It was an apt comparison. "I am sure most women would not care for the comparison, Your Grace."

"But you do." Ware raised his arm and pulled their clasped hands in his direction to press a kiss to her knuckles.

"Yes," Tamsin agreed, heat flowing over her skin.

"You need no adornment for me to see your light, Tamsin Sinclair." The soft timbre settled inside her. "No jewels. Nor fancy silks. Nothing at all required. You aren't even a beetle. Yet you shine brighter for me than a thousand glow worms until I see nothing else."

"Ware—" She turned to him, bowing her head. Her heart stretched and reached for him, wanting the solidness of Ware to surround her.

A breath released from him. "I beg you, stay silent. Do not pull apart my words so that you may take whatever meaning you desire from them." He pressed his forehead to hers.

Tamsin nodded, brushing her nose to his. "A superior probiscis. I vow I will not damage it in any way." She tentatively pressed her mouth to his.

A groan left him, a low seductive sound of hunger. Ware pulled her down into the grass, rolling so that she lay half beneath him, one of his legs tossed over hers.

"You've pinned me for your collection, Your Grace."

Ware sucked at Tamsin's lower lip, nipping gently at the flesh. "So I have, Tamsin." He bent to her mouth once more, stealing the very breath from her lungs. She moaned, threading her fingers through his thick strands of his hair, pulling free the silly ribbon he insisted on wearing. Waves of inky black spilled over her hands as she pressed herself to his chest.

Her mind barely whispered at her to stop.

Ware's hand moved beneath Tamsin's skirts, skimming up her leg with deliberation, worshipping every inch of her skin with his fingertips.

"I want to put my mouth on you, Tamsin." The words were rough. Commanding. As a duke's should be. The tip of one finger trailed along the slit of her underthings while his nose sensuously traveled down the length of her body, inhaling her skin. Slowly, Ware pushed up her skirts until the night air caressed her legs.

"I nearly ravaged you in my aunt's garden. I wanted to."

Tamsin's heart beat wildly in her chest at his confession. When his mouth pressed against her thigh, a sound erupted from her lips. The entire lower half of her body lay waiting impatiently for him to touch her.

"Hold still."

Ware's fingers tore at the cotton of her underthings, tugging and ripping the delicate linen methodically until Tamsin lay bare beneath him. Balling up what remained, Ware shoved the torn linen into his coat pocket.

"I may need that back." Her voice caught as his figure trailed over her wet, swollen flesh.

"You won't," he grunted before blowing a puff through the hair of her mound. "I promise." His tongue licked delicately at her slit.

"Oh." She grabbed at his hair.

Tilpin had done this to her. Once. A wet, damp affair that had Tamsin feeling as if she were being licked by a dog. Nothing like the careful way Ware savored her, as if he were taking the last bit of ice off a spoon. His tongue drew through her folds, avoiding the one spot, the one place—

A moan left her as two enormous fingers slid inside her.

Tamsin's hands fell to her sides. She grabbed at the grass, pulling up the blades, barely noticing when a glow worm landed on Ware's back.

He sat up slightly, grabbing Tamsin's buttocks, lifting her up more fully to his mouth. His fingers inside her curled, dragging slowly along her inner walls, rubbing gently at a spot that—

"Ware," she panted. "Please. I'm—"

He sucked at the small, engorged button of flesh hidden inside her folds, his mouth warm, tongue moving in an agonizingly slow fashion.

"Hayden." She moaned his name. The pleasure was so intense she thought she might faint. "Did they teach you this at Oxford," she panted, "while you were studying moths?"

A low amused hum against her slit was the only response.

Her impending climax tightened every muscle in Tamsin's body before erupting in a glorious wave of sensation. Her hips lifted and fell back down as she shattered, Ware's mouth still on her. His fingers, still lodged inside, never stopped their relentless assault, twisting and curling until another wave crested, breaking across her body.

Dear God. What *did* they teach him at Oxford?

"Again," he whispered against her mound before using his tongue until Tamsin unraveled once more. She had never thought—her mind went blank as yet another blaze of pleasure ripped through her. He held her to his mouth the entire time, coaxing every last bit of bliss from Tamsin's body until she lay limp and panting, staring up at the stars above their heads.

If any other woman in London knew what Ware was capable of, he'd soon be inundated with young ladies all vying to be his duchess.

Ware withdrew his mouth and fingers from her, pausing only to press a tender kiss on the inside of one thigh.

Tamsin grabbed at him, pulling him close to her side. She took his hand, pressing a kiss to his palm. Her tongue, of its own accord, wound along his finger.

Ware drew a sharp breath. "Tamsin."

She sat up, tugging at his coat. Pulling at his cravat. She pressed a kiss to his jaw, feeling the hair along his jaw chafe her lips.

"No," he caught her wrist, sounding pained.

"You *can't* ruin me, remember?" she blurted out. "I'm already ruined." She plucked at the buttons of his waistcoat before pausing. "Do you not want me?"

"I have wanted you since I was seventeen. It is a stupid question," he said in a broken voice, pulling her to her feet. Turning her, his big fingers carefully undid each button of her gown, pausing at intervals to press an open-mouthed kiss to the skin of her back. "I'm not strong enough to resist you another moment."

Since he was seventeen. "When I broke Thompson's nose." Tamsin's heart ached.

"Yes," he grunted. "Undone by a beautiful girl with a strong right fist."

Easing the garment off her shoulders, the gown fell away to her feet. The laces of her corset were pulled at, snapping in half with a growl from Ware. He tossed the corset into a shrub at the edge of the garden. "You don't need that contraption." He nibbled at the back of her neck, pulling at her chemise. "You are perfect as you are."

Tamsin stood perfectly still, allowing him to disrobe her, idly wondering if anyone had noticed they were both missing from the drawing room. "What did you say when you left my brother to his brandy?"

"That I had work to do. Research." His big hands palmed her naked breasts, fingers rolling and gently pinching her nipples until they peaked. "You have the most magnificent bosom."

Tamsin turned in his arms, her fingers tugging at his clothing, urging him to discard it. He was so much bigger than she, so powerful compared to her own slender curves. "I once considered you a bear, Your Grace."

"I don't disagree." He pushed her hands away and took off his coat, fingers halting at the buttons of his shirt. "Are you—?"

"Certain? Yes." Her hands tugged at his shirt until it lay discarded on the ground.

Ware was broad and muscled where her fingers touched, with just the slightest bit of extra flesh around his midsection. The rumpled clothing hid a thickly muscled torso and the wealth of wiry hair covering it.

Her fingers fell to the waist of his trousers, jerking them down over his hips. Tamsin ran her hands over the edge of his hips and down his heavy thighs. A rush of arousal lit once more thinking of having him atop her. Crushed beneath all of Ware with him inside her.

The mop of tangled hair fell over his eyes and cheeks, obscuring his face more efficiently than the darkness. The moonlight, pale and shimmering, glanced over his form. She tried not to stare at the jutting length of him.

There was quite a lot of Ware.

He wrapped his arms around Tamsin and lowered her to the grass with gentle care, covering her with his larger form. It was a delicious feeling, the sensation of being dominated by someone much bigger than yourself. She felt the press of him along her thigh, hard and thick, and hoped she could take all of him.

Ware settled between her legs, careful not to put his full weight on her. His mouth embraced hers once more, tongues licking and twisting about each other until Tamsin moaned. He moved down her body, teeth circling each nipple.

He raised his head, watching her with the same fascination she'd seen him show a moth.

"Ware?"

"The image of you, naked with your hair spilled about the grass surrounded by glow worms all blinking like stars will live inside of me, Tamsin, for the remainder of my days." Ware pressed one massive palm to his heart. "It will be the last thing I remember before I leave this earth."

"Oh." Tamsin's breath caught. It was, without a doubt, the most profound thing anyone had ever said to Tamsin. She'd never thought herself capable of inspiring anyone to such—"You are very good with words," her voice hitched, "for a man who claims not to be."

"I try for you." He thrust inside her, carefully at first, letting her become accustomed to his size and weight.

Tamsin inhaled slowly, feeling the painful stretch of her muscles. She had nothing to compare him to besides Talpin, but Ware was...larger than she'd anticipated. Had she still possessed her virtue, Tamsin might well have screamed. Her body fluttered and clasped around his.

"I won't break, Ware." Her fingers sank into one muscular buttock. "I promise."

His fingers sunk into her hair, tugging at the strands to bare her throat. Kissing along the slope of her neck, he thrust hard inside her, sliding Tamsin along the grass.

A strangled gasp left her. "More," she moaned. "More. Harder."

Ware's strokes became more forceful. His fingers wrapped around her throat, just beneath her chin, while his other hand grabbed her hip, holding tight as he thrust inside. She writhed beneath him, catching her body on his with a whimper.

Ware paused and gave her a thoughtful look. He adjusted his hips, testing her pleasure with each thrust until she moaned and gasped. Satisfied he'd found the right spot, Ware took her rather savagely, making sure each stroke drew out her pleasure. The sensation coiled deep inside her, tightening to a pinpoint before spiraling out, taking the breath from her lungs. Her back arched, his name on her lips as she climaxed, nails raking his back.

"We have an attachment," he growled out at her with one powerful thrust.

"Yes," Tamsin sobbed as the ripples of bliss ebbed and floated over her limbs.

Ware stiffened. His teeth sunk into her shoulder. A low rolling sound came from him as his own release found him.

"Tamsin," he breathed against her skin.

CHAPTER TWENTY

H AYDEN OPENED HIS eyes to see a wren staring at him. The bird hopped about, cocking its head, and came closer before chirping and flying away.

He sat up with a whoosh of air from his lungs.

Another bird flitted by. A tiny grasshopper leapt over his leg. Mist lay low to the ground. It was morning. Early. But broad *bloody* daylight. Hayden was naked and sleeping in at the very edge of the Earl of Emerson's garden. And he wasn't alone.

Tamsin shivered and swatted at Hayden, snuggling closer to his warmth. Her dress was thrown over her, but she was as naked as he beneath. This was not a situation Hayden had—anticipated. He'd meant to do this properly.

Well, he had done things properly. Three times by his count.

But he hadn't meant to fuck her in a garden all night as if she were some trollop mere steps away from her brother and the rest of the family.

Emerson was known to have a temper. Hayden was bigger but the earl was a brawler.

He had only meant to convey how much Tamsin meant to him. How much he desired her. Would protect her. Care for her. But maybe this was for the best. Cut to the chase, so to speak. Logically, Tamsin would have to wed him now. Last night had been very different than just plucking a bloody moth off her knee. And he wouldn't need to concern himself anymore that she would refuse him.

"Tamsin."

"Are you always this loud?" she mumbled. "It is far too early to be up." Her eyes opened to meet his sleepily. One glorious naked breast stared out at him.

I hope I wake up every day like this for the rest of my life.

There was a half-smile on her face before it froze on her lips. "Oh, good lord."

Hayden regarded her calmly, but with the most magnificent happiness blossoming inside him. This gorgeous, wondrous creature was *his*.

"Good lord indeed."

"We've got to get dressed," Tamsin sat up, realized she was naked, then pulled her discarded dress to her chest. A strand of chestnut hair fell over her eye, and she blew a puff of breath to dislodge it.

"It's too late, Tamsin. I saw most of you last night, and what I didn't see, my mouth and fingers touched."

A deep flush drew up her cheeks. She leaned over and thrust Hayden's trousers at him. His shirt billowed through the air and landed on his shoulder. "Hurry, Ware. Get dressed." A worried glance was tossed at the house.

"There isn't anyone about. Listen to me, Tamsin."

"We'll sneak in through the kitchens," she said in a panicked voice. "We'll tell everyone I was helping you collect insects. Early morning moths." She snapped her fingers. "I can't recall the name in Latin and—"

"Tamsin."

Tamsin was really the most stunning woman. Breathtaking, in fact.

"Why aren't you getting dressed?" She looked up at him in confusion. "Hurry." She picked up her dress and threw it over her head.

"We aren't going to sneak into the kitchens," Hayden said calmly.

"And I absolutely refuse to tell everyone, yet again, that I've been gathering moths with the most beautiful woman in London. I can't believe anyone who has ever seen you would believe it." Hayden tilted his head. "Or that I'm so obsessed with my work that I would prefer a moth to you."

Ware preferred *nothing* to Tamsin.

"Do you have a better idea, Ware?" Tamsin crawled over to where he'd tossed her corset the night before and simply pulled the garment down further into a patch of bramble. "I'll come back for that. You'll never get it laced up properly. I think my dress will button without it." She gave him her back. "Hurry."

Hayden leaned over and kissed her shoulder. "I do have a better idea."

Tamsin's eyes widened. "Yes, of course. The small door on the other side, close to that parlor you've taken over and filled with beetle legs. We'll go in that way. You can go straight to your work." She looked him up and down. "You are usually rumpled. Your shirts often have grass or dirt stains given your research. No one will even notice. I can sneak up the servants' stairs—"

"No." Hayden took firm hold of her hands. "We aren't doing any of that."

"But—" Understanding filled her eyes and she tried to pull away. "*No.* You cannot be serious. We just finished a ridiculous ruse to avoid this very thing."

He leaned over, rubbing his nose along the top of her head, smelling jasmine and grass. "Yes."

"No. Absolutely not. I—" She took a choking breath. "I—am not suitable as you well know. Good lord, Ware. I just allowed you to tup me in my brother's garden. I understand you feel you must—make such an offer given your past—but it isn't necessary. You need not sacrifice your future. I am hardly an innocent. My virtue was lost some time ago."

"Mine was still intact."

Tamsin burst into nervous laughter. "Very amusing, Ware. A man of your age and status, well—" she stuttered. "You are far too skilled at..." She waved a hand at the lower half of her body. "The idea that you might never have bedded a woman before is patently ridiculous. Now, button me up and we'll sneak inside."

"A long time ago, when my mother was presented with yet another one of my father's bastards, all of whom I support because their birth isn't their fault, I decided I was not going to be anything like the Duke of Ware. My brothers took after him, and I deemed that enough. No bastards or even the chance of one. There are other ways to take one's pleasure, Tamsin. I had female companions and I've done a vast amount of research."

"Dear God," she dropped one of her stockings. "You certainly did."

"So in answer to your earlier question, I *did* study quite a few more things other than insects during my time at Oxford. You'd be surprised at the variety of ways one can climax. But only one sure way to produce a child, who will not be a bastard because we are going to wed."

"You're serious." Tamsin paled.

"I am."

She pressed a hand to her throat. "I've deflowered a duke."

I AM THE Deadliest of Sins.

Had anyone told Tamsin that she would one day take the virtue of a duke, she would have accused them of having had one too many brandies. It had to be a jest of some sort, though Ware didn't look amused in the least. Mostly annoyed. But that wasn't unusual.

All I did was try to cool myself off at Lady Curchon's and look what happened.

This was what Lady Curchon had so feared. Why a ridiculous charade was deemed necessary, and Tamsin exposed to the sight of untold pinned insects. His honor, so tied up in a wealth of complicated feelings about his father, would compel him marry her whether it was the right thing to do or not.

Tamsin instructed herself to faint. Swoon. Have an attack of the vapors.

But she had never fainted. Not once. Not when Captain Talpin blithely informed her just after a good tupping that he couldn't wed her because he already had a wife. Not even when she found Mama after a coughing fit, a spray of blood ringing her lips and the bed like a halo. Not during all the horrible things Lady Longwood tossed at her or Lady Curchon's vile threats.

"We will wed. Promptly," Ware stated in a chilly tone. "It is the right thing to do."

How she hated that phrase. And the part of Ware who was so used to being obeyed commanded her without a second thought.

She had never been good at obedience. Dictating to Tamsin had never once produced a beneficial result. It was unlikely to do so now. Her temper flared sharply at his arrogant manner.

"Yes, Your Grace," Tamsin drawled a bit sarcastically. "Because it is the right thing to do."

"Haven't I just said so?" he growled back at her.

She looked around, searching for something to toss at his snobbish, moth-loving head, angry both at herself and Ware for creating this situation though the previous night had been nothing short of spectacular. "No one has been compromised, Your Grace."

"I disagree. I have."

"Oh, dear. Am I interrupting something?" Aunt Lottie peered at them from behind a poorly trimmed shrub, hands clasped, surveying the entire situation with one raised brow.

Ware jumped at the sight of her, and quickly put himself behind a large, untrimmed hawthorn with as much dignity as a large, naked duke could muster. He pulled a thick spray of leaves over his pertinent parts.

"Goodness, Your Grace. You've grown up, haven't you?" Aunt Lottie said with no small amount of female appreciation. "I believe the last time I saw you in such a state you were all of seven. You decided to go swimming in the fountain at Angus Whitehall's home in Reading. Do you recall?"

"I do," Ware snarled, cheeks pinking. "I have compromised Lady Tamsin, Miss Maplehurst."

"I see."

"Three times over. I took not an ounce of precaution." He glared at Tamsin. "She may even now carry my heir. We should wed in all haste."

Tamsin didn't care for his blunt, unwelcome recital. He'd reduced the previous night to something that reminded her of scientific observation. "I disagree." She glared back.

Aunt Lottie "That you have been compromised?"

"No, on the marriage. It isn't necessary."

"I see." Aunt Lottie nodded slowly. "Your brother may demand satisfaction of some sort, Tamsin."

"I need no one to fight my battles," Tamsin stated. "And duels aren't fought anymore."

"This is not a battle," Ware bit out in a disgruntled tone. "The outcome has been decided."

"Lady Curchon will be most disappointed," Aunt Lottie mused. "All that scheming on her part and yet you are in the same position as you were in her gardens." She walked forward and picked up Ware's trousers to fling at him. "You might seek Odessa's council before you speak to Emerson."

Ware stayed behind the shrub as he dressed, cursing when his shirt caught on one of the branches. Finished, he stepped out from behind the leaves, looking rumpled as usual. He picked up his coat and slung it over one arm.

Tamsin's torn underthings fell out of one pocket along with several tiny glass vials.

"Goodness." Aunt Lottie's eyes danced with amusement at the torn bits of muslin. "A bit of advice, Your Grace. Best not to discuss your intentions to Emerson with his sister's underthings in your coat pocket."

"Or rather not at all. I insist you stop this nonsense." Tamsin marched forward and placed a hand on Ware's chest. "You will not speak to Jordan." If Ware went marching in there in his current state Jordan was just as likely to throw a punch as listen. "Not at present."

"Perhaps I should wait until you are with child?" Sarcasm laced his words.

"Just—wait." Tamsin took a shaky breath, her mind fired in a dozen different directions. Her. Ware. The threats Lady Curchon held over her head. Aurora. Dunnings and the coal. "If there is no child—"

"Damn you, Tamsin," Ware insisted. "Child or not, I *was* beneath your skirts at Lady Curchon's." The striking lines of his face pulled taut with anger. "I *put my mouth* on the inside of your thigh. The right thing—"

"Stop talking," Tamsin nearly screamed at him, the fragile hold on her temper finally snapping. "There is no *right* thing to do. I was not a maid."

"Yes, but I—" he shot back.

Tamsin stomped on his foot to silence him. The last thing she needed was Ware's confession to Aunt Lottie that he had been a virgin. An extremely well-educated, talented with his mouth *virgin*.

"I am an avowed spinster," Tamsin insisted. "I am permitted to take lovers. Have indiscretions. None of which dictates wedding you."

A snarl came from Ware. The very tops of his cheeks were a deep rose color, a sure sign of his discomfort and unhappiness with this discussion. "There will not be any other lovers. We are to be married."

He ran a hand through his hair, making the ends stick up.

"You cannot force me, Your Grace. And I do not care to be dictated to." Tamsin lifted her chin.

Why would he not give her a moment? Just one bloody second to make sense of this. There had been no profession of deep affection last night, aside from the comment about her and the glow worms, which was lovely indeed. Nor was Tamsin ready to give credence to her own feelings. All of which left her with the growing suspicion that while Ware did care for her, his proposal had less to do with caring for her than it did his constant desire to not be his father. And Tamsin had never considered the reality of what a marriage to Ware might be; there had been simply too many reasons why such a thing was impossible.

I don't even know the right fork for fish.

"Try me, Tamsin." Ware turned from her and Aunt Lottie, marching back to the house, fists clenched, shirt flapping against his back. "If you do not inform Emerson," he said over his shoulder, "I will."

"He does not care to be dictated to either, Your Grace."

Ware halted. "Good. He may be a brawler, but I'm far larger. And a bloody duke." Then he continued, stomping viciously at the grass as he made his way to the side door.

"Goodness, Tamsin." Aunt Lottie touched her arm. "What stubborn creatures you both are."

"I did not mean for us to argue in such a way." She watched Ware's retreating back.

"You refused him. Did you not account for his temper when doing so?"

"I am not refusing him exactly. I only wished time to assess the situation."

"He has changed greatly since the episode with Odessa's father, and he is nothing like the scholarly Ware I used to know before the death of his father and brothers. Imagine, there has been a duke hiding all this time behind all those insects and wrinkled clothing. According to Odessa, Ware has recently taken up the reins of his estates, a vast undertaking and one he had no interest in for years. Lord Curchon has welcomed his nephew into political circles, increasing Ware's influence. The duchess will be most pleased."

More reasons why she must not allow Ware to force her into this. Tamsin would be an encumbrance in the life of a duke.

"There is much about him that is appealing, especially out of his clothes, I imagine." She wiggled her brows. "All that wild hair. I've always had a weakness for big, brawny men."

"You've a weakness for any man." Aunt Lottie was a shameless flirt for an elderly woman.

"I'm old. Not dead, Tamsin. There is no harm in admiration," she replied tartly. "I'll bring a mixture of herbs to your maid. For your bath. Be careful how you sit a horse."

"You are incorrigible."

"But correct." Aunt Lottie winked. "Why would you refuse him? Truly? You are afraid of something, Tamsin. I would help if I could."

"I think he will regret his hasty offer one day as it was made out of his desire to do the honorable thing."

"I've seen the way he looks at you. It isn't the least honorable."

Tamsin shook her head. "There are other matters which must be considered."

Aunt Lottie tilted her chin. "What other matters? That you were not a maid? I doubt Ware is concerned."

"My lack of virtue only makes my unsuitability that much more apparent. I became lovers with a ship's captain at the age of nineteen. What proper young lady does so?" Tamsin paced back and forth along the grass, her heart constricting painfully. "I'm not the sort of girl who should be a duchess, Aunt Lottie. You've said so yourself."

"I was wrong, dearest." Aunt Lottie reached out for her. "At the time you were so despondent over the fact you might have to wed him. It was more jest than anything."

"Think of the scandal should I wed him. The entire incident at Lady Curchon's would be taken in a different light, wouldn't it? Tamsin Sinclair would become a woman cut from the same cloth as her mother." She stopped and looked at Aunt Lottie. "Do you know how awful it is to hear my mother disdained in such a way? Constantly? Lady Longwood will smile and tell everyone she was right all along. Lady Curchon will be embarrassed, enough so that she withdraws her support from Aurora."

"Tamsin—

"Think what that will do to my family. To Aurora. Not to mention that Jordan is only now restoring the family to our rightful place. The—scandal is sure to damage or even halt the mining at Dunnings."

Aunt Lottie's lips pulled into a tight grimace. "What has she done? Alice. What did she say to you?"

"Nothing," Tamsin lied.

"Rubbish. I noticed how Ware looked at you during her dinner party, there is no doubt she did as well. Ironic, considering Alice is the one who devised the entire ruse to keep her nephew from having to wed you. She underestimated Ware. And now you doubt his sincerity. What did she do, threaten to have Lord Curchon make trouble for Jordan at Dunnings? Take back her sponsorship?" Aunt Lottie's brows drew together, furious on Tamsin's behalf. "Alice has overstepped."

Tamsin looked away, refusing to answer. "My family suffered once for my impetuous actions. I would not have them do so again."

"Dunnings was never your fault, but those assurances to you fall on deaf ears." Aunt Lottie spun on her heel and started back towards the house. "I'll leave you to make your own way inside as you need no one's assistance. How difficult must it be to carry the weight of responsibility for *everyone* on your shoulders. Frankly, I thought doing so would make you braver."

CHAPTER TWENTY-ONE

HAYDEN SAT AT the desk he'd commandeered at River Crest, the letter a footman had just delivered spread out before him. The Duchess of Ware was back in England. London, to be specific, and looking for her son. Well, not looking. She'd known exactly where to find him, courtesy of Lady Curchon. Lord only knew how Aunt Alice surmised his whereabouts. He meant to have a pointed discussion with her when they next met. She would attempt to interfere in events already set in motion and Hayden could not allow it.

Leaving Tamsin in the garden, he'd come to the parlor to find the letter from Mother waiting for him on the desk. She expected him to come to London immediately, which Hayden would. Today, as a matter of fact. He needed to put some space between himself and Tamsin for a short time. Most women would be overjoyed to have a duke compromise them and demand marriage. But not Tamsin. He wasn't sure it was him she rejected or what marriage to a duke would mean. Probably both.

He pinched the bridge of his nose. Ran his fingers through his too long hair, and pulled a twig out from between the strands. Glancing at the three perfect beetles he meant to pin to the board behind him, Hayden decided to just pack them away in a glass vial and store them in a trunk. Chapman, Emerson's butler, had already been informed to pack the rest of Hayden's things and have the coach readied.

He was a great, wounded creature sitting here in this parlor surrounded by beetles and considering whether it was far too early to have a brandy. Tamsin had pushed him away once more, even after he'd expressed the depth of his feeling for her the previous night. Words of affection had never come easy, so he'd tried to show her what was in his heart.

Perhaps she simply didn't want him for more than a decent tupping.

"Your Grace."

Hayden looked up to see Tamsin standing at the entrance to the parlor, looking much as she had when dismissing him earlier in the garden. She hadn't even changed before coming to speak to him.

Can't wait to rid herself of me.

A well of pain opened inside Hayden. A familiar one. Stupid to equate this sensation with the treatment of his father towards him. But it *felt* the same. Which put Hayden in an incredibly foul mood, each emotion sharp and distorted.

Chestnut hair fell about Tamsin's shoulders in a glorious riot of curls. There was a flower petal stuck in the strands. She crossed her arms, which did nothing but push up her magnificent bosom. Nibbled on her bottom lip while her eyes shifted from his.

"Tamsin," he greeted her, not caring to be addressed as *Your Grace* by a woman he'd spent the night bedding. If she dared to refer to him so formally once more, Hayden might well toss one of the beetles before him at her. An arsenal of insect parts were at his disposal.

She looked down at her hands, but not at Hayden. "I appreciate your offer to do the honorable thing, Your Grace."

Hayden picked up a dead beetle and tossed it at her. "Honorable?" The word sunk into his bones. "You think I want you out of honor?"

"I think you feel the need to be unlike your sire keenly." She brushed the insect off her sleeve without a qualm. "And as a spinster—"

"Are you?" *Spinster.* At the exalted age of twenty-six.

"You said yourself I was ancient," she reminded him. "A spinster may have an indiscretion, or a dalliance which does not result in marriage."

"Am I the indiscretion or a dalliance in this instance? I'm not sure I understand the difference." A chill lit the air, frost covering his words at her rejection. Last night had been an expression of his bloody heart.

"In addition," Tamsin finally looked up, "I also think that the *first* time—that is the loss of one's virtue—can cause one to feel an overabundance of affection for the more experienced partner." She stuttered slightly. "One which fades because—"

"Of all the ridiculous reasons I thought you might give me." Hayden stopped her. "This is by far the most insulting." Icy anger filled the hollows of his chest. "Forgive me, Tamsin, but putting my cock in you was not enough to cause me to become cow-eyed. Nor did the smell of your quim drive me to distraction like some schoolboy."

Tamsin reddened and looked down at her bare feet. She hadn't even bothered to recover her stockings in the mad dash to vanquish Hayden. Which made him more furious.

"Let us both agree that while I hadn't actually bedded a woman until you in the normal way, I'm far from innocent," he said. "I find it amusing you assume to be more experienced as your pretty little speech informed me. Do you think I learned how to do," he pointedly stared at the space between her thighs where his mouth had explored, "*that* at the Entomological Society?"

"No," she whispered, the color on her cheeks deepening. "I only meant—"

"I'm well aware of what you meant. But allow me to advise you that a good tupping is the *least* of the things I will do to you, Tamsin," he snarled, control snapping. "When we wed. Which we will."

"I have not agreed."

"I don't care," Hayden thundered back at her.

"Your Grace—"

He flung another beetle at her, angrier and more hurt than he had ever been in his life. Good lord, he sounded exactly like his father. If he hadn't been so *frustrated* with her, Hayden might have tried to rein in his rising ire. He rarely lost his temper, preferring to merely shutter himself away, but Tamsin—it was in his best interests to go to London today.

"I—you cannot wed me, Ware," she said with determination. "Surely you can see that. I am—not the sort of woman who should be a duchess."

Hayden stared at her for several moments, long enough to make her look away once more. "Very well," he said calmly. "I agree."

Tamsin's chin snapped up. "You do." Her hands dropped to her sides, fingers curling and uncurling while she looked at him, both surprised and chagrined he agreed with her. The sheen of tears glimmered in her eyes.

"Yes." Hayden nodded in agreement. "Truthfully, now that I'm over the magic spell of losing my virtue to you along with the taste of your quim, you've convinced me that I could never wed a woman of such poor background." His tone grew colder. More clipped. "One who isn't even pure. The daughter of an actress, for goodness sakes. A harlot in the making. You don't have proper table manners. The use of silverware seems to be a particular challenge."

A tiny, wounded sound came from Tamsin.

"You can't even manage the steps of a simple dance. I'd exist in a continual state of embarrassment with you by my side. I'd be pitied everywhere I went after falling for the charms of such an ambitious Deadly Sin."

Her fingers trembled as she clasped the doorjamb. Hayden almost stopped at her distress but did not. This was what she believed.

"Imagine the scandal were we to wed. London would speak of nothing for years. *You're* the sort of girl who would break a gentleman's nose. No wonder you were sent away."

Tamsin's slender form recoiled as if he'd struck her, clinging to the frame of the door. A lone tear ran down her cheek.

It was the worst thing to say to her, because Hayden knew she blamed herself for the Sinclair family's exile to Dunnings. But Hayden was in no mood to be charitable.

"Isn't that what you wanted to hear, Tamsin? What you have chosen to believe?"

A sob caught in her throat. "I am trying to do what is best for you."

"*You*, Tamsin. You are what is best for me. Only you are blind to it."

"Tomorrow," she assured him in a quaking tone, "we will speak again. You will feel differently."

"Doubtful. I'm leaving River Crest." Hayden sat back. "In about an hour."

"Leaving." Tamsin cleared her throat, swallowing several times. "You're leaving?"

"Don't pretend to be distressed. You've wanted me gone from the moment I arrived. I came with a ridiculous notion of courting you." Hayden watched the shock of his words pull at her features. "But I cannot dissuade you from your own beliefs."

"Ware—" She wiped at another tear rolling down her cheek.

"I will not change the course of action I have set forth. If you think me arrogant now, Tamsin, you've only to wait. We are going to wed. So, any ridiculous notion you have of hiding a child from me and stoically raising it in a cottage by the sea can be banished. Now," his tone was curt. "Leave, I beg you." He dipped his chin in the direction of the door. "If I speak to you further today, Tamsin, we will both regret it."

She continued to stand by the door for some moments, fists clenching and unclenching so that he thought she might hop on the table and box his ears. Hayden half-hoped she would. Anything would be better than this terrible, ugly discussion.

He hoped some time apart would give Tamsin perspective. Maybe allow her to miss him. Come to her own realizations. Staying would worsen the situation. She wasn't ready to let go of the truths she'd held onto for so long.

Hayden had recent experience in that area.

When she finally slipped away, he did not go after her, though his heart, broken as it was, screamed for him to do so. Instead, he carefully packed up his specimens and stored them in a waiting trunk. He was still an entomologist. But he was also a bloody duke.

One who *loved* every improper, uncivilized bit of Tamsin Sinclair. He wasn't about to wed anyone else.

Hayden nearly shouted so at her, but given Tamsin's mood, it was unlikely she would have believed him. Not in the state she'd put herself in. Not today.

Stopping the footmen who'd come for his trunks, Hayden asked, "Where might I find Lord Emerson?"

CHAPTER TWENTY-TWO

T AMSIN WENT DIRECTLY up to her room, refusing to waste another tear on the Duke of Ware. She changed and went directly to the stables and asked for Teach to be saddled. Taking off in the direction of the meadow at the edge of River Crest, she halted, her breath coming in pained gasps. Tamsin turned in the saddle to look back at her brother's estate in time to see the ducal coach pull away.

Isn't this what I wanted?

She had. Tamsin had prayed for him to leave River Crest for weeks. Been irritated by his presence. Wished for him to go before Lady Curchon got it into her head that Tamsin had lured him here. A hysterical wail bubbled up her throat. Her head fell over Teach's neck. Tamsin Sinclair, who never cried, now exploded in a torrent of weeping the likes of which she'd never known.

Hayden, her mind screamed.

She didn't feel better at his leaving. Anguish pounded through her body, the physical pain at Ware's loss. At the sheer ugliness of the words he'd hurled at her. Tamsin deserved every one. She'd called him a *dalliance*. Demeaned his feelings for her by equating them to some green lad who'd never bedded a woman.

A sob left her. Then another. She dismounted, holding on to Teach's reins. She shuddered against his side as the tears fell from her eyes. Falling back on the grass, Tamsin sobbed as if she would never stop.

"I did," she hiccupped between tears, "what was best for him."

"You are best for me, Tamsin."

Staring up at the sky, she listened to Teach munch on the surrounding grass, wiping at her nose and cheeks, wishing she could go back to that conversation in the parlor and explain herself better, but it was far too late.

"In time, I think he would regret me," she said to Teach. That fear, more than Lady Curchon's threats or the gossip Lady Longwood might spread was at the forefront of her reasoning. She would carry the blame for ruining Ware's life just as she had her family.

The next hour, Tamsin spoke softly to Teach and explained her reasoning. She and Ware did not belong together, no matter how much she might wish it. Some distance would make him reconsider his hasty proposal and he would be grateful. They would be friends, she assured herself. Ware would see reason. Eventually.

Tamsin slipped in the side door, the one closest to the parlor Ware had been using. She paused as she passed, the sight of the now empty room sending a fresh wave of pain through her. Her lip trembled as she searched for any sign of his trunks or insects. But there was nothing. No sign that Ware had ever been at River Crest except for small love bites and marks along her body and the soreness between her thighs.

She pressed a hand to her mouth lest she start weeping once more. It was done. He hadn't suddenly decided to turn around the coach and return to River Crest.

"This is what I wanted," she whispered. "It's for the best."

"Lady Tamsin." Chapman's voice startled her from his place a few feet away. "The duke has gone to London and is not expected to return."

"Thank you, Chapman. I was aware." She gave him a semblance of a smile.

"Lord Emerson would like to see you in the drawing room, my

lady. I've brought tea."

"I believe I'll go upstairs first, Chapman. Would you let my brother know—"

"Apologies, Lady Tamsin, but his lordship requested you attend him the moment you returned." Chapman bowed and waved her forward.

This couldn't possibly be good.

Tamsin wiped at her face, trying to compose herself before she faced her brother. Slowly making her way down the hall behind the butler, her stomach curled into knots. She caught sight of herself in the mirror, tear-stained with swollen eyes.

Chapman knocked on the drawing room door before swinging it open. "Lady Tamsin, as you requested, my lord."

Tamsin stepped inside to see Jordan, Odessa, Aurora, and Aunt Lottie all gathered. No one looked especially pleased to see her, nor were they enjoying the enormous tea tray Chapman had placed on the table. Aunt Lottie was sipping brandy and there was a glass of whiskey at Jordan's elbow.

No, this wasn't good at all.

"There you are. I wondered if you would sleep in the field with Teach instead of returning. According to the information at my disposal, you are accustomed to sleeping out of doors."

Her hope that Ware hadn't gone to Jordan before his departure faded. Now she was faced with her family knowing of the nature of her relationship with Ware.

"Please sit, Tamsin." Jordan nodded to the chair across from him. He didn't seem especially angry, which was good because her brother possessed a temper. But neither did he appear overly pleasant.

Odessa sat beside him, fingers twisting in her lap, slate blue eyes peering into Tamsin's soul.

"Go ahead," her brother said, catching sight of Tamsin eyeing his glass of whiskey. "This discussion might merit a whiskey. I know it did for me."

She squared her shoulders and marched to the sideboard, pouring out a fingerfull of the amber liquid into a crystal glass. Taking a swallow, Tamsin returned to sit in the chair facing her brother. Taking a deep breath she said, "Ware had no right to speak to you. There wasn't any need. I would have told you myself.

"He had every right. As I'm sure you can appreciate, Ware can be exceptionally blunt and to the point when he chooses, which was today, as a matter of fact. I found myself blushing at the sight of your torn underthings."

Tamsin cringed, fingers tightening on the glass.

"He did not want to give the opportunity for anything else to be assumed." Jordan peered at her over the edge of his whiskey. "Nor his intentions made unclear."

"Is this a conversation that everyone must be present for?" She cast a glance in Aurora's direction. "Perhaps we might discuss this in your study."

"I am not a child, Tamsin." Aurora stated abruptly with more than a touch of anger. "Stop behaving as if I'm barely out of the nursery. Or in need of your constant protection. You are *smothering* me."

Tamsin straightened, lips parting in surprise. "I only meant that this is a delicate matter." She glanced at Jordan who merely raised a brow. Aunt Lottie calmly sipped her brandy. Odessa stood and went to the sideboard, returning with a glass of whiskey for herself.

None of this could be good if she'd driven Odessa to the sideboard.

"Delicate?" Aurora said in an affronted tone. "You are concerned that whatever you say will cause me to faint as most young ladies? Me?"

"No, Aurora. I only meant—"

"I grew up at Dunnings," Aurora stormed. "A stone's throw from Spittal. Jordan raised pigs that *bred*, which resulted in piglets."

"God, I wondered why you kept wandering over to the pens,"

Jordan said under his breath.

"Didn't you notice me standing outside the window when Drew regaled you with tales of his latest escapades at the house parties he was always attending? Goodness, the things I learned listening to Malcolm describe his adventures soldiering. But suddenly I'm a perfect lady, living in London, and I'm to pretend I have no knowledge of," she waved her hands about, "*sexual congress*? Good grief, Tamsin. Aunt Lottie is my chaperone."

The older woman looked affronted. "Well, you haven't been ruined, have you?"

Jordan pinched the bridge of his nose. "This is why I prefer my pigs."

"Do you think us all blind?" Aurora continued, warming to her tirade. "I watched you dance with him. Ware. I'm not an idiot. I stopped playing a full ten minutes before the two of you ceased your wiggling against each other. He was sniffing your neck, Tamsin. *Sniffing.*"

Odessa took a large swallow of the whiskey in her glass and sputtered.

"Who do you think took your boots off after Ware carried you to your room a few hours later? *Me.* You reeked of Jordan's good whiskey."

"I knew I was missing a bottle," Jordan grumbled.

"All we did was share a glass of whiskey." Tamsin tried to defend herself even as heat washed up her cheeks at remembering his hands caressing her through the leather breeches.

"The duke is an exceptionally large person, Tamsin. Impossible to miss. Especially when he's dragging your foxed sister about."

"This has been going on far longer than Ware allowed me to believe." Jordan stood, went to the sideboard, took up the entire bottle of whiskey, and set it on the table before him.

Denial useless, clearly. Taking a sip of the whiskey, she wondered how much it would take to blot out this unsettling conversation. "I see."

"I never wrote to my cousin about beetles," Odessa stated. "Ware appeared without advising me of his arrival. A lovely surprise, though it wasn't meant for me. You realize he endured a too-small bed for your sake? As to his compromising you in the garden—"

"I am twenty-six." Tamsin sputtered. "On the shelf. A *spinster*." She shot a glance at Aurora. "I really do not think she should be present for this conversation."

"My room faces the pond, but also the edge of the garden," Aurora stated blithely. "I saw more of Ware than I wished. I advised Aunt Lottie immediately."

Tamsin drew in a breath, horrified that her entire family knew she'd been tupped by Ware, outside and in full view of the house. "A spinster is permitted her indiscretions."

"Unfortunately, Tamsin," Jordan said, "Ware doesn't see things that way. He has stated his intent."

"No does my cousin consider himself an indiscretion," Odessa said firmly, eyes narrowed on Tamsin.

This was terrible. Tamsin might awake to find Odessa on the bed, staring at her with those knowing eyes of hers, perhaps with a bucket of wax. Ready to create a death mask.

"Fine. Not an indiscretion. Lovers, if you will. Briefly." Tamsin flung back at her.

Odessa made a puffing sound.

"I think the duke is wonderful. Yes, he's overly large and a bit odd, but none of us can claim to be paragons of society. Well, perhaps I can," Aurora said.

"Give it time," Aunt Lottie said under her breath.

"There is nothing at all wrong with *him*," Tamsin said loudly to make her point. "But there is a great deal wrong with me. Do I look like a duchess? I'm getting foxed in the middle of the day. I wear breeches to ride." She waved a hand down her breeches, shirt, and boots.

"I told you," Aunt Lottie said quietly.

Tamsin glowered at her. "You all know what will happen if I marry Ware. It will be the only thing anyone speaks of for months, possibly years. I will be branded the ambitious harlot Lady Longwood has been declaring me to be." She took a shaky breath. "Our family is finally starting to regain our place. Aurora is coming out. Jordan has Dunnings and the coal to consider. I—made a rash decision last night, but it does not need to result in an unwanted marriage that society will despise me for. Or you." Her gaze lit on each of them. "I can't allow you all to suffer once more for my recklessness. I will not be the cause of my family's misery again." A tear ran down her cheek. "I will not."

"Stop it," Jordan said quietly. "Stop it this instant, Tamsin. I have listened to you berate yourself for our exile to Dunnings for years."

Another tear ran down Tamsin's cheek. "But it *is* my fault, Jordan. Bentley sent us away directly after. I think we might have been able to change his mind if I hadn't—been me. I'm the worst of us. You know that. So does all of London. I'm the reason you all had to live on cabbage and Mama—"

"Enough," Jordan yelled furiously. "Your guilt over something that was never your fault has consumed you. Bentley sent us to Dunnings, not you." Jordan stormed at her, so loudly Aurora's teacup rattled. "His plans were made well before you broke the nose of Ware's brother at Gunter's. I've told you so a dozen times, but you refuse to hear me. You don't want to hear me." He raked his fingers through his hair. "The truth is that *our parents* created a scandal, Tamsin. Mother was an actress and then Father's mistress before they wed. *That* is why Bentley sent us to Dunnings. *That* is why he bankrupted the estate. He hated us because Father loved our mother and *not* his. It was never your fault." He stood before her. "And frankly, I don't need your sacrifice."

"Nor do I," Aurora piped in.

"Or me," Odessa interjected. "Goodness, do you think I care if anyone ever receives me?" She set down her glass. "Your unsuitability is what garnered the affections of the Duke of Ware. I understand it is daunting, Tamsin. The gossips, Lady Longwood, and doubtless Cousin Alice will make things difficult for you."

"Alice threatened her," Aunt Lottie said firmly, ignoring Tamsin's pointed look to be silent.

Odessa sat back. "Dear God. She threatened the mines at Dunnings, didn't she? I expected her to promise to withdraw her support of Aurora, but suggesting she would tamper with Jordan's business? Ware will be *furious*."

"Please, you must not tell him. I don't want to be the cause—"

Jordan rolled his eyes. "If you say such a thing again, I will make you sleep with the damn pigs."

"You realize," Odessa continued, "it was Ware who demanded she sponsor Aurora to begin with, don't you? Cousin Alice wouldn't have offered on her own. Well, I hope you're prepared, Tamsin, for the havoc you've wrought."

Tamsin's eyes widened. "I've been trying to avoid havoc." She glanced at Jordan who made a noise at her.

"Far too late for that, my dear." Aunt Lottie pushed an opened letter across the small table holding the tea tray. "The messenger was instructed not to deliver it to Jordan until the Duke of Ware's coach left River Crest. He was paid quite a large sum to first deliver a note to Ware then hide and deliver the second message once Ware departed."

Tamsin looked at the creamy vellum; a terrible pitching in her stomach occurred, upsetting the whiskey.

"We're all going to London. Oh, I suppose the correct word would be commanded to go." Jordan finished his whiskey and poured another, obviously not pleased. "Sooner than I would have liked, but when you are summoned by a *duchess*," his words raised an octave, "you must appear."

Dread took root inside Tamsin as she looked down at the elegant script, so stark against the creamy paper. Her name was underlined. More than once. "I see."

"Note the signature, Tamsin. The Duchess of Ware has a flair for the dramatic," Aunt Lottie said. "She wishes to make your acquaintance. You have been instructed to call upon her in one week. I'm sure Lady Curchon has filled the duchess with all sorts of tales about you. I doubt Ware knows, although he might by the time you arrive."

Tamsin picked up the letter and read over the Duchess of Ware's carefully crafted words, noting the thinly veiled intimidation and the absolute arrogance that she would not be refused. Possibly someday Tamsin would know what that was like.

"You should know, Ware asked Jordan to bring you to London at the end of the month," Odessa said. "Even if you were kicking and screaming."

"Apparently he knows you well," Jordan informed Tamsin. "I would have punched him except I thought it would be similar to hitting a stone wall."

"It is very much like that." Tamsin dropped the letter to the table, seeing the looks they threw her way. A sort of odd relief filled her at having this choice taken away. She had not deterred Ware.

"No more blaming yourself, Tamsin." Jordan pressed a hand to his chest as Aurora squeezed into the chair with her.

A sob bubbled up her throat. Guilt had been her constant companion for so long.

"I think I speak for Drew and Malcolm as well when I say," her brother's voice thickened, "we cannot bear it any longer."

Aurora placed her head on Tamsin's shoulder. "You must let go of it."

Tamsin stared once more at the letter from the duchess. Lady Curchon had no doubt whispered a great many things to Ware's mother, or possibly the gossip had reached the duchess in Bavaria. No matter the reason, her purpose calling them all to London was to warn Tamsin away from Ware. Tamsin would be studied and intimidated by the Duchess of Ware.

Let her try.

Indeed, if Tamsin agreed to Ware's proposal, poorly given though it was, she would suffer a great deal of scrutiny. Most of it not good.

"Tamsin." Odessa took her hands. "Ware will never allow anything to happen to Dunnings. Aurora's come-out will not be ruined. Ware simply won't allow it. I think," her sister-in-law whispered so only Tamsin could hear, "that you and Ware are an oddly perfect match. And not even honor would compel him to wed a woman he didn't want. But the choice is yours."

Her heart, which had been a weight in her chest for the better part of the day, suddenly felt light. "I would hate to disappoint the Duchess of Ware." She lifted her chin.

CHAPTER TWENTY-THREE

T AMSIN TOSSED A shawl over her shoulders, intending to take one final early morning walk around River Crest before departing for London. The weather had already started to turn, the air growing chillier with each passing day.

Drew had never made it to River Crest over the summer months. According to the letter he'd sent to Jordan, he was in Lincolnshire. He'd won a farm in a game of cards. Or an estate. Drew wasn't very clear about it and had to settle things with the previous owner's widow. He wasn't certain how much longer he'd be away, apologized for not coming to River Crest, and promised they would all be together in London by the time Malcolm arrived and Aurora made her debut.

Good. Tamsin thought marshaling the troops to be in the Sinclairs' favor. There was strength in numbers. She had no idea how things would proceed in London other than the duchess was sure to be a trial. There was also the possibility that Tamsin's fears were correct and Ware had reconsidered his hasty proposal to her in the garden.

He won't. Her heart thudded.

Ware, hands outstretched in the park and surrounded by Blues flitted before her eyes. Blue fluttering wings surrounding him as he stood, appreciating the sun and the butterflies. A place he'd chosen to take her without knowing about the Blues at River Crest. It had been a sign, but Tamsin didn't want to see it. She'd found him so shockingly beautiful. And then he'd kissed her and—it had been glorious but also terrifying.

I love him.

A hard thing to admit, nearly as difficult as letting go of the guilt over Dunnings. Tamsin's entire purpose had been to protect and sacrifice for the Sinclairs because she had convinced herself she was the cause of their ruin. Jordan and she had walked out across the field the other day, Tamsin talking, her brother just listening. The guilt was starting to ease, as if she'd been weighed down by dozens of pebbles which were slowly being taken off her chest.

She missed Ware desperately after that walk with Jordan, wanting so much to talk to her odd duke.

"I hope he forgives me." There was a great deal of worry inside Tamsin that he would not.

Just as she turned the corner to make her way to the waiting coach, Tamsin caught a flash of blue from the corner of one eye. A blue butterfly floated in the air above a patch of still-green grass near the gardens. Her brow wrinkled in consternation. It was far too late in the year for the Blues to still be out. There were certainly no flowers to tempt the butterfly. If Ware were here with her, she would mention such an oddity to him so he could make a note in his tiny book.

Tamsin pressed a palm to her heart, struck by the sight of the Blue.

New beginnings, Mama's voice whispered in her ear. *A fresh start.*

She blinked, trying to still the moisture gathering in her eyes. It was a sign, Tamsin was sure of it.

Alone at night, Tamsin relived making love with Ware amid the glow worms. The weight of her eccentric duke pressing her into the grass, their naked bodies intertwined. How could she possibly have underestimated what that night meant to Ware, especially after his rather pointed explanation of events later? That night had been a declaration of his intentions and Tamsin, so wrapped up in her past, hadn't seen it.

I just didn't want to see it.

She would open her eyes, not seeing the canopy above the bed, but Ware above her, the dark strands of his hair spilling over his shoulders and cheeks, far too long.

I love him, her heart whispered once more.

"The coach is ready. Jordan is cursing and wondering where you are. Odessa has promised to read to us from a particularly gruesome book Ware bought her in London. There is a creature living in the Thames. Apparently, this monster will snatch you off while you merely stroll by or even from a passing barge. I imagine after that, you are eaten." Aurora came up beside her.

"Sounds fascinating." Tamsin had been so lost in her thoughts of Ware she hadn't even heard Aurora's approach.

"Don't be worried, Tamsin." Aurora took her hand. "Ware loves you. I'm certain of it." She tugged her in the direction of the carriage. "Though I don't know how you're going to go about pinning poor insects for the remainder of your days."

"I'll get by."

Tamsin's future was before her, and she wanted Ware to be part of it.

CHAPTER TWENTY-FOUR

T AMSIN STOOD AT the entrance of the drawing room as the critical eye of the Duchess of Ware fell upon her. She kept her spine ramrod straight, hands perfectly clasped before her, just as Aunt Lottie had instructed her repeatedly before leaving Emerson House. The duchess had sent her own carriage to retrieve Tamsin, a sleek, black conveyance which dripped with an excess of power and wealth.

She had climbed in having no idea where the ducal residence was located and hoping she wasn't being kidnapped and sent away. Wales perhaps. Or America.

Residence. Such a bland word for the enormous gray stone structure taking up the entire left side of the street. Tamsin likened it more to a castle of sorts. A wall of ancient stone and mortar surrounded the towering edifice covered in strands of curling ivy. Tamsin had no idea how illustrious or how far back Ware's pedigree reached, but considering his home was larger by far than any of the others in London and situated near the park, it was safe to say that the Dukes of Ware had been prominent in society for a least a century.

Tamsin's stomach pitched during the entire journey through the London streets, though the carriage was well-sprung.

Not a moment later after arriving at the Duke of Ware's London residence, an elderly butler who introduced himself as Hobbs ushered Tamsin into the elaborate drawing room so full of understated elegance and quiet wealth, Lady Curchon's home seemed no more than a cozy cottage in comparison. Curtains of deep blue, two shades darker than the walls, greeted her. A fireplace so large an entire orchestra could sit inside. Furniture richly appointed. Every available surface was covered with a vase, a figurine, or a snuffbox of exquisite quality.

And cats. A great deal of them. They circled around Tamsin as she made her way into the room, drawing down in a curtsey before the woman seated on a tufted striped settee.

"Your Grace." Tamsin murmured in a low, respectful tone, though she didn't care for the duchess having summoned the Sinclairs to London just so Her Grace could inspect Tamsin over tea. She had no idea if Ware knew her family was in London. There had been no note from him upon Tamsin's arrival, nor anything since.

She frowned a bit, smoothing her skirts, trying to appear unruffled.

The modest day dress selected for today's meeting was the color of bluebells and chosen specifically because the duchess favored blue as evidenced by the décor of the drawing room. Tamsin had disagreed, but Aunt Lottie insisted she'd need every advantage when dealing with the old dragon. The neckline of the dress was higher than any other Tamsin owned and did a decent job of hiding her generous bosom. Mostly.

"Hmmm." The imperious sound came from duchess. "Sit." She waved at a blue damask chair directly across from her.

Tamsin lifted her chin higher, careful to take small steps and not her usual wide strides across the Persian rug beneath her feet. The design was intricate. Rather lavish. Made one dizzy if you looked too long.

The duchess cleared her throat.

Her Grace looked *nothing* at all like Ware, except for her height, which was evident even though she remained seated. Her angular form was garbed in rich amethyst silk, a hint of jewels sparkling beneath the artful sprinkle of ash blonde curls hovering above her ears.

Very few lines marred her features and Tamsin had difficultly discerning her age. But not her haughtiness. Under more friendly circumstances, she might have referred to the duchess as stately. Regal. But considering this was more interrogation than a social call, Tamsin decided to be unkind and refer to Her Grace as *The Giantess*.

A tiny smile pulled at Tamsin's lips.

The duchess studied Tamsin from the slope of her thin, aristocratic nose. "I recall your mother." Her accent was brutally clipped, the words freezing in the air. A shiver went down Tamsin's spine. "You resemble her most strongly."

Tamsin didn't dare look away. The duchess might be inclined to take a bit out of her if she did. "How kind of you to say."

"It was not a compliment. Lady Emerson was far too beautiful for her own good. As I you are." Her eyes flicked over Tamsin's bodice, inclining her head at the froth of lace. "I suppose that is why you broke Thompson's nose."

This was going splendidly thus far. She'd been here less than a quarter hour and already the punch at Sokesby had reared its head.

"His admiration was not appreciated, Your Grace." Tamsin was not about to apologize for Ware's brother even if he was dead. Thompson had groped her at Gunter's more than once before she punched him.

Silence settled between them. A clock ticked away the minutes, though Tamsin couldn't see the timepiece. Purrs reached her ears as the cats inspected Tamsin's person. She reached down and idly scratched the ears of the tabby curling about her ankles while listening for Ware's heavy tread, wondering if he was somewhere in this monstrosity of a house, but heard nothing. Surely, Ware was here, wasn't he?

The tabby, happy for Tamsin's affection, purred loudly, brushing its head along her leg.

Another cat roamed along the bookcases on the other side of the room, deftly moving around a delicate vase. Two others, no more than kittens, rolled about beneath the table.

Ware had said his mother adored cats.

"That is Aset." The duchess raised a brow at Tamsin.

Tamsin nodded. "Also known as Isis. Goddess of fertility, magic, and healing." She scratched Aset under the chin. "An apt name." Tamsin might be uncivilized according to society, but she did read a great deal. The museum was a welcome excursion for her.

A pang of longing struck her for Ware.

"Hmm," the dowager duchess intoned once more.

Aset climbed into Tamsin's lap, where she curled into a ball and batted a paw at the lace edging Tamsin's neckline.

"I must confess," the words dripped with icy disdain, "I am somewhat disappointed."

"Disappointed, Your Grace?" Tamsin looked up from the tabby.

The cool gaze of the duchess flicked over her. "I've been informed, by various sources, of your bold manner. Indeed, it is all that was spoken of at the small gathering I attended. I understand you once threw a tart at Lady Longwood."

Tamsin lifted her chin. "It was sponge cake, Your Grace, with jelly in the center, though I do not remember the kind only that the lady in question deserved it."

"There is also a rumor you like to strut about in breeches."

Tamsin stroked the tabby, deciding how to respond. What had Ware said about her to his mother, if anything at all? He was probably out collecting beetles and had no idea she was enduring the Duchess Inquisition, which was somewhat distressing. "I like to ride astride," she finally returned.

"A lady uses a sidesaddle."

"That is why ladies are always in danger from falling from their horse," Tamsin said politely. "I am not one for a sedate gallop." It was probably the wrong thing to say to Ware's mother, though there was nothing improper in her answer, but Tamsin could only think of how she'd ridden Ware in the gardens.

Warmth crept up her cheeks.

"Yes. You used to race for a fat purse." A bored sigh came from her. "I don't find you to be overly appealing." The duchess curled her lip. "Honestly, I don't see what all the fuss is about."

"Perhaps," Tamsin ran her hand over Aset's back, "my appeal is lost on you, Your Grace."

An overly fat Persian leapt onto a blue silk pillow next to the duchess.

"I doubt it. I'm very discerning." She tilted her head in the direction of the cat who settled on the pillow. "Khonsu."

"I'm certain you are. Discerning, that is." Aset was purring and attempting to climb up Tamsin's shoulder. "The moon god. Are you testing my knowledge of the Egyptian gods for a reason, Your Grace? Will Greek mythology be next?"

"Impertinent," the duchess responded.

"Did your sources not mention that?" Tamsin replied.

"Lady Curchon's theory is that you were in the gardens intent on garnering my son's attention while he was focused on his research. She claims you to be a young lady of much ambition."

"Clever as well to know the duke was in the gardens, then discern what moth he was looking for *and* to coax such a moth to land on my knee. I suppose I also arranged Lady Longwood to come upon us suddenly. Truly, Your Grace. I am most cunning."

Tamsin was not about to shrivel before Ware's mother. She sensed it would be an enormous mistake. Most of the *ton* was terrified of the Duchess of Ware. She would not be counted in that number.

The duchess's lips rippled. "According to Lady Curchon, had she not intervened, things might have become that much worse."

"I do not see how, Your Grace."

"I'm aware of the lengths Lady Curchon went to in order to make it appear you and the duke were merely acquaintances of a sort to protect your reputation."

"More Ware's, begging your pardon, Your Grace."

"Do not dare correct me, Lady Tamsin. Nevertheless, very few believe that a girl of your reputation did not put herself in the right place at exactly the correct moment. Did my son compromise you, Lady Tamsin?"

Tamsin thought of Ware's lips on the inside of her thigh. Of his mouth on her while she writhed in the grass at River Crest. "No, Your Grace. Nor have I ever claimed such."

The duchess peered at her, studying Tamsin for any flaw or tic. "But why not say he did? You could have become a duchess if not for the intervention of Lady Curchon."

Tamsin gently disengaged Aset's claws from the lace. "Because Ware did not."

"He tells me differently."

Her fingers froze in the cat's fur, mind searching for the correct words. So, Ware had told his mother something about Tamsin. Hope and dread mixed together in equal measures. "Does he, Your Grace?"

"I find your habit of answering my question with one of your own to be incredibly impertinent. I am not amused."

"Nor am I." Ware's baritone boomed from the door moments before his heavy tread entered the drawing room. "Cease your examination of Lady Tamsin." He shot Tamsin a glance, but his attention remained on the duchess. "While I enjoyed the errand you sent me on, Your Grace, I believe my time is better spent here."

Tamsin drank in the sight of him, the longing for Ware nearly making her jump from the chair. There was so much she must say to this man, her moth-loving duke. He'd cut his hair; where before it nearly brushed his shoulders, now the dark strands merely clung to his ears. Clothes neat and tidy. Not a leaf or bit of dirt anywhere. A nicely tied cravat. He looked very much like a duke as he stood before her. A shame. She loved her rumpled entomologist.

I love this version of him as well.

"Ware." The duchess glanced between the two of them, arranging her stern expression into one of penitence. "I invited Lady Tamsin for tea."

"Invited or demanded, Your Grace?"

The duchess gave a delicate shrug. "Aset likes her quite a bit. I suppose that may have to do. But she *is* impertinent."

"Lady Tamsin or the cat, Mother?"

"Both." Her gaze landed on Tamsin. "Breeches. It will cause quite a bit of gossip, Ware."

Ware turned to regard Tamsin, eyes soft where they landed on her. "She looks quite splendid in breeches."

Tamsin's heart constricted painfully. Gratefully. Had his mother not been present, Tamsin would have jumped into his arms.

"I'm not pleased, Ware."

"You rarely are, Mother."

Ware was smiling at the duchess, belying their stern conversation. A look of deep affection passed between them before his mother came to her feet. "I must find Hobbs, though it shouldn't be difficult. He's probably listening at the door."

"Hobbs is nearly deaf."

"Pah. Hobbs, do you hear me? There is much to be done."

Shuffling footsteps came from the other side of the drawing room door. The duchess gave Ware a look. "I told you. Ear pressed to the door." A dramatic sigh came from her. "I will be forced to endure Charlotte Maplehurst. Saints preserve us." She paused before Tamsin but addressed Ware. "You are certain, Ware."

"Absolutely."

"Lady Curchon may have a fit of apoplexy. Very well." She presented Ware with her cheek for a kiss before turning to Tamsin. "Do not try me, Lady Tamsin."

Tamsin bobbed. "I will endeavor not to, Your Grace."

"She's impudent, Ware." Her fingers brushed his arm. "This will be a trial for me," she said over her shoulder. "Charlotte Maplehurst." The duchess sailed out, cats trailing her before she closed the door with a click.

"That went well," Ware grumbled looking down at her.

Tamsin caught a whiff of bergamot, but no wet earth, and struggled to contain her emotions. The duchess was obviously speaking of arrangements for her and Ware to wed, and Tamsin should be furious that he hadn't asked her properly or merely assumed she would agree. But she couldn't find it in herself to be angry.

"I'll assume the hostile invitation to tea was an approval of sorts," Tamsin replied. "Though I don't recall agreeing to anything."

Ware shrugged. "The fact that you are here means at the very least you haven't refused." He reached out with one finger to trace the line of her knuckles. "I expected a fist. A kick. Possibly a punch to the stomach."

That beautiful hum started once more along her skin, the one that came only from Ware. She lowered her eyes, feeling horribly exposed.

"I love you," Tamsin blurted out before she lost her nerve. She backed away from him in an instant, shocked at her words, and paced over to the fireplace. "This is a very large fireplace." Studying the mantel, she moved yet another cat out of the way to view the small collection of figures atop it. "These are lovely. Does your mother collect them?" Why wasn't he at least making some sort of comment? Perhaps he didn't love her. It was only lust and honor. Which would make a horrible marriage now that she'd decided—

"Please," he said, the deep rolling baritone wistful. "Say it once more."

Her heart clenched in her chest at hearing the longing in his words. Tamsin spun around and came within a few feet of him, stopping before him. "I love you, Hayden Redford, Duke of Ware. And I am sorry that I—well, I am just sorry." She toed the carpet with the tip of her slipper, blinking back the tears attempting to form. Ware had made her a watering pot. "I didn't even know you were here. I—was sure you'd come to the conclusion that your proposal had been hasty. That I was more trouble than you wished and—I was awful to you, Ware. I said terrible things I didn't mean."

"As did I." His fingers took hers. "We will always have disagreements, Tamsin. Horrible rows, I expect. I will retreat to my specimens and notebooks. You will ride about the park in breeches scandalizing everyone." He brought her hand to his lips and pressed a kiss to her knuckles. "But my attachment to you, Lady Tamsin Sinclair, is firmly fixed and cannot be undone."

"You are often unpleasant," she murmured, pressing herself into his chest. "You will deserve the occasional kick from my half-boots."

Ware pressed a kiss to the top of her head. "You cannot dance. I don't think you are capable of forcing your body into obedience. So, no balls."

Tamsin pulled his hand up, pressing it against her heart. "I don't mind going if only to sit in the gardens with you and listen to the musicians."

A rumble came from him. "No breaking of noses, my love. Especially mine." He took a deep breath. "There will be a great deal of gossip when we wed. And while you are quite capable at defending yourself, you must know that I am your shelter from such things, Tamsin." Ware's thumb tilted up her chin to look at him. He lowered his mouth to hers in a gentle kiss. "I will not let anyone or anything," his voice grew steely, "touch the wife I love."

"I am not used to having such a shield. I may balk at times."

"I am overprotective where you are concerned. You must allow me to be."

Tamsin sniffed. As a declaration of affection, it was quite lovely and very much Ware. Her fingers curled into the lapels of his coat.

"Nor will I allow any harm to come to my wife's family, who is now mine. You will be a duchess. If Lady Longwood so much as glances in your direction, I will smite her."

Tamsin nodded, pressing her forehead into his chest once more, content to be in the circle of his arms and comforted by the sound of his breathing. Her nose bumped against a glass vial in one of his many pockets. "I did not realize dukes could smite."

"It is only a fraction of our power." Ware laughed "You need not worry over Aurora. Lady Curchon has rescinded her sponsorship in favor of my mother's. Did you know, gorgeous creature, that I am a silent partner in Dunnings?"

No, she didn't. Jordan probably didn't know either. How foolish she'd been to allow herself to be threatened by Lady Curchon who held far less power than she assumed.

"I think the duchess likes me." Tamsin gave him a saucy look.

"Like is a rather strong word, my love. It is better to say the Duchess of Ware does not *dislike* you."

"Well," Tamsin looked up at him, running her fingers along his jaw, "that is something I suppose."

⋙✦⋘

THE CROWD WAS sparse at the museum today; still, Tamsin and Ware drew looks from nearly everyone present as he escorted her in the direction of the cat mummies.

"Thank you for bringing me, Your Grace." She looked up at him with look of worship and batted her lashes. "Is this the proper way to adore you?"

Ware gave a derisive snort. "Stop that. You look ridiculous. And as to the cat mummies, you finally found the correct incentive to get me to agree."

When Ware arrived earlier at Emerson House, he did so in a

closed carriage. Rain had started, a light drizzle at present which would eventually become a downpour. Tamsin made the proper preparations. Closed carriages made excellent venues for assignations, according to Odessa.

"The look on your face when you realized I possessed no under-things, Your Grace, was priceless," she whispered.

Their engagement had been the talk of London for weeks. The Duchess of Ware hosted a small gathering at her home to celebrate her son's impending marriage, which featured the performance of an Italian soprano and a French acting troupe. The champagne flowed freely. The buffet was lavish.

But there wasn't any dancing, per Ware's request.

Ware's eyes darkened to pewter as they approached the wing housing the Egyptian exhibits and his palm slid dangerously low along her back. "I will have to double my driver's pay. I'm sure he and half of London heard you scream out your pleasure, Tamsin."

"Undoubtedly." She wasn't the least embarrassed. Just happy.

Lady Longwood, true to form, had attempted to spew her usual vile opinions when Tamsin visited the modiste. She was stopped in her tracks by the sight of the Duchess of Ware, who would tolerate no disparagement of her future daughter-in-law.

But Tamsin had no doubt Lady Longwood was only temporarily vanquished.

"We've had a letter from Drew." Tamsin hurried to keep up with Ware. "Stop walking so fast."

"I am *strolling*. Your legs are far too short. I can't imagine what holds his attention in Lincolnshire. Didn't you tell me he hated the country?"

"He does." Or at least he did. Tamsin wasn't sure what was delaying him.

Ware paused before the exhibit of cat mummies. "Behold, my almost duchess. But after, the pinned bodies of insects." He winked. "We'll take the long way back to Emerson House. Through the park."

About the Author

Kathleen Ayers is the bestselling author of steamy Regency and Victorian romance. She's been a hopeful romantic and romance reader since buying Sweet Savage Love at a garage sale when she was fourteen while her mother was busy looking at antique animal planters. She has a weakness for tortured, witty alpha males who can't help falling for intelligent, sassy heroines.

A Texas transplant (from Pennsylvania) Kathleen spends most of her summers attempting to grow tomatoes (a wasted effort) and floating in her backyard pool with her two dogs, husband and son. When not writing she likes to visit her "happy place" (Newport, RI.), wine bars, make homemade pizza on the grill, and perfect her charcuterie board skills. Visit her at www.kathleenayers.com.

Printed in Great Britain
by Amazon